GARDEN OF EVIL

GARDEN OF EVIL

A Jim Rook novel

Graham Masterton

This first world edition published 2012
in Great Britain and 2013 in the USA by
SEVERN HOUSE PUBLISHERS LTD of
19 Cedar Road, Sutton, Surrey, England, SM2 5DA.
Trade paperback edition first published
in Great Britain and the USA 2013 by
SEVERN HOUSE PUBLISHERS LTD.

All rights
The mora

British Li

Masterton
Garden
1. Rook
tales.
I. Title
823.9'2-

ISBN-13: 978-0-7278-8249-3 (cased)
ISBN-13: 978-1-84751-468-4 (trade paper)

Except where actual historical events and characters are being
described for the storyline of this novel, all situations in this
publication are fictitious and any resemblance to living persons
is purely coincidental.

All Severn House titles are printed on acid-free paper.

Severn House Publishers support the Forest Stewardship Council [FSC], the
leading international forest certification organisation. All our titles that are printed
on Greenpeace-approved FSC-certified paper carry the FSC logo.

MIX
Paper from
responsible sources
FSC
www.fsc.org   FSC® C018575

Typeset by Palimpsest Book Production Ltd.,
Falkirk, Stirlingshire, Scotland.
Printed and bound in Great Britain by
MPG Books Ltd., Bodmin, Cornwall.

ONE

The smog was so thick that Jim didn't see the dark figure walking up the college driveway until the very last moment, and he had to stamp on the brakes and swerve sharply to the left to avoid hitting him. His car slewed around with its tires screaming in a shrill, panicky chorus.

For a few seconds afterward, he sat behind the wheel of his car, his heart palpitating. The CD player continued to thunder out Beethoven's *Piano Concerto Number Five* at deafening volume, but the Swiss-cheese-and-pastrami sandwich that he had been eating had dropped into his lap.

'*Jesus*,' he said. He knew that he had probably been driving too fast, and that he should have had his headlights on and been paying less attention to eating his sandwich and more attention to where he was going. All the same, the figure had been walking right in the middle of the driveway, dressed entirely in black.

Jim picked up the slices of rye bread and cheese and pastrami and pickle that were scattered over his navy-blue chinos and cupped them in his hand. Then he climbed out of his car and looked around. The figure had vanished into the smog, which Jim thought was deeply strange. Like, if somebody almost runs you over, what do you do? Either you scream and shout at him and accuse him of driving like a fricking maniac, or else you tell him that he missed you by inches and that you're fine. What you don't do is simply walk away as if nothing had happened.

'Hey!' Jim shouted. 'Hey! Are you OK?'

No answer. And no sign of him, either. Only a suffocating wall of yellowish smog, which muffled the constant roaring of traffic from the San Diego Freeway.

'Hey! *Hallo*? I'm sorry if I scared you! I just want to know that you're OK!'

His voice was flat and didn't seem to carry at all, as if he were shouting in a soundproof booth. Again, no answer. Jim tossed the bits and pieces of his disassembled sandwich on to the grass, smacked his hands together and returned to his car. He started up the engine, and then crept up the driveway, hunched over the wheel, peering intently ahead of him in case the figure was still walking in the middle of the road.

He reached the top of the slope, where the driveway widened into a large circular turning area in front of the college's main entrance. The college buildings themselves gradually appeared out of the smog like some phantom castle. It was still early, around seven thirty, and only a few students were walking to and fro, although more than twenty of them had gathered under the huge cypress tree in front of the college, which was a favorite meeting place for gossip and banter and flirting before class.

Jim drove very slowly past them, staring at each of them in turn, but not one of them was a match for the dark figure that he had nearly run over. At least a half dozen of them were dressed in black sweaters or black T-shirts, but they all wore jeans or cargo shorts, and four of them wore baseball caps, while three of them had sports bags slung over their shoulders, bulging with books. Apart from that, most of them were far too chunky. The dark figure on the driveway had been tall and very thin, like a stretched-out shadow.

Jim gave up his search and circled around to the faculty parking lot. As usual, he maneuvered his green metallic Mercury Marquis into the space reserved for Royston Denman, the head of mathematics. The Mercury was eighteen feet long and six feet wide and Royston Denman's space was adjacent to the entrance and much larger than any of the others.

He climbed out, took his briefcase out of the trunk, and then crossed over to the students under the cypress tree.

'Any of you see a guy walking up the driveway a couple of minutes ago? Dark top, dark pants.'

'*Walking*?' said one of the students.

'Sure, you know. That thing when you put one foot in front of the other and it miraculously gets you from one place to another.'

Almost all of the students shook their heads. 'Woulda noticed some dude *walkin'* to college. Jeez.'

'OK,' said Jim. 'Just asking. Any of you here in Special Class Two?'

Three of them put up their hands – a very tall African-American boy in a droopy gray tracksuit, a baby-pretty blonde with scraggly curls and a tight pink T-shirt with sparkly silver sequins on it, and a red-headed boy with a buzz cut and raging red acne and a bright green sweatshirt.

'Good. My name's Mr Rook and Special Class Two, that's my class. So I'll be seeing you characters later.'

Just then, he caught sight of Sheila Colefax mounting the steps to the college's main entrance. He jogged across to catch up with her. Sheila taught Spanish in the classroom next to Jim's. She was a petite, perky brunette but she always wore heavy-rimmed eyeglasses, a blouse that was buttoned right up to the neck and fastened with a brooch, and knee-length pencil skirts. Ever since he had first met her, Jim had harbored a fantasy that she wore a black bustier and black stockings underneath those formal outer clothes, and that once she had taken off her eyeglasses and shaken her hair loose, she would be a tigress in bed.

'Hi, Sheila! *Cómo está usted?*'

'Very well, thank you, Jim.'

'*Cuál es le precio de la salchicha hoy?*'

Sheila didn't even turn to look at him, but continued to hurry up the steps. 'I suppose you've been practicing that,' she said, sharply.

'Well, yes, I admit it. Spanish isn't actually my second language.'

She reached the top step and now she confronted him. 'Sometimes I don't know whether you're ignorant, Jim Rook, or juvenile, or crude, or all three. It isn't exactly seductive to ask a woman how much a sausage costs.'

'You're kidding me! Is that what it means? I thought it was a compliment. Like – "to me, o my darling, you are more precious than sapphires."'

There was a moment when Jim seriously thought that Sheila was going to slap him. But then her lips pursed tightly to stop herself from laughing and her eyes brightened up behind her eyeglasses and she shook her head from side to side.

'You really are one of a kind, aren't you? "More precious than sapphires." You didn't think it meant that for a moment, did you?'

'No,' Jim admitted. 'But it tickled you, right? And I could tickle you all evening, if you let me.'

She pushed her way in through the college entrance, and Jim followed her, catching his briefcase in the revolving doors as he did so. He had to forcibly tug it out, breaking the handle.

'Shit,' he said.

Sheila turned and said, 'It's a strict rule of mine, Jim. No dating fellow teachers under any circumstances, ever. I'm sorry.'

'Ehrlichman doesn't have to know.'

'That's not the point. It happened to me once before, when I was teaching in San Luis Obispo. No matter how discreet you are, it always ends in tears.'

'Sheila—'

'No, Jim.'

With that, she walked off along the corridor toward the faculty room, her heels rapping on the polished vinyl floor. Jim was left standing there for a moment, with his briefcase in one hand and the broken handle in the other. Three students went past and gave him goofy grins. He looked back at them fiercely, and said, '*What*?'

He was still standing there when the principal, Dr Ehrlichman, came bustling out of his office. Dr Ehrlichman was short and round shouldered, with a bald head peeling from sunburn and bulging green eyes and a nose that always made Jim feel that he wanted to *parp*! it like an old-fashioned motor-horn. Jim thought that if he hadn't been appointed principal of West Grove Community College, he could have easily found an alternative career as a clown.

'Jim! Just the man!'

'Doctor E. How was your summer vacation? You went to Bora-Bora, didn't you, or was it Bolivia?'

'Bulgaria. My wife has relatives in Sofia. It was very cultural. Well, to tell you the truth, it *could* have been very cultural. But my wife's relatives are a little earthy, if that's the right word.'

'Earthy. Yes, I know what you mean. I have an earthy uncle,

up in San Francisco. Uncle Ned. Swears like a longshoreman, drinks like a dolphin, but he always picks the winners at Golden Gate Fields, I'll give him that. Doesn't have to work for a living, like you and me.'

Dr Ehrlichman lifted the clipboard in his hand and flipped over three pages. 'Ah, here it is. You have an extra student joining Special Class Two. Simon Silence.'

'Silence? What kind of a name is that?'

'He's the son of the Reverend John Silence.'

'Never heard of him.'

'Well, neither had I, until this morning.'

Dr Ehrlichman leafed through two or three more pages on his clipboard, and then he said, 'Yes, here it is. The Reverend John Silence is the Supreme Pastor of the Church of the Divine Conquest, 8136 Lookout Mountain Avenue, Laurel Canyon.'

'Still never heard of him. Nor the Church of the Divine Whatsitsname.'

'Conquest.'

'Whatever. But OK. What's his background, this kid?'

'Apparently he's been homeschooled up until now, but now the Reverend Silence is anxious that he mixes more with students his own age, and becomes a little more worldly.'

'Worldly? He'll get plenty of worldly in Special Class Two, I can promise you that.'

Dr Ehrlichman lifted up his hairy wrist and peered at his weighty gold Rolex.

'General assembly at eight thirty. You *will* try and be there, won't you, unlike last semester, and the semester before that? I have some very critical announcements to make.'

'Hey . . . seriously impressive watch,' said Jim. 'How much are they paying you these days?'

'This watch was fifty Bulgarian lev, at the flea market outside of the Alexander Nevski Cathedral in Sofia. That's about thirty-five US dollars.'

'OK, Dr E., I believe you.'

Jim walked along the corridor until he reached Special Class Two. The door was freshly painted a dull slate blue, which had obliterated the graffiti that had appeared at the end of last semester: HERE BE DUMMIES! He took hold of the door handle but for some reason that he couldn't quite understand, he hesitated before he opened it. He thought: *here I am, at the start of yet another semester. How long have I been doing this? How many more times am I going to be doing this? Is this all my life is going to be about, opening this door year after year and facing yet another class of slackers and slow learners and kids who simply can't understand why 'cough' and 'bough' and 'ought' are all pronounced differently, and never will understand it, as long as they live.*

He hesitated a moment longer and then he opened the door and stepped inside. The classroom smelled strongly of lavender floor polish and through the windows Jim could see that the smog was gradually lifting, and the sun was shining through. Outside, students walked through the gilded haze like ghosts.

Sixteen desks stood in front of him, in four rows of four. He walked slowly up and down between them. In an hour's time, fifteen students would be sitting here – white, African-American, Chinese, Hispanic, who knew? Fifteen confused and reluctant young minds to be dragged out of the briars of semi-literacy and text-speak and slang. He didn't expect them to be able to write like Walt Whitman or Emily Dickinson, so long as they could fill out a job application, although now and then they surprised him.

Jim went back to his own desk, opened up his briefcase and took out a sheaf of papers on which were printed the first lesson of the day. It was a list of twenty sentences, and all his students had to do was underline any which were grammatically incorrect or misspelled. 'I are playing baseball tomorrow with my freinds.' 'Me and Kim wented out and us et cheseburgers at Burger King.' 'My Dad went fishing and court a sammon and a cold.' 'I ran through hoards of people looking for my mom.'

He walked up and down between the desks again, placing one questionnaire on each desk. In the distance he could hear the bell ringing and the sound of doors banging and scores of sneakers squeaking and shuffling as the students poured in from outside. Before long, he would be meeting this year's Special Class Two, face to face. *If I were religious*, he thought, *this is when I would cross myself. Spectacles, testicles, wallet and watch.*

He returned to the front of the class to take out the list of students. As he did so, however, he heard a sharp *plip!* like water dripping. Then another. He looked around and saw that on the sheet of paper which he had just placed on the third desk from the front, in the second row, there were two crimson spatters, almost like two large poppy flowers.

He went back and picked up the questionnaire and frowned at it. The two spatters were wet, like paint, or blood. He sniffed them. They didn't *smell* like paint, so he could only assume they were blood. But where the hell had they come from?

At that moment another drop landed on the back of his hand, warm and viscous – and yet another, almost simultaneously, on the sleeve of his pale blue linen coat. It was then that he looked up and saw what was nailed to the ceiling.

He opened and closed his mouth, but he couldn't speak. He didn't know how he had walked into the classroom and not seen them immediately, but then he had been too busy handing out papers and thinking about this year's students. Not only that, they had been fastened in between the two long fluorescent light fittings which hung down about two feet from the ceiling, so when he had been standing at the front of the class, they had mostly been masked from his view.

In the center of the ceiling, a naked girl had been pinned face downward, with her arms and her legs spread wide. Nails had been driven through her hands, her elbows, her thighs, her knees and her ankles. She had been whitewashed all over with some kind of thick distemper, which had made her all the more difficult for Jim to see her when she had first walked in. Her eyelids were closed and her hair was stiff and fanned out. She looked more like a stone statue than a human being, but the blood that had been dripping down had fallen from her cracked but partly open lips.

Around her, in a circle, had been fastened eight pure-white Persian cats, each with at least four nails through their bodies, so that their legs were splayed out like hers. The whole grisly arrangement of girl and cats had the appearance of a ritualistic black-magic symbol.

But on the *ceiling*? In a college classroom? For the past few days, the entire college had been undergoing cleaning and refurbishment for the new semester. Jim couldn't even begin to imagine how anybody could have done it, or when, without being seen or heard. Or, for God's sake, *why*.

He stood staring up at the girl and the cats for nearly half a minute. He felt totally numb. He had seen all kinds of apparitions and spirits in his life, but he had never seen anything like this.

Very slowly, he walked backward toward the door, lifting his cellphone out of his inside coat pocket as he did so. Just as he reached the door, however, it burst open, and the girl with the scraggly hair and the pink T-shirt pushed her way in.

'This is the right room, yeah? Special Class Two?'

Jim immediately turned around pushed her back out again, so that she collided with the spotty red-haired boy who was right behind her.

'*Out!*' he told them. His voice was much higher than he had meant it to be, almost a scream.

'What? We was told to come in and find our classrooms!'

'Out! Something's happened. You can't come in. Go back outside for a while and wait until I come to talk to you.'

'What's happened? What?'

'I don't know, to tell you the truth. I don't have any idea.'

He gave her arm a last push, firmly but gently, and then he closed the door, and locked it. He could see the lanky African-American boy peering in through the circular window, his nose flattened against the glass.

'I don't know what's happened,' Jim repeated, under his breath, and then he dialed 911, and said, 'Police?'

TWO

'Lieutenant Harris told me about you,' said Detective Brennan, with a thumping sniff. 'You remember Lieutenant Harris? Retired now. Runs the pro shop at Rancho Park Golf Course. Nine bucks for a bucket of balls.'

'How could I forget him?'

'You know what he told me? "If anything really weird ever happens at West Grove Community College, you can bet your ass that the first name that comes up will be Rook." Those were his exact words.'

'I hope you're not trying to suggest that I had anything at all to do with this.'

Jim was sitting at a paper-cluttered table in the faculty room. Dr Ehrlichman's secretary Rosa had brought him a mug of strong black coffee, but he still felt badly shaken. All he could think of was that dead girl's alabaster face, with a skein of blood slowly sliding out of the corner of her mouth.

The police had arrived within fifteen minutes of his calling them. Now the college parking lot was crowded with five black-and-white squad cars and two Humvees, as well as four assorted panel vans from the county CSI, the LA Coroner's Office and the Department of Animal Care and Control; and TV trucks from KABC and Fox 11 News.

All five hundred and sixty students and most of the faculty had been sent home, leaving Dr Ehrlichman pacing up and down the corridor in frustration, a diminutive king, like Lord Farquaad in *Shrek*.

'You didn't happen to see nobody around who didn't have no legitimate business being there?' asked Detective Brennan. He was a big, sallow man, with skin like candle wax, who looked as if he never went out in daylight. He had an iron-gray widow's peak and glittery near-together eyes, which made him appear to be permanently suspicious. He was wearing a crumpled khaki suit with pants that were two inches too short for him, and saggy beige socks. His belly hung over his belt.

Jim put down his coffee mug and shook his head. 'I didn't see anybody at all, apart from Ms Colefax. And let's face it, nobody could have nailed that girl up on to the ceiling on their own. Not to mention all of those cats. They would have needed two or three guys at least, and some kind of a platform.'

'Maybe it'll help when we can identify her,' said Detective Brennan. He took out a crumpled Kleenex and fastidiously began to unfold it.

'Maybe it will, maybe it won't. I certainly didn't recognize her.'

Detective Brennan blew his nose and then folded up his Kleenex again. 'I hate this spooky shit. You don't know how much. Couple of weeks ago we had a call from the Whispering Palms Hotel. The chambermaid went into one of the rooms to turn down the beds and found two heads lying on the pillows. Two heads, a man and a woman. We still don't know who they are or where the rest of them's at.'

He paused, and made a gesture toward the ceiling. 'But this . . . this is a hundred times more spookier. I really hate this shit.'

Jim said nothing. To him, it was more important to understand *why* the girl and the cats had been nailed to the ceiling like that, rather than how. He was sure that the way in which they had been arranged was symbolic, but he couldn't begin to think what it symbolized. He had seen pentacles and spirals and inverted crosses. But a girl smothered in whitewash and surrounded by eight white cats?

Just then, there was a soft knock at the faculty room door.

'Come!' said Detective Brennan. But the door remained closed, and nobody answered.

After a while, there was another knock. Soft, again, but insistent.

Detective Brennan went across the room and opened up the door and said, 'Yes?'

A tall, skinny boy was standing outside. He had long blond hair tied back in a ponytail, and a very pale, angular face. He was quite handsome in a bloodless, bleached-out, hippie-ish way. He was wearing a loose white open-necked shirt with the sleeves rolled up, and loose white linen pants, and Jesus sandals. Over his shoulder he was carrying a white canvas bag, like a gunny sack.

He said, 'Excuse me, sir, I'm looking for Special Class Two.' Jim would have placed his accent as Louisiana or Mississippi – Deep South, anyhow. Soft, like his knocking at the door, but insistent.

'College is closed for today, son,' said Detective Brennan. 'Didn't nobody tell you that when you was coming in? They should of.'

'Closed?'

'There's been an incident. You'll see it all on the TV news.'

'We don't have a TV, sir. My father doesn't approve.'

'Oh. Well, you'll read all about it in the papers.'

'We don't have any papers delivered. My father—'

'Your father don't approve of papers, neither. I see. Well, no news is good news, that's what they say, ain't it, although I don't see no harm in the funnies.'

Jim said, 'Wait up. Let me guess. You're Simon Silence, right? And your father is the Reverend John Silence.'

'Yes, sir. That's absolutely correct, sir.'

Jim stood up and walked across to the door. 'In that case, welcome to the wonderful world of mass education. You and I should be meeting each other tomorrow morning, if and when the police have finished combing the college for forensic evidence. My name is Mr Rook and Special Class Two, that's my class.'

'Pleased to meet you, sir. I've never been in a class before. Well, I've never even been in a *school* before. My father taught me, mostly, although I did have outside tutors for physics and math. I'm sure that I'm really going to enjoy it.'

'You are? Good. I'm glad about that. But before you get too ecstatic, why don't you wait until you meet your class-mates? Even *I* haven't met them yet.'

'Go on, kid,' said Detective Brennan. 'Push off home now, come back tomorrow.'

Simon Silence ignored him, and said, 'May I just ask you one question, Mr Rook?'

'OK, go ahead. What?'

'You teach English, I know.'

'*Remedial* English, if you want to be accurate. English for students who don't see anything wrong in saying "this pizza's good – but this pizza's a whole lot gooder – and *this* pizza's gooderer than any other pizza I ever ate."'

Simon Silence gave Jim the faintest of smiles. 'What I actually wanted to ask you is whether you ever give your class any spiritual guidance.'

'Spiritual guidance? What kind of spiritual guidance? You mean religion? I don't do religion, Simon. Sometimes we talk about life and death, but only so far as they're part of a poem, or an essay, or a story we happen to be studying. "*Because I could not stop for death, He kindly stopped for me. The carriage held but just ourselves and immortality.*" Discuss.'

'I didn't really mean that kind of spiritual guidance. I meant, do you ever give your class the benefit of your . . .' He paused, his right hand circling around and around, as if he couldn't quite find the word for it.

Jim waited patiently, but eventually he said, 'Yes? The benefit of my what?'

'I'm sorry, sir. I should be going, shouldn't I?'

'No, come on, Simon. The benefit of my *what*?'

Simon Silence looked at him. The last of the smog was clearing away and the sun suddenly shone on him through the faculty room window. It lit up his face so brightly that he appeared to have hardly any features at all. His eyes were very pale blue and his eyebrows were blond. He could have been a watercolor painting that somebody had tipped their paint water over, so that all the colors had washed away.

'My father says that we all have a gift, sir, every one of us. It is how we use our gifts that makes all the difference. I know *you* have a gift, Mr Rook. You have a rare and wonderful gift. That is why my father sent me here. I was simply asking how freely you share it with your students.'

Detective Brennan laid his hand on Simon Silence's shoulder. 'Come on, kid. That's enough. *Vamos*. Come back tomorrow.'

Simon Silence stayed in the doorway for a while, still staring at Jim with those pale blue eyes, as if he were prepared to wait for an answer for as long as it took. The smog momentarily drifted across the sun again, and as the room darkened his features became more definite. At the same time they appeared subtly to alter, so that instead of looking innocent he appeared strangely *knowing*.

'There's just one more thing,' he said, lifting the white canvas sack off his shoulder, loosening its drawstring, and starting to rummage around in it.

'You really should go home, Simon,' Jim told him. 'Whatever it is, it can wait till tomorrow.'

Detective Brennan began to close the door. But before he could do so, Simon Silence took his hand out of his sack and held out a shiny pink-and-green apple.

'This is for you, sir,' he said. 'We have an orchard near Bakersfield, and we grow our own.'

'An apple for the teacher?' said Jim. 'This isn't grade school, you know.'

'My father says that if somebody gives you a gift, you should always give them something in return. This is *my* gift, as a thank you for *your* gift.'

Jim took the apple and sniffed it. It smelled very sweet and aromatic, but it had a sourness to it, too – almost like a tamarind, more than an apple.

'It is a variety called Paradise,' said Simon Silence. 'We are the only orchard in the region to grow it. We bus down-and-outs and homeless people up to our orchard to pick them, and we allow them to eat as many as they like. Then we distribute them free to anybody who comes to our church to pray.'

'OK, then thanks,' Jim told him. 'Maybe I'll see you in the morning.'

Simon Silence gave Jim another faint smile, and then he turned around and walked away, his sandals slapping on the floor.

'Don't envy you, teaching that fruitcake,' said Detective Brennan, closing the door.

Jim said nothing, repeatedly tossing up the apple that Simon

Silence had given him, and catching it again. For several reasons, the boy had unsettled him. He was completely unlike most of the students that he had to teach in Special Class Two. He had seemed shrewd, and self-confident, and although he had a strong Southern accent he had spoken grammatically and without any slang whatsoever.

What had disturbed Jim was the way that he had wanted to talk about his gift. If he hadn't mentioned 'spiritual guidance', Jim might have thought that he was referring to nothing more than his talent for teaching semi-literate slackers to compose a sentence that almost made some kind of sense. But it was obvious that Simon Silence was already too fluent to need much guidance in the art of expressing himself.

When he was seven years old Jim had almost died from pneumonia. After he had recovered he had gradually come to realize that his close encounter with the other side had given him the ability to see spirits, and ghosts, and every other kind of supernatural presence, from poltergeists to demons. He saw them, and he could speak to them, too, when they appeared.

He was sure that this was the gift that Simon Silence had been talking about. But how did he know about it? Jim had learned to live with it, and sometimes to use it to help people who were plagued by vengeful or angry spirits, but he couldn't understand how the son of a preacher could have come to hear about it, and why he should be showing so much interest in it.

There was another knock at the door and this time it was a woman CSI, in a noisy white Tyvek suit, her cheeks still flushed from wearing her protective helmet.

'That's it, Detective. We're done here. We should have some preliminary reports for you by the end of the week. But at this stage I seriously don't think they're going to tell you a whole lot.'

'Any indications yet as to how it was done?'

The CSI shook her frizzy blonde curls. 'Not a clue, so far. No fingerprints, no shoe impressions, nothing. We have the nails, of course, and we'll be trying to trace where they came from, and we'll also be taking samples of the white paint that the vic was covered in. Animal Care and Control will be checking on the cats. They all look like pedigrees, so it's pretty certain they'll have microchips.'

'Well, that should help us,' said Detective Brennan. 'It can't be every day that somebody goes to a cat breeder and buys eight white Persians. Or steals them.'

'We still have no idea how the girl and the cats were physically nailed to the ceiling,' the CSI told him. 'If the perps used a scaffold, or stepladders, they would have had to make some kind of impression on the floor tiles. But there's zilch. No dents at all.'

Jim said, 'Did you ever see anything like this before? I don't necessarily mean on the ceiling. But a similar sort of pattern . . . a woman with her arms and legs spread out, and all the cats around her? Or anything even remotely like it?'

The CSI shook her head again. 'Never. And, believe me, I've seen some pretty far-out arranging, when it comes to bodies. A woman's head that was sewn on to a man's body, and the other way about. A guy who was stuffed into a race-horse, with his head sticking out from under its tail. We never found out who did it but I think we can guess what point he was making.'

Detective Brennan said, 'Thanks, Moira. I'll wait to hear from you. Mr Rook, you can go off home if you like. You gave me your cell number, didn't you? I might have to call you if anything new comes up.'

'Fine,' said Jim. He picked up his briefcase with the broken handle, dropped the apple into it, and left the building. Outside, it was warm now, and clear. Usually, if he was given an unexpected day off, he would head for 26 Beach Restaurant in Venice and order himself a beer and a prosciutto burger and exchange some banter with his favorite waitress, Imelda.

But today he was not in the mood for anything except going back home and trying to make sense of what had happened. He still couldn't quite believe that what he had witnessed was real.

He climbed into his car and backed out of the parking lot with a squeal of tires. He drove back down the driveway, still thinking about the girl and the cats on the ceiling; and about the dark figure he had nearly run over in this morning's smog.

He had told Detective Brennan about him (or *her*, or *it*, or whatever the figure might have been) but Detective Brennan hadn't shown too much interest.

'Like you said yourself, Mr Rook, no single person could have done this unaided.'

As he drove out between the brown brick pillars that marked the college grounds, his eye was caught by a white flicker among the trees, off to his left. He slowed down, and then he stopped, frowning, and backed his car up twenty or thirty yards and let down his window, so that he could see the white shape more clearly.

There was a small grove of shady oaks beside the road, just where it curved down from North Saltair Avenue toward Sunset. Standing under these oaks with his arms spread wide was Simon Silence, in his flappy white shirt and his flappy white pants. He had his back to Jim, so that it was difficult for Jim to tell exactly what he was doing. But what puzzled Jim most of all was that seven or eight young people were sitting around him in a semicircle, cross-legged, looking up at him with rapt expressions on their faces as if they were spellbound by something that he was saying.

From the way they were dressed, and the sports bags lying on the ground beside them, Jim could see that they were students. He backed up a little more and it was then that he recognized the lanky African-American student he had seen earlier this morning, under the cypress tree; and also the pretty blonde girl with the pink T-shirt and the scraggly hair.

Jim stayed where he was for a while, wondering if ought to go over and ask them what they were doing. He was well aware that what they got up to outside of college was none of his business. They could be jumping around stark naked or smoking crack, or both, and there was nothing he could do about it, except call the police. Besides that, he didn't even know their names yet, or how many of them were going to be joining Special Class Two. The last thing he wanted to do was to appear stuffy and censorious, even before he found out who they were. He wouldn't be able to teach them unless he earned their trust.

All the same, Simon Silence had set off his psychic

sensitivity, like a burglar alarm ringing unanswered in a distant warehouse. *Something wrong here*, although he couldn't begin to guess what it was. *Something very wrong here.*

He was still sitting there when there was a deafening two-tone blast on a horn. He looked into his rear-view mirror and saw that a huge black Dodge Ram was close up behind him, impatiently waiting for him to get out of the middle of the road.

He waved his arm out of the window to apologize, and pulled away. But as he did so, he saw Simon Silence turn around, and catch sight of him, and smile – that same knowing smile that he had given him before.

THREE

When Jim parked on the steeply sloping driveway outside his apartment block on Briarcliff Road, he found Ricky Kaminsky sitting on the steps, playing a Spanish guitar and smoking a hand-rolled cigarette.

'Hey man, you're back super early,' said Ricky, the cigarette waggling between his lips. 'Don't tell me – you took one look at your new class and totally freaked?'

Ricky was an artist and lived in the first-floor apartment. He was in his early sixties, with a wild mane of gray hair and a droopy gray moustache. His face was creased and leathery, as if it had been weathered by every outdoor rock concert from Woodstock to Altamont. His bare chest was brown and bony like a kipper, and he wore only a tan leather vest and jeans and six or seven necklaces of colored beads.

'We had some security problems,' Jim told him.

'Security problems, huh? What's that a euphemism for?'

'I found a dead girl in my classroom. And some dead cats, too.'

Ricky narrowed his eyes, but he kept on playing his guitar. 'No shit. What was that all about?'

'Wish I knew. It looked like some kind of ritual.'

'There's some fuckin' weird types out there, man. I tell you. I used to think the sixties were weird. Then I thought the seventies were weird. But today . . . whoa. The whole fuckin' world is weird. Here . . .'

He took the cigarette out of his mouth and offered it to Jim with a nod of encouragement. 'This is good shit, man. You want to try it. Ease your troubles, that's what it does.'

Jim shook his head. 'No thanks. I think there's enough happening in my head already, without that stuff. Anyhow, why aren't *you* working? I thought you had that commission to finish for the Westwood Library.'

'I'm working on it, I'm working on it. I'm having a little difficulty, that's all. It's like the paint won't behave itself.'

'What does that mean? You've bought some disobedient paint? Take it back to the art store and get your money back.'

Ricky stopped playing and propped his guitar up on the step. 'No – I'm serious, man. I mean, you write a bit of poetry now and again, don't you? You know what it's like when the words won't do what you want them to do?'

'Not exactly.'

'Well, let me show you.'

Ricky stood up and led Jim up the steps to his apartment. The faded red front door was open and there was a strong smell of incense and turpentine wafting out of it. The living room was chaos. Three easels stood at angles to each other, and there were dozens of unfinished canvases stacked up against the walls. A trestle table was crowded with paintbrushes and rags and dried-out palettes, as well as scores of half-squeezed tubes of oil paint, like a writhing nest of multicolored worms.

The walls were draped with Indian durries, in red and brown and green, and brass lamps hung from the ceiling, wrapped in red silk scarves. In the corner there was an oriental-style birdcage, with a red cockatoo perched inside it.

'This is the painting I'm supposed to be doing for the Westwood Library,' said Ricky. He nodded toward the easel on the right-hand side, on which was propped a large canvas depicting a man in a white cloak sitting in a chair like a throne, surrounded by small children. He had a thick leather-bound book on his lap, and he was obviously reading them a story.

The painting was only about a third completed, so much of the background was still sketched in charcoal. But Ricky had already painted the man's face in considerable detail. He was blond haired and very pale, with high cheekbones and pale turquoise eyes and the slightest suggestion of a smile. For some reason, though, he looked as if he were smiling at a private joke, rather than sharing his amusement with the children who were gathered all around him.

Jim stared at the painting for a long time without saying anything. He thought that the pale-faced man bore an uncanny resemblance to Simon Silence, although it had to be a coincidence. Like, it *had* to be. Either a coincidence, or Jim's psychic alarm bells still faintly ringing, in the back of his mind.

'Who *is* that?' he asked.

'He's supposed to be The Storyteller. The library have baby story-time and toddler story-time a couple of times a month, and they wanted a painting to put up in the corner where they hold them.'

'No – I meant who did you use as a model?'

'Well, that's the whole fuckin' point. *This* is the model.' He went across to the easel and picked up a dog-eared color photograph of a man's face. He handed it over to Jim and said, 'This is what The Storyteller was supposed to look like.'

The man in the photograph was round-faced and jolly-looking, almost like Santa Claus without a beard. His cheeks were red and his eyes were crinkly with good humor and he had a broad, cheerful smile.

'That's actually a guy called Morton Toft, who runs the Brouhaha Bar on Wilshire. I 'specially chose him because he's always telling tall stories, and he has a child-friendly face.'

'So – what happened? Your Storyteller looks completely different.'

'I can't paint him any other way, that's why. I sketch his features, I mix my colors, and that's how he always turns out. That face you're looking at there, that's the third fuckin' face I've painted, one on top of the other.'

Jim went close up to the painting and stared into The Storyteller's eyes. There was no question about it, he did look very much like Simon Silence, except he was at least twenty years older. His hair was thinner and there were crows' feet around his eyes.

'Can you explain it?' asked Ricky. 'Because I sure can't. I think it's something to do with the paint.'

Jim heard a rattling sound, like a bead-curtain parting, and then a woman's voice said, 'It's a message from the spirit world. I've told Ricky that over and over, but he doesn't believe me.'

'Oh for Christ's sake, woman! "A message from the spirit world," my ass! There ain't no fuckin' spirit world, otherwise your ex would be sleeping in between us every night just to keep us apart!'

A very emaciated woman with her white hair cut into a bob had entered the living room. She was wearing a silver Navajo necklace and several silver bracelets, but she was naked to the waist. Her breasts were small and flat, but with prominent brown nipples, both of which were pierced with silver rings. She wore gauzy brown harem pants and oriental slippers with curled-up toes. She was smoking a cigarette in a long black holder.

'Hallo, Nadine,' said Jim. 'How's the fortune telling?'

'Oh, I'm getting by. Business types mainly, these days, wanting to know when the next crash is coming.'

'So – this Storyteller – you think this is a message from the spirit world?'

Nadine came sliding up to Ricky and twined her arm around his waist. 'He *refuses* to believe me, but what else could it possibly be? All right, he's not Norman Rockwell, but he's not that crap at painting faces, are you, bunny-hugs?'

'It's the paint,' Ricky insisted. 'It's something to do with the paint, I'm sure of it. When it dries, it loses all of its pigmentation.'

Nadine blew out a long stream of smoke. 'You don't believe that any more than I do, do you? You just don't want to admit that there are forces in this world that you can't explain. Jim knows all about them, don't you, Jim?'

Jim deliberately didn't answer that question. 'What do *you* think this means, then?' he asked Nadine. 'This face, always turning out different from the way that Ricky wants to paint it?'

'I think it's a long-dead relative, desperately trying to communicate with him through the medium in which he is the most proficient – oil paint.'

'Oh, yes? Why not through music? Or why not simply *talk* to him?'

'Because he's high most of the time, and he would forget. But if the message is in a painting, then he *can't* forget. He needs to find out who this is, this Storyteller, and when he does, he'll discover something greatly to his advantage.'

'Nadine, will you cut that out? I don't believe any of your fortune-telling garbage!'

'But you could be rich without knowing it. This man could have left you an untold fortune, bunny-hugs, and then you and I could live in the lap of luxury for the rest of our lives!'

Ricky turned to Jim and spread his arms wide. 'Can you believe this drivel? This is what I have to put up with, every day of my life. I leave coffee grounds up the side of my cup, and that means I'm going to sell one of my paintings for a record price. I haven't sold a fuckin' painting in months, not at *any* price.'

Jim checked his watch. 'Listen – I'd better leave you two in peace. I have a whole lot of preparation work to finish up for tomorrow.'

'Stay for some chamomile tea,' begged Nadine, taking hold of his arm and pressing her deflated breast against it. 'We have so few visitors, don't we, Ricky?'

'I really must go,' Jim told her. 'I have to take my cat for a walk.'

As he turned to leave, however, the red parakeet suddenly ruffled its feathers and let out a harsh, high-pitched squawk. '*Silence!*' it screamed. '*Silence!*'

Ricky snapped, 'Shut the fuck up, bird!' Then he turned to Jim and said, '"Silence" – that's the only word he knows. I've tried to teach him a couple of good old-fashioned cuss words, but all he says is "silence"!'

'*Silence!*' the parakeet screamed back at him. '*Silence!*'

As he walked along the landing past Apartment 2, the door suddenly opened and Summer stepped out. She managed to time her appearances almost to the second. She was blonde, tall, and stunningly pretty, with enormous blue eyes and a little ski-jump nose and naturally pouting lips.

This morning she was dressed more demurely than she usually was, in a pink roll-neck sweater with short sleeves, which didn't quite manage to reach down as far as her navel, and a pair of white deck shorts with turned-up cuffs.

'*Jimmy!* I thought you'd be at college!'

Jim gave her a kiss on each cheek. 'How's it going, Summer? How's the pole-dancing job?'

'Oh, didn't I tell you? I quit. A guy came in from the Starstruck Model Agency and offered me much better money to do modeling. I have my first shoot Monday.'

'I thought you enjoyed the pole dancing.'

'It's OK, but it's much more tiring than you think. And those horrible old men . . . they can never keep their paws to themselves. Why aren't you at college?'

'Oh . . . there was some kind of health-and-safety problem. We'll probably be back to normal tomorrow.'

Summer reached up and twisted his hair around her fingertip. 'So . . . if you're not doing anything this afternoon, maybe you could take me to the beach or something?'

'Summer . . . you know how much I like you, and I think you're the most gorgeous girl I ever met. But let's just keep it that way, shall we? You know, friends.'

'Friends can go to the beach together, can't they?'

'I've seen your bikinis, when you've been sunbathing. How long do you think that we could stay just friends if you wore one of those?'

'Oh come on, Jimmy. I had a Brazilian only yesterday. I haven't had the chance to try it out yet.'

Jim gave her another kiss. 'Get thee behind me, Satan. I'll see you later, OK – round about eight? Maybe we can have a drink at Barney's Beanery, and a bite to eat if you're hungry.'

'I'm hungry for *you,* Jimmy. You know that.'

'Stop teasing me, Summer. I'm just a tired old college teacher.'

Jim climbed the last flight of steps to his own apartment. He opened the front door and Tibbles immediately jumped off the kitchen table, as if he had been caught doing something wrong.

He came up to Jim and rubbed himself against his legs and gave him two or three ingratiating mews.

'What have you been doing that you feel so guilty about?' Jim asked him.

He walked through to his living room and unlocked the sliding door that gave out on to the balcony. Below him, in

the garden, a warm wind was rustling through the yuccas, and
Santana the gardener was bent over the flowerbeds, trying to
dig out a gopher hole. He looked up when Jim scraped one
of the chairs on the balcony, and waved his frayed straw hat.
Santana was young and very handsome in a Mexican gardener
kind of way, and Summer thought he was 'durr-vine.'

'*Hola, Señor Rook!*'

'*Por que trabajo tan duro?*' Jim called down. 'Why are you
working so hard? *Se volveran solamente!* They will only come
back!'

'*No cuido!* I don't care! *Todavia consigo pagado!* I still get
paid!'

Jim went back into the kitchen and opened his briefcase. At
least he would have the chance to finish preparing his lesson on
the poetry of Rachel X. Speed. He tipped the contents of his
briefcase on to the counter, and along with all of his files and
folders, the Paradise apple that Simon Silence had given him
rolled out, too, and almost dropped off the edge of the counter.

He caught it, and sniffed it again. Its pink and green colors
were slightly striped, almost like candy, and it had the most
enticing aroma. He took it across to the kitchen sink and
washed it, and then he picked up his file on Rachel X. Speed
and went back out on to the balcony, biting into the apple as
he went.

He sat down, opened the file, and spread out the poems in
a fan shape. Rachel X. Speed was a very edgy, difficult poet,
but he thought that her words would appeal to a class brought
up on rap and dubstep and grime.

He took another bite out of the apple. It was delicious, sweet
and crisp, but with a sharpness that reminded him of something
that he couldn't quite put his finger on. A person, more than
a taste. A person and a place. How strange was that? An apple
that brought back memories.

He was still reading and eating when Tibbles came out on
to the balcony. Tibbles mewed, and mewed again, and rubbed
himself up against his ankles.

'Tibbles for Christ's sake, you just had breakfast!'

It was then that Tibbles jumped up into his lap, crumpling
all of his papers.

'Tibs – what the hell are you doing?'

He lifted Tibbles up so that he could drop him back on to the floor, but then he saw the figure standing at the far end of his balcony. The same dark shadowy figure that he had seen in the smog this morning, and had almost run down.

It could have been made of black smoke, or black gauze. It seemed to float in tatters in the breeze. Tibbles crept slowly backward, his fur standing on end, and Jim himself felt a prickling sensation all the way down his back.

'*What*?' Jim demanded. 'What in hell are you?' He tried to sound stern, although his voice came out much weaker than he had intended. 'What are you doing here?'

There was a moment's pause, while the shadowy figure seemed to ebb and flow like a torn black cape caught on the tide.

Then it said, in a deep, vibrant voice, '*I have come for you. I have come for all of you. This time, none will escape me.*'

Jim wasn't sure if he had actually heard the figure talking, or whether the sound of its voice had vibrated through his bones.

The shadowy figure spiraled around, and then it seemed to flow off the balcony into the air, and vanish. Jim dropped what was left of his apple, which rolled across to the edge of the balcony and fell down into the garden.

FOUR

He leaned over the railing and called down to Santana, '*Usted vio eso*? Did you see that?'

The gardener looked up from his gopher-digging again and took off his hat. '*Qué*?'

'*Esa sombra* – that shadow.'

Santana stuck out his bottom lip and shook his head. '*Veo solamente la tierra, señor*. I see only the ground.'

Then, however, he crossed the neatly cropped grass and picked up Jim's half-eaten apple. '*Aqui – usted cayó su manzana.*'

'Here,' said Jim, holding out his hands. 'Throw it up to me, will you?'

Santana frowned and said, '*Usted lo quiere realmente*? You really want it?'

'Here,' Jim repeated. The gardener shrugged, and swung his arm back, and tossed it up to him.

Jim took the apple through to the kitchen and rinsed it. He doubted if there was any connection between his eating the apple and the shadow that had appeared on his balcony. But the apple's sweet-and-sour taste had provoked such a strange, elusive feeling – partly happiness, partly regret, like a song that unexpectedly brings tears to your eyes, and he badly wanted to know what it was.

He bit into it again, and slowly chewed it. Tibbles came up to him, sat down on the kitchen floor, and looked up at him with undisguised resentment, as if to say: *why can't you ever let me live a normal life, like every other cat, filling my belly with Instinctive Choice Shrimp Dinner and then allowing me to sprawl on the balcony in the afternoon sun, without some shadowy spirit appearing out of nowhere and making my fur stand on end*?

Jim finished the apple and dropped the core into the trash can under the sink. He closed his eyes for a moment, but he still couldn't think what memory it had evoked. He thought he could sense a warm wind, and a woman talking to him, and maybe some faraway music, like a calliope, but that was all.

He spent the rest of the afternoon sketching out his lesson on Rachel X. Speed, and her poem *Street Life*.

> 'Wherever I walk, whoever I meet
> They turn their back and won't catch my eye.
> Love on the street? No such thing.
> It's all suspicion. It's all mistrust.
> It's all graffiti and wrecks and rust.'

He hardly noticed the sun going down, but suddenly his doorbell jangled and he realized that it was almost dark. Tibbles raised his head and looked at him with his eyes narrowed. *Don't answer that. It might be a shadowy specter.*

He went through to the hallway, switching on the light. Through the hammered-glass porthole in his front door he could see a heap of blonde hair, with two pink ribbons in it, so he knew at once who it was.

He opened the door and said, 'Summer – come on in. You're early.'

'I know, Jimmy. But I was bored. Life is so boring sometimes. I blame God.'

'You blame *God*?'

'Well – He didn't think of enough things to keep us entertained, did He? He was resting on the seventh day when he should of been making up stuff like different funny animals and upside-down rainbows and birds that flew backward.'

'Even if He'd done that, Summer, you would have grown used to them by now, and you'd still be bored. Nice outfit, though. Very unboring. We're only going to Barney's Beanery, though. Not space.'

Summer was wearing a silver short-sleeved jacket with a high collar and a zipper down the front that was open as far as her navel. She also wore tight silver pants and little silver boots with turned-down tops and very high heels.

'That's what I love about you, Jimmy. You're so iconic.'

'Laconic, sweetheart. But, good try.'

He spooned out the last of Tibbles' shrimp dinner, and refilled his bowl of milk. Then he shrugged on his tan leather coat and he and Summer left his apartment and went down the steps to his car. The evening was unusually humid, and over the Santa Monica Mountains they could see flickers of lightning, like snakes' tongues.

'I had such a scary nightmare last night,' said Summer, as they drove southward on North Gower Street. She shifted herself closer to Jim and her silver pants made a squeaky noise on the vinyl seat. 'I dreamed that I was standing in line with all of these hundreds of people and it was all dark all around us. Up ahead, though, I could see this orange light, like a bonfire? And it was *hot*, too, like a bonfire. Well, more like a furnace. I said to the guy in front of me, why are we all standing in line like this? I don't want to be here. I want to be home in bed.'

'So what did he say?'

'He said, "We have to be here. It's the end." So I said, "The end of what?" And he said, "It's the end of all of us. It's arrived."'

Jim looked at her for about two seconds too long, and almost rear-ended a Toyota Prius at the intersection with Hollywood Boulevard.

'That was some nightmare,' he told her. 'Maybe you saw something on TV that triggered it off? Or it could have been something you ate? I always have nightmares when I eat fajitas.'

Summer shook her head. 'It was more like, *Biblical*, if you know what I mean.'

'Yes, I think I do. Like Armageddon, the end of the world as we know it.'

As if to emphasize what he was saying, the lightning flickered again, much closer this time, and they heard the indigestive rumbling of thunder.

They parked outside Barney's Beanery on Santa Monica Boulevard and pushed their way in through the double doors. Although it was only 7.30, the bar was crowded and the music was playing at top volume. They made their way through to the big room at the back and found themselves a seat in the corner. Heads turned as Summer walked past, and there was an appreciative chorus of whoops and whistles.

Every inch of the inside of Barney's Beanery was covered in beer advertisements and license plates and Route 66 signs and newspaper cuttings, even on the ceiling. The two pool tables were already taken, so that their conversation was punctuated by the intermittent clacking of balls.

Jim ordered a mimosa for Summer and a Fat Tire beer for himself, and asked to see the eight-page newspaper-sized menu, which boasted that 'If we don't have it, you don't want it.'

'Listen – I wouldn't worry about that nightmare,' Jim said to Summer. 'I don't think the end of the world is coming any time soon. Not in our lifetime, anyhow.'

'I don't know,' said Summer. 'I *never* have nightmares like that. All I dream about is sex, mostly. And dancing.'

Whenever Jim came to Barney's, he usually chose the Fireman's Chili, but this evening for some reason he didn't feel at all hungry. In fact he felt completely full, and slightly nauseous, too, as if he had been eating and drinking too much all day, and needed to go to the men's room and stick his finger down his throat.

Summer asked for the Mediterranean Salad, but with seasoned fries on the side. She cupped both breasts with her hands and said, 'I can't give up the carbs altogether. I don't want to get flat chested.'

'Summer, the Mojave Desert will freeze over before you get flat chested.'

'So what are you eating?'

'I don't know. Nothing for now.'

It seemed to Jim that the talking and laughing and music was growing progressively louder. He found himself having to shout at Summer to make himself heard, and he could hardly hear what she was saying back to him. He began to feel more and more nauseous, and when he took his first swallow of beer out of the bottle, it immediately came back up again and filled up his mouth, so that he had to swallow it a second time, flat and warm and far too sweet.

A large balding man in a horn-rimmed eyeglasses and a pea-green suit was sitting on his left, and talking very loudly with his friends. 'This script is shit, that's what I told him. *The Second Coming*? Jesus is working as a mechanic for American Brake and Muffler? If that had been Satan, working for Century Twenty-One, then I could have believed it!'

Summer was frowning at him. 'Are you OK, Jimmy? You're looking kind of bloopy.'

'I'll be all right. My stomach's a little upset, that's all.'

As he said that, however, something drew his eye toward the long wooden bar at the front of the restaurant. All of the twelve red-leather bucket seats were filled with drinkers, most of them laughing and leaning on the counter. But almost at the far end, one of them had turned his seat around so that he was staring directly in Jim's direction.

Jim stared back at him. There was no question about it – he was the same man whose face kept appearing in Ricky's painting. He was blond, and very pale, and dressed entirely in white. White linen shirt, white linen pants, and sandals. He looked very much like Simon Silence, except that he was older, like The Storyteller. He was smiling at Jim as if he were taunting him.

The waitress came up with Summer's salad and her bowl of seasoned fries. Jim said, 'Give me a moment, Summer, would you? There's somebody here I have to talk to.'

'Jimmy – are you *sure* you're OK? You're acting so antsy.'

'I'm fine. I really am. I have to talk to this guy, that's all.'

As he got up from the table, however, he knew that he wasn't fine at all. He felt suddenly hot, and very angry. He had never felt so angry in his life about anything. He elbowed two customers out of the way as he made his way through to the bar, and one of them said, 'Hey – watch who you're pushing, dude!' Jim ignored him and headed straight for the man in white.

The man in white stayed where he was, still smiling that calm, taunting smile. Jim went right up to him and said, '*What?*'

'I'm sorry, my friend,' the man replied. 'Is something troubling you?' His accent, like Simon Silence's, was distinctly Southern. The pupils of his eyes were so pale that they were like blue glass pebbles that had been washed for years in the ocean. Jim noticed that around his neck he wore several gold chains, with medallions and stars attached to them. The largest medallion had the face of a woman on it, with staring eyes.

Jim could hardly catch his breath, as if he had run all the way to the restaurant. He didn't know this man at all, except that he looked like Simon Silence, and could well have been his father, the Reverend John Silence. Yet for some reason he had provoked him into such a boiling fury that, when he spoke, he was almost incoherent.

'You were looking at me,' he panted. He turned around and pointed to the table where Summer was just starting to eat her salad. She smiled at him and give him a little finger-wave. 'I was sitting over there, right? – and you – you were *looking* at me.'

The man ran his fingers through his thinning blond curls. 'I think you're mistaken, my friend. I was miles away. I was looking into the future, not at you.'

Jim grasped the man's shirt and twisted it, pulling him closer. 'You – were – fucking – *looking* – at me.'

The man said, 'All right. Supposing I was. This is a restaurant, open to the public. There's no law that says the customers can't look at each other.'

'*You were looking at me!*' Jim screamed at him, right into his face. '*Don't pretend you weren't! You were looking at me and I want to know why!*'

The barman said, 'Hey, buddy. That's enough. Go back to your seat and shut up or I'll throw you out.'

Jim turned to the barman and screamed at him, too. 'What the *fuck* do you know? This man – this man here – he's in a painting! My friend wants to paint The Storyteller and what happens every time he tries to paint this jolly old man? He gets *him*! Him and his creepy white face! And now I come in here for a drink and here he is again – looking at me! How did he know I was coming here? Ask him that! And ask him why he's looking at me! *Ask him!*'

A dark-haired, smooth-looking man in a red shirt came up

behind Jim and gripped his arm, very hard. 'OK, sir, let's head for the exit, shall we?'

Jim tried to twist himself free, but the smooth-looking man was extremely strong.

'Ask him,' Jim insisted. His chest was heaving with rage and breathlessness. 'Ask him why he was looking at me, go on!'

'I'm sorry, sir, I don't know who you're talking about. Now, let's go quietly, OK? I'm sure you don't want me to call the cops.'

Jim turned back to the man in white, but there was no man in white, only an empty barstool. He looked around the bar in bewilderment, and then toward the exit, to see if the man in white was walking away down the street. But the sidewalk was deserted, apart from a woman with an undulating bottom walking her over-clipped poodle.

'You didn't see him?' said Jim. 'He was sitting right here, and you didn't see him?'

'Let's go, sir. Please.'

Conversation and laughter in the restaurant had completely died, with curious customers craning their necks to see what was going on. There was only the music playing, *Werewolves of London*. Summer had obviously heard Jim shouting and now left her seat and came tripping up to him in her little silver boots. 'Jimmy, what's *wrong*? Jimmy?'

'This gentleman is just leaving, ma'am,' said the smooth-looking man. His grip on Jim's arm was unrelenting.

'I *told* him he looked bloopy,' said Summer.

The smooth-looking man escorted Jim outside. 'Whatever you ordered, it's on the house,' he said. 'Just one thing, though. Don't ever come back. Either you or your girlfriend *or* your imaginary enemy.'

Jim and Summer walked back to his car. Jim didn't start the engine at first, but sat behind the wheel with his head bowed, trying to make some sense of what had just happened to him. Summer stroked and tugged his hair at the back of his neck.

'You'll be OK, Jimmy. It's stress, that's all. Starting a new semester and everything. You're a very sensitive man, that's what I love about you. You can't help it if you go nuts now and again.'

'Oh, thanks,' said Jim. 'So you didn't see him, either? That man in white, sitting at the bar?'

'I saw you there, but nobody else. I wasn't really looking, to tell you the truth. I dropped an olive down the front of my jacket and I was trying to hook it out.'

Jim drove back to Briarcliff Road, and walked Summer back up to her apartment. Thunder was still banging away, over the mountains, but it was further east now.

'I'm sorry I spoiled your evening,' he said. 'Maybe you're right, and I am going nuts.'

'I could always come up for a drink,' Summer suggested.

Jim kissed her cheek and said, 'Not tonight, sweetheart. Tonight, I think I need Pepto-Bismol and Pachelbel's "Canon in D", in that order.'

Summer put her arms around him and kissed him on the lips. 'One day,' she whispered, in his ear.

Jim trudged up the last flight of steps. He felt exhausted, as if he had been teaching a rowdy class all day. He didn't turn around as he unlocked his front door, or else he would have seen the man in white standing on the opposite side of the road, his linen pants flapping in the evening breeze, smiling at him still.

'I'm very, very pleased with you, Mr Rook,' he said, under his breath, although he may not have been talking entirely to himself. 'You're coming along famously.'

FIVE

Next morning he was woken up at 7.11 by Tibbles jumping up on to his chest.

'*Aaahhh*!' he shouted, and sat bolt upright. Tibbles weighed over six pounds, and had badly winded him, but more than that, he had abruptly jolted him out of his dream.

He had been wandering around the college parking lot in a dense yellow smog, trying to find his car. It was no longer in his usual parking space – or rather Royston Denman's space – but he couldn't imagine who would have wanted to move it, apart from Royston Denman. On the other hand, Royston Denman had given up complaining about it years ago, especially since these days he had become a climate-change fanatic and usually came to college by bicycle, wearing a streamlined helmet.

Jim couldn't imagine who would have wanted to *steal* it, either. A 1971 Mercury Marquis, in metallic green? Hardly a collector's car. You could pick one up online for less than twenty-five hundred dollars.

He was almost about to give up looking for it when he heard the low whistling noise of its 7.1-liter engine. Someone had moved it, but they were parked somewhere close by, as if they were patiently waiting for him to find them.

He followed the sound of the engine until the car gradually took shape through the smog. It was parked at an angle close to the entrance to the parking lot, with exhaust smoke billowing out its tailpipe. Its passenger door was wide open. It reminded Jim of the folk story told by the Irish poet W.B. Yeats about the death coach that arrives outside your house when you are about to die, the *cóiste bodhar*, and waits outside with its door open to take you away, because it cannot return to the underworld empty.

Jim approached his car warily. As he came nearer, he bent down so that he could see who was sitting in the driving seat. When he did, he immediately felt a crawling sensation all over his scalp, as if he had lice.

It was the shadowy figure that he had almost run over, and which had appeared on his balcony. He was shocked to see it sitting there, but for some reason he felt less afraid of it now than he had been when he had seen it yesterday. It seemed more solid now, more definite, although its cloak still seemed to flow and ripple as if it were being blown by an unfelt wind, and its face was concealed by a deep, floppy hood. Its left hand was resting loosely on top of the steering wheel, covered by a gray suede glove. On top of the glove, on its wedding finger, it was wearing an elaborate silver ring, like a mass of intertwined snakes.

'*Where would you like me to take you, Mr Rook?*' the figure asked him, in that reverberating voice. '*A man with your gift – he could go anyplace he chose, believe me.*'

'Who are you?' Jim demanded. 'What do you want? This is my car, Charlie, not yours. If I want to go anyplace, I'll drive there myself, thanks.'

'*Aha – but you can never go to the places to which I can take you,*' the shadowy figure replied. It turned its head slightly, and as it did so, Jim saw two glittering eyes inside the darkness of its hood.

At that moment, Tibbles sprang on to his bedcover and he sat up in shock.

He called Dr Ehrlichman's secretary, Rosa, and asked her if college was going to be open today.

'Absolutely,' she said. 'You won't be going back to your usual room, though, until the crime-scene people have finished with it, and it's all been cleaned up and redecorated. We've relocated you to Art Studio Four, on the second floor.'

'Art Studio Four? *Art Studio Four*? That's nothing but an expletive deleted storeroom.'

'I'm sorry. Dr Ehrlichman said to tell you that the college is oversubscribed this year and we don't have any other class-rooms free. By the way, you won't miss his assembly this morning, will you?'

'Of course not.'

'You *will* miss it, Jim. I know you.'

'I'll try my best, Rosa. But I've always been allergic to Dr

Ehrlichman's inspirational speeches. And his academic fore-
casts, too. They bring on my asthma, and I don't even suffer
from asthma. I can't even predict what I'm going to have for
lunch, let alone what grades my students are going to get a
year from now.'

'Please try, Jim. It will make him so much happier.'

'Rosa – you can only be happier if you're happy to begin with.'

'Well, all right. It will make him marginally less grouchy.'

Jim made himself a Swiss-cheese-and-tomato sandwich for
breakfast. He would rather have had pastrami, but he had used
it all up yesterday and there was nothing else left in the fridge.
He would almost have preferred to share Tibbles' turkey dinner,
which actually smelled quite tasty. Tibbles didn't even look
up at him, even when he tucked his briefcase under his arm
and went to the front door and said, 'Later, you obscenely fat
cat.' Tibbles had his head in his dish, gobbling.

As Jim drove to college, his thoughts kept going around
and around like some nauseating carousel ride that wouldn't
come to an end, no matter how much he wanted to get off.
Again and again he saw that dark shadowy figure, twisting
off his balcony like smoke; and the same shadowy figure in
last night's dream about his car. Those glittering eyes, inside
that hood. Again and again he pictured the nightmare that
Summer had described to him, about lines of people shuffling
toward the final fiery furnace. Then he saw the pale self-
satisfied face that kept appearing in Ricky's portrait of The
Storyteller, in spite of all his efforts to paint him differently,
and the same man in white, sitting at the bar yesterday evening,
mocking him.

He didn't want to think about what had happened at the
restaurant because it was too embarrassing. You had to be seriously off your head to get yourself barred from Barney's Beanery.

All the same, he couldn't help thinking that all of these nightmares and all of these incidents were somehow entangled with
each other, like the tangled-up snakes on the shadowy figure's
ring. It was impossible to distinguish where dreams ended and
reality began. Or maybe they weren't dreams. Maybe they were
all real – the shadowy figure and the man in white and Summer's
nightmare about Armageddon. Or maybe *none* of them was real.

Or maybe they were just coincidences and Summer was right and he was going nuts.

It required some complicated maneuvering, but he managed to park his car in the space marked J. ROOK. Somehow he didn't feel like tempting fate by parking in Royston Denman's space. It wasn't smoggy this morning, unlike his dream, but you never knew. He made sure he locked his car, too, because he never usually bothered. He didn't want to come back at the end of the day and find some shadowy character in a hood sitting in the driver's seat, offering to drive him to God alone knows where.

He was too late for Dr Ehrlichman's assembly, of course, which was partly due to the crawling traffic along Sunset, and partly due to the fact that he had deliberately left his apartment about ten minutes too late to make it in time.

He climbed the two flights of stairs to the second floor and walked along to the end of the corridor to Art Studio Four. Assembly hadn't finished yet, so the building was empty, and his footsteps echoed.

Before he opened the battered, blue-painted door, he peered through the porthole. Instead of the separate desks of Special Class Two, there were four long benches, all of them spattered with inks and paints of every conceivable color. The walls were hung with scores of paintings and portraits – landscapes and abstracts and odd-looking animals by students who seemed to believe that horses had legs as thin as golf clubs and bodies the shape of overstuffed couches.

There were shelves on either side of the studio, too, crowded with sculptures and pottery in various stages of completion. Most of the human figures were lumpy and misshapen, more like trolls than people, and the jugs and bowls looked as if they been molded during a disastrous out-take of the pottery scene in *Ghost*.

Jim did one thing more before he opened the door. He craned his head and looked up toward the ceiling. If there was anybody nailed up there, with or without cats, he wasn't going to go inside. All he could see, however, was a grubby plastered ceiling with cracks in it, and a small lizard, and two fluorescent tubes hanging down.

He went in. Art Studio Four smelled strongly of oil paint and dried clay and damp dishrags, so he went across and opened the windows. From the second floor, he could see the windows of his own classroom, Special Class Two, and three figures in white protective suits moving around inside it. Outside Special Class Two, there was a grassy slope, which rose gradually up to a small grove of five or six eucalyptus trees, surrounded by a scattering of dry fallen leaves.

To his surprise, Simon Silence was standing underneath these trees, his arms spread wide. He was wearing a white shirt and white linen pants and sandals, just like yesterday, and his white canvas sack was lying by his feet. It was difficult for Jim to see clearly at this distance, but he looked as if he had his eyes shut, and he was chanting, or singing.

Whatever he was doing, Simon Silence too had missed Dr Ehrlichman's assembly, but then Jim reckoned that *he* wasn't in any position to complain about that. And Simon Silence was the son of a pastor, after all. Maybe this was the way he always started his day, by praying or singing hymns. Just because Jim thought that praying to God was futile, that didn't mean that he disapproved of anybody else doing it. Jim thought that buying lottery tickets was equally futile, but that didn't mean that some people didn't occasionally get lucky.

He laid his briefcase down on his desk, opened it up, and took out fifteen freshly printed copies of his grammar questionnaires. He thumbed through them, ready to hand them out, but then he had second thoughts and tucked them back into his briefcase again. After seeing at least some of his new class sitting outside the college grounds yesterday, listening to Simon Silence, he thought that he might start the morning differently, and read them a poem by Rachel X. Speed instead. He didn't quite understand why, but he had a feeling that he might learn more about them by listening to their reactions to *A New Language of Love* than he would by watching them struggle to work out the difference between 'pour' and 'pore' – as in, *'DuWayne poured over his books all evening.'*

He sat down at his own desk. It was antique, and made of pine – small and square and covered with almost as much ink and paint as the students' four benches. Some bored art teacher had used felt-tip pens to draw a highly detailed doodle of a naked woman on it, with a large green snake entwined around her. The woman was blindfolded, so that she couldn't see how the snake was triumphantly leering at her.

Underneath, the doodler had written the letters πειρασμός, but even though Jim knew a smattering of words in Greek, like κεμπάπ (which meant kebab), he had no idea what this meant. Beware of blind bends?

He tried to open the desk drawer. It was jammed at first, but he managed to wrench it from side to side and at last it came out. Inside was a roll of Scotch tape, a half-finished pack of fruit Life Savers, and a dog-eared copy of *Hustler* magazine for June, 2009.

He was just leafing through the center-spread pictorial of a bosomy young woman named Alexis Ford when the studio door burst open and a diminutive girl with frizzy black hair and upswept eyeglasses came staggering in, carrying in her arms an oversized, grubby white teddy bear with the Star of David on its T-shirt. She was wearing a pond-green cardigan over a drab gray dress, and brown shoes that looked almost like hiking boots.

She stopped and stared at Jim and his copy of *Hustler* and said, in a very nasal voice, 'Oh, *zay moykhl*! I'm sorry. I guess I shoulda knocked.'

Jim tossed the magazine back in the drawer but then he had to struggle for a few seconds to close it again. 'Don't even think about it. That was research, that's all.'

'Oh, research. OK,' said the girl, although she clearly didn't believe him. Then she said, 'You don't mind my bringing Nudnik into class? It's only for today. I'm going to auction him this evening for Lev LaLev – you know, the charity for orphan girls in Israel.'

'Your bear's name is *Nudnik*?'

'Because that's what he is, he's a nuisance. My grandfather called him that because he's so big and he was always tripping over him.'

'I see. So what's *your* name?'

'Rebecca Teitelbaum. My mom and dad were both killed in an air crash in Israel when I was only three so I was brought up by my grandparents who are very kind people but their English is pretty *schlecht*. That's why they put me in Special

Class Two. I want to do international charity work so I have to learn English real good.'

'That's very laudable, Rebecca. You and Nudnik, find yourselves a couple of seats anyplace you like. Mind if I call you Becky?'

'Yes.'

'Yes you mind, or yes I can call you Becky?'

'Yes, I mind.'

As she went to sit down, Jim pulled a sad clown face behind her back. Then he pushed back his chair and went over to the dusty old blackboard on the wall behind his desk and started to write out *Rachel X. Speed, born 1981 in Schaumburg, Ill. Winner, Ruth Lilly Poetry Award, 2007.*

Before he had finished, the door opened again and more students came jostling their way in, swaggering and laughing. Jim recognized at once the tall African-American boy he had seen outside, under the cypress tree. Today he wasn't wearing a droopy gray tracksuit but a droopy pale-blue tracksuit. He walked with a shuffling lope, swinging his arms, as if he could hear hip-hop music in his head. He had an unusually tall head, too, with a haircut that rose straight up from the top of it like a cylindrical black smokestack.

'Good morning,' said Jim. 'Want to tell me who you are?'

'Sure,' the boy grinned at him. 'Soon as you tell me who *you* are.'

Jim gave him a tight, puckered-up smile. 'I think you already know who I am. I'm the man who can have you kicked out of this class so fast you won't even have time to learn A for Asshole.'

The boy stared at him for a very long time, and then said, 'OK. DaJon – DaJon Johnson.'

'Go find yourself someplace to sit, DaJon. Right at the back, preferably, so that your lofty coiffure doesn't interfere with anybody else's line of sight.'

'My *wha'* choo say?'

'Your hair, stupid. Go sit down.'

DaJon lope-shuffled to the very back of the studio and sat down on the opposite end of the fourth bench, as far away from Rebecca Teitelbaum and Nudnik as he could, and sprawled out his legs.

The remaining students of Special Class Two came through the door, including the girl with the scraggly blonde curls, who was wearing an even tighter T-shirt today, in turquoise this time, with shiny silver sprinkles; and the red-haired boy with the raging acne. In all, Jim counted eight boys and five girls. He would namecheck them all later, but he was always forgetting his students' names, even when he had found out what they were. Most of the time he privately gave them nicknames, like Crater Face and Jolie Lips and Clarissa Broad-ass and Sammy The Squint, although he tried hard not to use them to their face.

'OK,' he said, raising his hand for silence. 'Any one of you here know what "zythum" is?'

Almost all of the students shook their heads, and shrugged, and said 'zythum?' 'zythum?' until the classroom sounded like a beehive. But after a few moments, one boy hesitantly lifted his hand and said, 'Yes, sir. Me.' He wore round spectacles held together by a Band-Aid on the bridge of his nose, and a maroon T-shirt that looked as if it had been attacked by a swarm of ravenous moths.

'You do?' said Jim. 'That's pretty amazing. What's your name, son?'

'Kyle Baxter the Third, sir.'

'All right then, Kyle Baxter the Third, what's the answer?'

'Zythum is a type of malted beer, sir, that used to be brewed in ancient Egypt.'

Jim was completely taken aback. 'How the *hell* do you know that, if you don't my asking?'

Kyle Baxter blushed, and glanced quickly around him in obvious discomfort. 'I read dictionaries, sir,' he said, his voice dropping to a mumble. 'I read dictionaries and I learn all the words.'

'You read dictionaries and you learn all the words? You certainly don't have to be embarrassed about that, Kyle. Well done. That's great. *Unusual,* I admit – but highly commendable.'

'Yes, sir. I really like words.'

Jim waited, and then said, '*But*? There has to be a "but", Kyle, or else you wouldn't be here in Special Class Two.'

Kyle blushed even redder, and began to tug at his T-shirt. 'I *know* the words, sir. I know all of the words. It's just that I find it hard to put them in the right order. Especially when I'm trying to write them down.'

'Hey, man!' called out a Hispanic boy sitting at the end of the third bench, 'I find it hard to put them in the *wrong* order, and I don't even know them to begin with, like what you do!'

Everybody laughed, and Jim said, 'Don't you worry, Kyle. By the end of this year, you'll be writing like Herman Melville.'

'Herman who?' asked a pretty African-American girl sitting right at the front, with her hair crowded with colored beads. 'Is he that cookery guy on TV?'

Jim smiled and shook his head. 'Herman Melville was an author who wrote a classic novel called *Moby Dick*.'

'What's that about?' sang out one of the boys. '*Moby Dick*? Sounds like an STD to me. Gotta go to the clinic, man, I got this real moby dick.'

Jim suddenly realized that Simon Silence hadn't yet appeared. He walked slowly down the right-hand side of the art studio toward the window, to see if he was still outside, under the eucalyptus trees.

As he walked, he told his class, abstractedly, 'To be honest – I didn't actually *expect* you to know what "zythum" is. In fact, even *I* didn't know that it was some kind of beer. All I *did* know was that it's the very last word in the dictionary.'

He reached the window and looked out. There was nobody there, apart from one of the groundskeepers, on a ride-on mower.

'The last word,' he repeated, turning around and walking back toward his desk. 'That's why you're here in Special Class Two – so that *you* can have the last word. You won't only be learning how to spell words, and how to arrange them into sentences that really sing. You'll be learning how to use words in such a way that nobody will ever be able to put you down again for the way you speak or the things you write.

'You won't have to win arguments by yelling louder than anybody else, or threatening to beat up on them. You'll win them because you'll know how to express yourself clearly, and dramatically, and well. Gene Kelly sang *I Got Rhythm*. I'm going to give *you* "zythum" – all of you. I'm going to give you the last word.'

'Gene Kelly?' frowned the African-American girl in the front row. 'Who's she?'

As Jim reached his desk, the studio door opened, and Simon Silence made an entrance.

'Ah, Simon,' said Jim. 'Glad you could join us.'

But Simon Silence stood in the doorway with his arms spread wide, in the same way that he had been standing under the eucalyptus trees. His eyes were bright and unfocused, as if he were staring into the distance, and he was smiling a beatific smile. In his white shirt and white pants and sandals, he looked almost like Jesus.

Jim was about to tell him to find a place to sit down when the African-American girl clasped her hands together as if she were praying and lowered her head until it almost touched the workbench in front of her. Then, one after another, the remaining students did the same, even Rebecca Teitelbaum, as if they were all paying homage.

Jim stared at all of his students in disbelief. Then he turned back to Simon Silence to ask him if he knew what the hell this meant.

For a fraction of a second – and it was so quick that he couldn't be sure that it wasn't an optical illusion – he thought that Simon Silence's sandaled feet were actually *floating* about a half inch above the floor. But then Simon Silence looked at him, and took a step forward, and said, 'Mr Rook – I'm so sorry I'm late. I had to have a word with my father.'

Jim turned back to the rest of the class. They were all sitting up now, or slouching, or leaning back in their chairs and chewing gum, as if nothing had happened.

'Not the *last* word,' Simon Silence added, still smiling. 'It's not quite time for the last word yet. But it will be soon. Sooner than you think.'

With that, he lifted his white sack off his shoulder, reached inside it and produced another pink-and-green apple.

'This is for you, sir. Paradise.'

SIX

For a moment, Jim didn't know if he ought to accept the apple or not. But Simon Silence continued to hold it out to him, with that strange radiant look on his face, and Jim thought: *it's only an apple, for Christ's sake.* And besides, he was really interested to find out if it had that same sweet-and-sour taste as the apple that he had eaten yesterday, and what it was that taste brought to mind.

A woman talking, a warm wind blowing. A calliope playing someplace far, far away. And for some reason, a feeling of infinite regret – regret for something that he should have done, but never had.

'OK, Simon, thanks,' he said, taking the apple and placing it on his desk. 'Now, why don't you find yourself a seat so that we can get on with what we all came here to learn – English for people who are not too good at it?'

Simon Silence made his way to the third bench back. The Hispanic boy who was sitting on the end immediately stood up so that he could make his way to the middle of the bench. *Almost the geopolitical center of the classroom,* thought Jim. All the other students turned around as Simon Silence sat down and opened up his sack, and he gave a benign smile to each of them in turn.

Jim said, loudly, 'Any of you people want to tell me what all that kowtowing was all about, when Mr Silence here came into the room?'

Simon Silence was setting out a neat row of different-colored felt-tip pens. 'It was not "kowtowing", sir. They were simply showing their friendship and respect.'

'This isn't downtown Kyoto, Simon. This is West Hollywood. In West Hollywood, we show friendship and respect by shaking hands, or punching fists, or high fiving. We don't *bow* to each other, OK?'

Simon Silence gave an almost imperceptible shrug, 'My

father said that if a person is a living representative of a higher power, sir, then there is nothing demeaning in bowing one's head. You are bowing to the higher power, not to the person himself.'

'Oh, I see. So you think that you're the living representative of a higher power? And which higher power would *that* be, exactly?'

Simon Silence looked around at his fellow students. They were all smiling back at him. 'Yesterday I talked to almost all of my new classmates, sir – together and individually. I think most of them already share a similar vision.'

'OK,' said Jim, 'enough of this spiritual malarkey. In this class, Special Class Two, there is only one higher power, and that higher power is called M-E, me. My name, for those who don't already know it, is Jim Rook, and if you want to express my purpose here in a spiritual way, I will be doing my best during the coming college year to lead you out of the wilderness of street slang and text speak and general illiteracy into the promised land of nouns and verbs and adjectives and sentences that actually make some kind of sense.'

A pale-skinned African-American boy sitting right in front of Simon Silence put up his hand. He had a long face and bulging eyes and wing-nut ears with at least half a dozen gold earrings in each of them.

'Hate to say this, sir, but that sound to me like a whole shitload of hard work for nothing. Nobody never has no trouble understanding me now. I make good enough sense.'

'What's your name, son?' Jim asked him.

'Jordy Brown, sir.'

'Whose face is that on your T-shirt, Jordy?'

'Snoop Dogg, sir.'

'Well, to give him his proper name, it's Calvin Cordozar Broadus, Junior. But do you know what Calvin Cordozar Broadus, Junior, is most famous for saying?'

Jordy Brown grinned broadly. 'Yes, sir, he say that Britney would make a better prostitute than Christina cause she's thicker.'

'Yes, he said that. But he also said that if the only job you can get is flipping burgers at McDonalds, make sure that you're the best burger flipper that ever was. Like, *ever* – in the whole history of burger flippery.'

'I ain't goin' to flip no burgers at McDonalds, sir. Not never.'

'Maybe not. Don't count on it. But you *are* going to be speaking and writing English for the rest of your life, so make sure you're the best English speaker and writer you can possibly be.'

Jordy Brown twisted around to look at Simon Silence, as if he were appealing for a second opinion, but Simon Silence simply raised one of his blond, almost-invisible eyebrows, and shrugged. Jim thought: *at least somebody in this classroom knows that I'm talking sense, even if he doesn't talk much sense himself.*

'Right,' he said, turning to the blackboard. 'Here we see the name of Rachel X. Speed, an award-winning poet who made her name by writing very gritty, in-your-face kind of poems. She wrote about stuff that poets don't usually write about, like losing babies and falling in love with other women and falling in love with all the wrong men.

'This poem is called *A New Language of Love* and when I've finished reading it to you, I want you each to write down what you think of it. One sentence will be enough. Three sentences will be plenty, but – hey – don't think that I'm stopping you from writing more if you want to. You can write me a whole book if you like.'

He opened the slim, black-bound collection of Rachel X. Speed's poetry and started to read.

'You came home last night.
My love, my lover.
You came up the stairs and I opened the door wide to
  welcome you.

You hit me.
You said not a single word, not even that you hated me.

I sit here now, watching you sleep.
My love, my lover.
Trying to understand what you were telling me.

It's three a.m.
On the other side of the room hangs a portrait of me
An oval portrait that moves when I move.
And writes, whenever I write.
A portrait that shows what you have done to me by
    hitting me so hard
Both of my eyes are crimson, like a clown's, and my
    lips are split
My love, my lover.

I always believed you when you said you loved me
So, when you stopped talking to me –
When you started hitting me instead
What was I to think?
You didn't leave me, so you must have found
A new way to tell me how you cared.
A new language of love, called "hit".

I am trying so hard to learn it
My love, my lover.
But, please, give me time.

No other language, as you learn it, makes you cry like
    this.'

Jim closed the book and looked around. Some of the class
were obviously baffled. Some looked completely indifferent,
staring up the ceiling or frowning at their fingernails as if they
hadn't really been listening. A few of them, though, appeared
to be upset. The pretty African-American girl with the beaded
hair who was sitting in front of him had tears sparkling in her
long false eyelashes, and was rummaging around in her beaded
purse for a tissue.

   Jim dragged his chair around and sat close to her. 'Hey,' he
said, 'The poem wasn't meant to make *you* cry. What's your
name, sweetheart?'

   'Jesmeka,' she told him, dabbing her eyes. 'Jesmeka Watson.
Oh, shoot, there goes my frickin' eyelash again.'

   Jim waited while she carefully peeled off her upper-left

eyelash, and then he said, 'So, Jesmeka – how did that poem make you feel? If you were to write down something about it, what would you say?'

'It's the same as my sister Donisha and this guy she's living with, exceptin' Donisha has a little baby boy to take care of, too.'

'Really?'

Jesmeka nodded, and sniffed. 'Every night he comes home and either he's high or he's drunk or else he's both, and he hits her just like the guy in the poem. And she's always the same, with the split lips and the swelled-up eyes, and I keep telling her, kick the frickin' loser *out*, girl, or else call the cops on him. But she always says he can't help it, he's depressed because he don't have no job to go to, and him hitting her, that shows at least that he cares about her. She says she loves him and couldn't bear to lose him – or worse still, if he just ignored her, like she didn't even exist.'

Jim laid his hand on top of hers and patted it. 'I'm sorry, Jesmeka. I hope things work out all right for her. I didn't mean to distress you like that. If you ever need any help – or your sister does – I'm always here. I know a whole lot of counselors of various kinds and I know a whole lot of cops, too. Tough cops, with nightsticks, who don't particularly care for men who beat up on women. They call themselves the Nosebreakers.'

He stood up and dragged his chair back behind his desk. He scanned the classroom for a while, as if he were searching for survivors at sea, and then he pointed to the boy who was sitting directly behind Jesmeka. This boy was white, and skinny, with a dirty-blond pompadour that stuck right up in the air, like a cartoon of somebody who had been scared by a ghost. He was quite good-looking in a starved, James Dean way. He was furiously chewing gum and texting on his iPhone.

'What's your name?' he asked him.

The boy kept on texting until he realized that the classroom had gone silent and that everybody was staring at him. He looked around and said, 'What?'

'I hope that message is of vital national importance,' said Jim.

'This message?'

'*That* message.'

Jim walked around and picked up the boy's iPhone. On the screen, he had written: 'BTD CU 2nite @ Rage AEAP maybe 8 we can do sum 420 then find sum kitty.'

'I see,' said Jim, putting the iPhone down. 'You're bored to death, are you?'

The boy pulled a face and said, 'Doing this medium English stuff, that wasn't my idea. My old man said I had to, so I didn't wind up like him.'

'*Remedial* English,' Jim corrected him. '"Remedial" meaning special teaching for people who can't tell the difference between angel and angle, and think that dirt gets pushed around in a wheelbarrel, and who can't tell kitty from pussy, for that matter.'

The boy shifted in his chair and said, 'I listened to the poem.'

'That's good. It's good that you listened. Listening is always a pretty good first step in learning something. What's your name, son?'

'Rudy Cascarelli.'

'Any relation to the pizza-making Cascarellis?'

'Like, second cousins or something. I don't know. My old man's a bus driver.'

'OK, Rudy. You listened to the poem. What did you think?'

Rudy Cascarelli stayed silent for so long that the class began to shuffle their feet and talk amongst themselves. At last, he said, 'She musta done *something*. I mean the woman that wrote it, just because she don't tell you in the pome what it was, that don't mean she didn't. Maybe she gave him this real crap sandwich to take to work. Like baloney or something. My old man hates baloney. He hit my mom once, when she made him a baloney sandwich.'

'Your mom made your father a baloney sandwich so he hit her?'

'Yeah. I mean it wasn't a punch or nothing, more like a push, but she fell over and hit her head on the kitchen counter, so it looked like it was worse than it was, which it wasn't. He told her, just because his name's Italian, that doesn't mean he likes Italian sausage. Like, he won't eat nothing pink. If it's pink, he won't put it in his mouth.'

'Not gay, then,' put in the Hispanic boy sitting next to Simon Silence. There was a burst of laughter from all around the classroom, but Simon Silence turned and gave the boy a disapproving stare that froze his face in mid-grin.

'What about you, Simon?' asked Jim, walking up the side of the classroom until he reached the third row of benches. 'Did that poem do anything for you?'

'Oh, for *sure*,' said Simon Silence. 'That poem clearly shows what happens when you disturb the natural order of things.'

'Unh? What do you mean by that? What "natural order of things"?'

'Who was Adam's first wife, in the Garden of Eden?'

'OK . . . some legends say it was Lilith.'

Simon Silence nodded. 'That's quite correct, Mr Rook – Lilith, who was fashioned out of the same clay as Adam, and not from Adam's rib, as his second wife Eve was.'

'So what does this have to do with hitting women?'

'It has everything to do with hitting women. Why was Lilith cast out of the Garden of Eden? Because she was Adam's equal, and refused to be subservient to him. And after she had been cast out of the Garden of Eden, she became the lover of the angel Sammael, sometimes known as the Angel of Death, and even God could not persuade her to return.'

Jim said, 'What you're saying here, Simon, is that if Lilith hadn't been booted out of Eden, and she and Adam had stayed together, men and women would have been equal, right from the get-go?'

Simon Silence gave his radiant, illuminating smile. 'Exactly, Mr Rook. The sexes would have been balanced, as they were meant to be. Men and women, good and evil, life and death. Very few people believe it, but if it hadn't been for God, and God's intolerance, and the ignorance of his priests and his earthly representatives, the world would have been a far safer and a happier place, all the way down the centuries.'

'Where the *fuck* you get all that from, man?' asked DaJon Johnson, in bewilderment. 'I thought I heard a poem about some dude disrespectin' his old lady, not some Bible story. Or maybe I fell asleep there for a while. Maybe I went into some mini-coma and missed out on all of that Bible-y bit.'

Simon Silence lifted his hand to him, like a priest giving him a benediction. 'You *will* understand, DaJon, I promise you. And sooner rather than later.'

'Well I sure as fuck hope so, man, cause I'm gettin' real confused back here.'

'*Language*, DaJon,' Jim cautioned him. 'There are ladies present.'

'Oh, yeah. Sure,' said DaJon. He tilted back in his chair and said, 'Sorry, Simon.'

Jim started to walk back to the front of the class to ask Kyle Baxter what *he* had thought about the poem when there was a brisk rapping at the door, and Detective Brennan walked in. He was closely followed by a woman detective with dyed-black, pixie-cut hair, a snub nose, and bright scarlet lips. She had eyes as a green as a cat's, and there might have been some whistling and feet-stamping if she hadn't had a gold LASD badge on the pocket of her blouse and a large nickel-plated SIG Sauer automatic holstered at her waist.

'Mr Rook?' said Detective Brennan. 'Real sorry to break into your class like this. This is Detective Carroll. May we have a private word with you, please?'

'Sure,' Jim told him. He turned around to Special Class Two and said, 'I won't be more than a couple of minutes. Try and write me that one sentence about *A New Language of Love*, OK? Don't try to impress me. Don't worry about your spelling, or your grammar. We're going to be tackling all of that later. Just try and express how you feel. Make it come from the heart.'

He followed Detectives Brennan and Carroll out into the corridor, and closed the door behind him. Immediately he heard talking and laughter, and he didn't hold out much hope of his class actually writing anything.

Detective Brennan said, 'We have some information on the young girl who was nailed to the ceiling of your classroom.'

'I see. Really?' For some reason, Jim felt suddenly breathless, as if he was about to be told something matter-of-fact but terrible at the same time. He had experienced the same breathlessness on the day that the nurse had come out of that room at Cedars-Sinai and told him that his father had died. He could see his father through the open door, lying in bed with the sun shining on his silver hair, and he didn't *look* dead.

'Did you check your class register yet, Mr Rook?' Detective Carroll asked him.

Jim shook his head. 'I usually like to kick off with something a little more lively, before I do that. I'm not too good with names, as a matter of fact. I'm like, *visual*, more than categorical.'

'Special Class Two is supposed to number fifteen students this semester, including a student called Simon Silence who was enrolled only the day before yesterday.'

'That's right. Yes. I think so, anyhow. I've only counted fourteen so far, but it's not unusual to have one or two fail to turn up, especially on the first day.'

Detective Carroll said, 'Do you know a woman called Jane Seabrook? She currently resides at three seven one zero nine, Stone Canyon Avenue.'

Jim stared at her. His breathlessness was growing worse. 'Jane Seabrook? Jane Seabrook is just a girl. Well, she was when I knew her. And she was living in Santa Monica in those days.'

'Jane Seabrook is thirty-nine years old, Mr Rook.'

'Thirty-nine? Yes. Jesus. I guess she must be. What about her? Nothing's happened to her, has it?'

'No, Mr Rook. Ms Seabrook is fine. But Ms Seabrook had a daughter, Bethany, and Bethany Seabrook was enrolled in Special Class Two this semester.'

'She had a daughter? I didn't know. She told me she wasn't going to keep it.'

'Apparently Ms Seabrook always told her daughter who her father was, and how much she still loved him, and that was one of the reasons why Bethany wanted to join Special Class Two – to get to know her father without her father realizing who she was.'

Without any warning at all, Jim found that he was crying. His throat felt as if it were choked up with thistles and tears were pouring freely down his cheeks. He found it almost impossible to say anything.

'It wasn't . . . don't say that . . . please don't tell me—'

Detective Carroll took hold of Jim's hand in both of her hands and squeezed it in sympathy. Detective Brennan laid a hand on his shoulder. Jim had never known that it was possible to feel so bereft.

'The girl who was nailed to the ceiling, Mr Rook. Ms Seabrook has made a positive ID, and the coroner has also taken DNA samples in case you want to question your own parenthood.'

Jim gave the slightest shake of his head. It was all he could manage. He couldn't speak any more. He walked off slowly along the corridor until he reached the window at the end, which overlooked the grassy slope that led to the athletics track.

As they sailed overhead, the clouds cast shadows which fled across the grass like the souls of people who were once loved, hurrying to go wherever they have to go, or wherever the wind takes them.

SEVEN

Outside Jane Seabrook's house, Stone Canyon Avenue sloped steeply uphill, and the driveway leading up to 37109 was even steeper, so that Jim had to park his car at an awkward tilt, with its rear end protruding into the road, and he had to push his door open with his feet in order to climb out.

It was midday, and still breezy, with the clouds tumbling overhead like a speeded-up movie. He felt completely unreal as he climbed the steps that led up to the front porch. Ocher-colored dust blew up from the flowerbeds on either side, as if he were a spirit who caused whirlwinds wherever he walked.

The house was modest: a cream-painted two-story family home, with Spanish-style windows, and a heap of flowering pink bougainvillea hanging over the porch. As Jim reached the top of the steps, a small dog began to yap, and he heard a clear woman's voice call out, 'Tessie – hush up, will you!'

He didn't recognize the voice. Are you supposed to recognize somebody's voice after eighteen years? He went up to the varnished oak front doors and rang the bell. He waited, biting his lower lip. He looked around. An old man in a frayed Panama hat was standing in his front yard on the opposite side of the road, staring at him suspiciously. Jim almost felt like giving him the finger.

The doors opened and there she was. No longer brunette, but blonde, with a shoulder-length bob, with bangs. But still the same hazel-colored eyes, and the slightly feline cheekbones, and the pink lips that looked as if she had just finished blowing somebody a kiss goodbye.

She was wearing a simple black linen dress, and a string of black beads around her neck, and a plain silver bracelet.

'Hallo, Jane,' said Jim.

She gave him a tight, complicated smile. 'You'd better come in,' she told him.

He followed her across a wide, cool hallway with a brown-tiled floor. On the left-hand wall hung a large mirror, with a brown wooden frame; and on the right-hand side hung a garish amateur oil painting of a lake, with disproportionately giant ducks flying over it.

They came out into a conservatory, with calico blinds drawn down to keep out the sun. It was furnished with brown wicker armchairs, and a glass-topped coffee table, and a variety of frondy potted palms. It smelled of dry heat, and plant fertilizer, but it also smelled of Jane. She was still wearing the same perfume, after all these years. Light, and flowery, with an underlying muskiness, although he had never known the name of it.

'Can I get you something to drink?' she asked him.

'I'm good, thanks.'

'Please – why don't you sit down?'

He hesitated for a moment, and then he sat. She sat, too, with her knees tight together and her back very straight, although she ceaselessly fiddled with her bracelet.

'I guess the police have been keeping you up to date,' said Jim. 'They still can't work out how anybody could have done it. You know, up on the ceiling like that. Or why they would have wanted to.'

Jane said, 'They told me that they found her clothes and her bag in the changing rooms. That's how they found out who she was.

Jim nodded. Detective Carroll had told *him* that, too.

'They had washed her before I identified her,' Jane went on, 'but they showed me a photograph of what she looked like when they found her, with all of that white paint all over face. You know, just in case it meant anything significant.'

'And did it?'

'I don't know, Jim. If it did, I can't imagine what. It made her look like a statue.'

'Yes,' said Jim.

There was a very long pause between them, and then Jane said, 'She was looking forward so much to seeing you. To getting to know you.'

'Did she plan on telling me who she was?'

'Eventually, yes. I think so.'

'But not if I turned out to be some obnoxious bastard who smelled of liniment and always gave her bad marks?'

'Now you're being unfair.'

'Oh, I see. And it was fair of you to give birth to her without even letting me know?'

'Jim, please. That was a long time ago. We were both a lot younger then.'

'Yes,' said Jim. 'I guess I should have stood up to your mother, shouldn't I? What a wimp I was.'

'Oh, God, Jim, you weren't to blame. Nobody could *ever* stand up to my mother, not even my father.'

'I thought she was hell-bent on you getting rid of it.' He paused, and then corrected himself. 'Getting rid of *her*, I mean. Of Bethany.'

Jane nodded. 'She was at first, but she was a very twisted woman, my mother. I think she got more pleasure out of my keeping our baby, and you not knowing about it, than you believing that I had had an abortion.'

Jim shook his head in disbelief. 'She hated me as much as that?'

'It wasn't *you* she hated, Jim. It was *me*. She was jealous of me from the moment I was born. But she knew how much I loved you. And she knew that everything that hurt *you* hurt me just as much.'

'Jesus. Where is she now? I should go round and tell her what a goddamned bitch she is.'

'You can if you like. She's in the Union Cemetery in Brentwood, next to her own mother, who was even more of a bitch than she was. You want the plot number?'

'So, what?' said Jim, after a while. He looked around the conservatory. 'You married now?'

'Yes. My married name's Edwards.'

'Happy?'

'That's a question you should never ask a married woman. You know that.'

'Oh. OK. What was she like? Bethany?'

Jane's eyes began to glitter with tears, but she managed to smile. 'Pretty. Very pretty. Very petite. She always had messy hair, just like you. She loved poetry and she loved music and she loved to dance.

'You got some pictures?'

'Of course. I'll give you some that you can take away with you. I have some new ones which were taken only a couple of weeks ago, at her church summer fair.'

'She belonged to a church?'

Jane stood up and went across to a brown wicker bureau. She opened one of the top drawers and took out a folder of photographs. 'I always brought her up to be God-fearing, Jim. We used to go to communion every Sunday and she would sing like a little angel. Lately, though, she found this new church, and she's being going two or three times a week. Well – she *was* going two or three times a week.'

She was silent for a few moments and Jim knew that she couldn't speak.

'I know,' he said. 'It's been a terrible shock for you.'

Jane handed him some photographs of a young girl in a long white muslin dress and flowers in her hair, dancing barefoot through an apple orchard. She wasn't just pretty, she was beautiful, and she looked so happy.

When he came to the third photograph, however, he saw a group of young people standing in the background, between the trees. They were all dressed in white, too, even the boys. He peered closer, and one of them looked distinctly familiar, even though his face was turned away from the camera.

He looked at the fourth photograph, and the fifth, and the sixth, and there he was – staring directly at the camera this time, with a shining smile on his face. It was Simon Silence.

Jim said to Jane, 'What church is this? Did you ever visit it yourself?'

'No,' said Jane. 'Bethany said they had a chapel on Lookout Mountain Road, in Laurel Canyon, but they also had a country place near Bakersfield. That's where these pictures were taken.'

'The Church of the Divine Conquest,' said Jim.

'You *know* it?'

'I've heard of it, let's put it that way.'

Jane frowned at him. 'You don't think that what happened to Bethany had anything to with her church, do you? She always loved going there. It always seemed to give her such a buzz, you know? Such confidence. She always seemed to have so much more confidence than I ever did at her age. Especially with boys.'

'The natural order of things,' said Jim. 'Men and women, both equal.'

'That is *so* strange,' Jane told him. She was standing against the muted sunlight with the folder of photographs in her hand. 'That's exactly what Bethany always used to say, over and over. "The natural order of things."'

After Detective Brennan and Detective Carroll had told Jim about Bethany, Dr Ehrlichman had told Jim that he could take the rest of the day off, but Jim didn't really see the point of that. What was he going to do, go home and drink five cans of Fat Tire Ale and talk to Tibbles about the meaning of life? And, what was even more painful, the meaning of death?

Before he left, Jim stood on the doorstep and said to Jane, 'Maybe I can come around again sometime? We both have a whole lot catching-up to do, don't we?'

'I don't think so,' said Jane. 'But of course I'll send you an invitation to the funeral.'

'Jane—'

'No,' she said. 'When you and I were together, that was one of the very best times of my life. But – it was also the worst. I don't want to relive it.'

She came up to him and wrapped her arms around him and held him tightly. He kissed her hair, and her forehead. That perfume, it brought it all back. From the opposite side of the road, the old man in the frayed Panama hat stared at them intently. *What's the matter, you nosey old fart*, thought Jim. *Don't you know what regret looks like?*

He gave Jane one more kiss, and then turned away and went down the steps and climbed into his car. He drove back to college feeling numb. He wondered if time travelers felt as numb as he did, after they had been back to stop Lincoln being assassinated, or to watch the Battle of the Little Bighorn.

He switched on the car radio and it was playing *Big Yellow Taxi* by Joni Mitchell. *'Don't it always seem to go,'* she was warbling, '*You don't know what you've got till it's gone.*' He switched it off again and drove in silence.

When he turned in through the gates of West Grove Community College, he saw the squad cars and the ambulance and the coroner's vans immediately, all of them clustered in the turning area outside of the main college buildings. There were two fire trucks, too. TV vans were parked all the way up the left-hand side of the driveway, and he passed knots of news reporters and technicians, talking and smoking and unraveling yards of black cable.

He drove slowly up to the top of the slope, until he reached a yellow wooden police barrier that had been set up across the driveway from one side to the other. A gingery sheriff's deputy approached him and he put down his window.

'You have any business here, sir?'

Jim took his college ID badge out of his shirt pocket and showed it to him. 'What's going on here?' he asked.

'There's been an incident, sir. If you want to make your way to the parking lot and go directly inside. For the time being the students and faculty are confined to the interior of the premises.'

'What's happened? Is it one of the students?'

'There's been an incident, sir. Please make your way to the parking lot and go directly inside.'

'What are you? A recording?'

The gingery deputy stared at him without blinking. 'Please make your way—'

'Yes, OK. I heard you. I'm going.'

He drove into the parking lot and parked in Royston Denman's space. As he climbed out of his car, he saw that there was a crowd of deputies and paramedics and firefighters gathered around the large cypress tree. Two of the firefighters were carrying an aluminum ladder on their shoulders, but at the moment it looked as though there was more discussion going on than action. Jim could see Detective Brennan and Detective Carroll, too, and for some reason they were talking to Father O'Flaherty, the college chaplain, who was nodding repeatedly so that his bald head reflected the sun like a heliograph message.

Nobody was looking. The gingery deputy was leaning over a bright green Volkswagen, repeating his message to one of the college lab assistants. Jim walked across the grass to where Detectives Brennan and Carroll were standing, and came up close behind them. They were too busy talking to Father O'Flaherty to notice him.

Shielding his eyes against the sun, he looked up into the cypress tree, with its grotesquely gnarled trunk and its wide-spreading branches. As he did so, he felt a cold, crawling sensation all the way down his spine.

High up in the tree, almost twenty feet up, where the branches began to divide from the trunk, a naked white figure was pinned, with its arms and its legs spread out. It was a young man, who had been painted all over with thick white paint, so that his hair stuck out in the same way that Bethany's had stuck out, when she was nailed to the ceiling of Special Class Two.

This young man, though, had been nailed to the cypress tree upside-down, head downward. All around him, four on each side, eight white cats had been nailed.

Pushing his way past Detectives Brennan and Carroll, Jim approached the tree and stared up at the young man with a growing feeling of dread. This had to be a symbol. Not only a symbol, but an omen. One young person nailed to a ceiling with eight cats around her might have been nothing more than some bizarre act of perversity. But here was a second, nailed up in almost exactly the same way.

Something supremely evil is on its way, thought Jim. *Something more evil than any of the ghosts or demons that I've ever come across before*. Almost all of the ghosts or demons that he had met before had been vengeful or wantonly destructive, but in their own selfish interest. Either they had wanted to punish people for what they had done to them while they were alive, or else they were trying to gain entrance into the world of the living from the world of the dead.

But Jim had the strongest intuition that this was very different. He couldn't yet understand why, but what was happening here felt a thousand times more powerful, and a thousand times more frightening, because this was a warning that life as we know it was soon going to come to an end. These young people were a countdown. Two so far. How many more would be nailed up to ceilings or trees to warn of the coming catastrophe? And what would happen when it finally arrived?

Jim couldn't help thinking of Summer's nightmare. '*I dreamed that I was standing in line with all of these hundreds of people and it was all dark all around us. Up ahead, though, I could see this orange light, like a bonfire? And it was hot, too, like a bonfire. Well, more like a furnace.*'

He was still standing there when a hand was clapped on his shoulder.

'Mr Rook! You shouldn't be here!'

He turned around. 'I think this is the one place that I *should* be, Detective.'

'Oh, yes? And why is that, exactly? Can you see something here that the rest of us can't see?'

'No, detective, I can't. But I can *feel* something. This isn't the work of some weirdo, or some gang of weirdos. This wasn't done by some serial killer with a penchant for white paint and Persian cats.'

'Meaning what?' asked Detective Brennan.

'Meaning that these killings aren't an end in themselves. They're a warning of something very much worse to come.'

'Now, why would anybody who was going to do something very much worse than this feel the need to warn us about it? After all, you never know, we might be clever enough to work out what it is that he's warning us about, and stop him before he can carry it out. We didn't get any warnings, did we, about the World Trade Towers? If we had, we might have been able to catch the bastards before they did what they did.'

He paused, and sniffed, and then he said, 'Besides, what the hell could be worse than this?'

Jim silently recalled what the man standing in line had said to Summer in her dream: *He said, 'We have to be here. It's the end.' So I said, 'The end of what?' And he said, 'It's the end of all of us. It's arrived.'*

Meanwhile, Detective Brennan said, ''Preciate it if you'd return to your classroom for now, Mr Rook. Detective Carroll and me, we'll come up to see you later. Meanwhile, we have to get this poor young guy down from the tree, and try to find out who he is.'

Jim was tempted to tell him about Bethany's membership of the Church of the Divine Conquest, but he decided against it for now. He wanted to find out more about Simon Silence and the Reverend John Silence before he did so. The church's beliefs seemed to be somewhat unusual – all this talk of Lilith in the Garden of Eden, and her equality to Adam – but there were plenty of other churches with beliefs that were ten times wackier than that.

He looked up at the whitewashed body nailed to the tree. The young man's mouth was partly open, and a thin string of blood was dangling from it, just like Bethany's. Jim couldn't imagine what they both must have suffered before they died.

'OK, Detective,' he said, 'I'll talk to you later.'

Detective Carroll looked at him sharply before he left and said, 'You *are* feeling OK, Mr Rook?'

'Sure. Just a little shaken, that's all.'

'Did you go visit Bethany's mother?'

'Yes, I did.'

'And?'

'You know what L.P. Hartley said, Detective. "The past is a foreign country: they do things differently there."'

'OK,' said Detective Carroll. It was obvious from the look on her face that she didn't have a clue who L.P. Hartley was, or what Jim had meant to tell her, but she grasped his arm and gave him a squeeze of reassurance, and that was more than he could have asked for.

Jim went upstairs to Art Studio Four. As he climbed the stairs, he passed Sheila Colefax coming down – dressed, as usual, in a high-necked blouse and a black pencil skirt.

'Jim,' she said. 'I thought you'd left for the day. I'm so glad I bumped into you.'

'What is it, Sheila? I'm kind of tied up right now.'

'Well, I suppose it can wait. But I was wondering if you'd like to come to a concert with me.'

Jim stared at her. 'Sheila – do you know what's happening outside? Do you know why the whole place is crawling with cops and paramedics and firefighters and media?'

Sheila looked confused. 'No. Not really.'

'Well, please, do me a favor and ask me some other time, would you?'

'Oh. All right,' she said. She still looked confused.

Jim carried on climbing the stairs.

'It's only a folk concert,' she called after him. 'The Woolspinners. It's just that I have two tickets and my friend can't come.'

But Jim was already out of sight. He walked along the corridor until he reached Art Studio Four and opened the door.

Usually, when Special Class Two was left alone, they would be playing classroom basketball or listening to hip-hop music or playing poker or polishing their nails. This afternoon, though, the class was almost completely silent. All of his students were sitting at their places, writing.

Simon Silence stood up as Jim came in. 'I didn't know if you were coming back today, sir.'

'Yes, well, I decided I would. You've lost enough time already this semester, and it hasn't even begun.'

DaJon Johnson stuck up his hand. 'What's happening out there, man – I mean sir? All those po-lice cars and fire trucks and stuff. I axed one of the other teachers but all she said was that nobody had told her squat.'

'I have no idea what's going on, either,' said Jim. 'All I know is that there's been some kind of an incident and we have to stay inside until the police say it's OK for us to leave.'

Jim didn't like to lie to his students, but he didn't want to upset them, either, before he knew more about the young man's body nailed to the tree. He looked around and said, 'What's everybody writing?'

Simon Silence gave Jim a challenging smile. 'I set them all a short essay, sir. I hope you don't mind.'

'You set them an *essay*?'

'Yes, sir. Only half a page. "My Idea of Paradise."'

'Oh. I see. OK, then. You might as well carry on. The results might be . . . well, interesting, to say the least.'

He paced up and down the classroom. He had never seen any Special Class Two writing with such concentration, even if Jesmeka Watson did seem to be rubbing out what she had written almost as fast as she was writing it, and the table around her was covered in thousands of gray eraser crumbs.

As he walked back toward his desk for a second time, he noticed that Kyle Baxter was missing – Dictionary Dude, as he had already nicknamed him, for his own benefit.

Kyle Baxter was missing, but on the table where he had been sitting this morning lay a pair of spectacles, with a grubby lump of Band-Aid holding them together.

EIGHT

J im sorted through his briefcase and found a letter that he had received last week from his mother in Mill Valley. He folded the envelope like a paper glove to pick up Kyle Baxter's spectacles from the bench.

'OK, I'm just going to take these down to the cops outside.'

'Hey, Mr Rook?' asked Rudy Cascarelli. 'You don't think that nothing's happened to that Kyle kid, do you?'

'I sure hope not, Rudy. But if he's missing, his spectacles may help the cops to identify him. You know – DNA.'

'You're not saying he's *dead*, are you, sir?' put in DaJon Johnson. 'Is that what all this emergency thing is all about? They found another student *dead*? Shit, man, this has to be most dangerous seat of learning I ever sat in!'

Jim said, 'I'm not saying anything, DaJon. Just let me take these down to the cops so that they can make absolutely sure.'

He went toward the classroom door, but as he did so it suddenly opened and Kyle Baxter walked in, blinking.

He frowned at his spectacles which Jim was holding up in his folded envelope; and then he frowned at Jim.

'I, ah – Kyle!' said Jim. 'Where the heck have you been?'

'I went to the bathroom,' Kyle Baxter told him, obviously baffled.

'Oh – I see. You just went to the bathroom! Sure, yes, OK. No problem with that! The only thing was, I didn't know if you were coming back or not, so I was taking these down to the lost property room, in case they got broken.'

'They're broken already, sir.'

'Yes, well, I can see that. But you still wouldn't want to lose them, would you?'

'I'll be getting my new ones tomorrow, sir.'

'Good. Great. Anyhow, why don't you sit down, Kyle, and finish off your essay about Paradise?'

Jim looked around the rest of Second Class Two, daring

them to tell Kyle that he had been thinking of taking his spectacles down to the CSI. One or two of them smirked and looked away. DaJon Johnson slowly tilted his chimney-stack hair from side to side in amusement, and Simon Silence smiled an even more self-satisfied smile than usual.

Jim sat down at his desk and took out the book that he had been trying to finish for the past seven months, *The Human Goldfish*, a novel about a man who wakes up every morning with no memory of what happened to him the day before. The trouble was, Jim had very little spare time to read any book that wasn't included in his curriculum, and when he did get time, he was usually too tired to manage more than two or three pages before he fell asleep. In the morning, just like the main character in *The Human Goldfish*, he had almost always forgotten what he had read.

After fifteen minutes, he checked the clock and said, 'Right . . . you should have had enough time by now. Let me take a look at what you've written, and get to know you people at the same time. I'm sorry we've had such a screwed-up start to this semester. Let's try to get back to normal, shall we?'

First he took her paper from Jesmeka Watson, the pretty African-American girl who sat right in front of his desk. Jesmeka had rubbed out her essay so many times that there was a ragged hole in the middle of the page, but she had managed to write 'Paradise 4 me is 2 B lik MIA singin n dansn n pantn picshuz n also bein mega famus.'

'So . . . paradise for you would be singing and dancing and painting pictures like MIA? She's very good, MIA, very original. Very talented.'

'Most of all mega famous, though,' put in Jesmeka, pointing at the words 'mega famus' in her essay with a purple-frosted fingernail. 'I just want to stand up in front of all of those thousands and thousands of people and they all, like, adore me.'

For some reason, Jim found himself glancing across at Simon Silence when Jesmeka said that. Simon Silence was talking to the Hispanic boy next to him, and both of them were grinning. Jim couldn't understand why he found Simon Silence so disturbing. He kept feeling that there was an undercurrent in this classroom, silent communications flowing from one student to the next – communications to which he wasn't quite tuned in.

Kyle Baxter was next. He had written, 'Paradise is happiness/ bliss/ ecstasy/ rapture/ cloud nine/ seventh heaven/ dreamland. Paradise is knowing words all where to put them. Paradise is me cleverer around me all than idiots/ fools/ cretins/ morons/ imbeciles/ halfwits/ clowns/ muggins/ boobies/ dopes/ dumb-bells/ boneheads/ saps.'

'So, Kyle. . . Paradise for you is being smarter than everybody else in the class, and all of them giving you full credit for it?'

'No, sir.'

'Oh. Maybe I misunderstood what you've written here. You want to explain it to me?'

'I don't just want everybody in the class to know that I'm smarter, sir,' he said, under his breath, but with fierce intensity. 'I want *everybody* to know that I'm smarter.'

'Like everybody on the planet?'

Kyle nodded so enthusiastically that his spectacles nearly dropped off. Jim gave him a reassuring pat on the shoulder and moved on to the next student, who was sitting at Kyle's right elbow. He was a Chinese-American boy whose glossy black hair was cut into a bowl shape, with a fringe so low that Jim could hardly see his eyes. He was wearing a black T-shirt with a large white number 8 on the back, and he had red-and-green dragon's-tail tattoos all the way up his left arm, disappearing into his sleeve.

His essay was five lines written in a strange spidery hand-writing. 'Paradise will come on the day when Wo Hop To is gone and Chung Ching Yee is gone and also Vietnamese Boyz and all is Wah Ching. On that day I will walk like a god.'

Jim said, 'What's your name, son?'

'Xiao Chang but everybody calls me Joe.'

'All right, Joe,' said Jim, holding up his essay. 'These Chinese names you have here – Wo Hop To and Chung Ching Yee, etcetera – these are all Chinese street gangs. Apart from the Vietnamese Boyz, anyhow, and half of *them* are Chinese.'

Joe Chang nodded, and kept turning his pencil over and over, end to end.

'Are you a member of Wah Ching?'

'Not any more, sir. When I live with my parents in Monterey Park I was Wah Ching. But now my father move to West Grove, I don't hang out with them no more.'

'But you'd still like to? That's your idea of Paradise?'

Joe Chang clenched his fist. 'In Wah Ching,' he said, 'I always felt like I got *strength*,' although he pronounced it '*strempf*.'

'Nobody stand in our way. Nobody. They dreaded us, is why. They dreaded us! Strength like that, *that's* Paradise.'

'Wow, OK. I see. Maybe it's Paradise for you. But how about the people who dread you? Not exactly Paradise for them, is it?'

'I was only asked to write about *my* Paradise, sir. Nobody else's.'

Jim was about to go on to the next student when there was a knock at the door, and Detective Carroll came in. She crossed straight over to Jim and cupped her hand around her mouth so that the class couldn't hear what she was saying, although her hair tickled Jim's left ear.

'Mr Rook? Everything's clear now, outside, although the primary crime scene is still cordoned off and we still have at least half a day of forensic work to do. We've consulted with Doctor Ehrlichman and we've agreed that college will close early today, and try to make a fresh start tomorrow morning.'

'Oh, OK,' said Jim. He turned around to Special Class Two and said, 'Looks like Paradise will have to be postponed for now. You can all pack up your books and beat it.'

They began to push back their chairs back and noisily gather up their belongings, and it seemed like all of their iPhones started warbling and ringing and playing music all at once. As they shuffled out of the classroom, Jim called out, 'Just one thing I want you to think of overnight! You're trapped in a space capsule, right? Going round and round the Earth with no prospect of being rescued for at least a year! You're allowed to take one book with you! Let me know tomorrow which book you would choose!'

As Simon Silence came past him, slinging his white gunny sack over his shoulder, Jim said, 'Shouldn't be a problem for you, Simon, choosing a book.'

Simon raised his eyebrows as if he didn't quite understand.

'Well . . . your father being a reverend and all. There's only one really good book, isn't there?'

'Oh. You mean the Bible. There are other good books. There is *one* good book in particular, which I would probably take with me.'

'Oh, yes?'

Simon smiled and touched his finger to his lips. 'I regret that its name is never spoken, sir. Some names, like the name of God, may be thought of, but never uttered out loud.'

With that, he walked off. Detective Carroll came up to Jim and said, 'That the fruitcake Dave Brennan was telling me about?'

Jim nodded. 'I don't know. At first, yes, I did think he was borderline bananas. Now . . . I'm not so sure.'

Traffic was stop-go all the way home on Sunset. The second apple that Simon Silence had given him was lying on the passenger seat next to him, rolling backward and forward every time he stopped for a traffic signal or to avoid rear-ending the vehicle in front.

He was trying very hard to resist the temptation to pick it up and bite into it. There was something about its pale pink-and-green color that just made it *look* as if it were going to taste deliciously sweet and sour, and if it tasted anything like the first apple, he knew that it would.

Yet, strangely, he felt almost virtuous for leaving it where it was. It rolled back, it rolled forward. It came close to rolling off the seat but still he didn't make a grab for it.

When he reached the Vine Street intersection, however, traffic up ahead of him had come almost to a standstill because of a burst water main underneath the Hollywood Freeway, and three lanes were merging left into one. He had to sit under the gloomy concrete pillars of the freeway for more than five minutes, half deafened by impatient car horns, drumming his fingers on the steering wheel and feeling hungrier and thirstier. Because he had gone to visit Jane this morning, he hadn't had time to stop for anything to eat or drink.

He glanced down at the apple. What had Oscar Wilde written? 'I can resist anything except temptation.' And if that was a good enough excuse for Oscar Wilde – why not for him?

He had bitten into the apple before he knew it, and it *was* just as good as the first one. In fact it seemed even juicier and even sweeter, with that distinctive hint of sharpness which gave it so much character.

Not just character, either. It had an immediate effect on his emotions. He had taken only two or three bites before he was sure he could feel that warm wind blowing again, and hear that faint calliope music playing.

Even though he knew he was here, in his car, in the shadow of the freeway, he also felt as if he were on a seashore someplace, although he wasn't sure exactly where. The sun kept disappearing behind the clouds, so that the day continually brightened and faded, brightened and faded, and seagulls were crying out like lost children.

Something had happened on that day, long ago, and he was being reminded of it. Something had happened but it wasn't something that he wanted to remember. It was something hurtful and humiliating. He must have buried it so deeply in his mind that he couldn't even be sure that it had really happened, or if it had happened not to him but to somebody else altogether.

As the traffic crept forward along Franklin, he began to feel more and more distressed, and his breathing became increasingly hard and harsh. He felt anger and embarrassment and an overwhelming urge to get his revenge, even though he didn't understand what for, and against whom, or why.

Just after he had turned into the narrow uphill slope of Briarcliff Road, he had to pull into the first driveway that he came to, because he was panting and sweating. He was gripping the steering wheel with both hands as if he were trying to wrench it away from the steering column. He was filled with such rage and frustration that he clenched his teeth tightly together and let out a roar like an angry beast.

He was still sitting there when an elderly man in yellow-and-blue Bermuda shorts came down the steps from the house and tapped with his knuckle on his passenger-side window.

Jim took three or four deep breaths and then let the window down. The elderly man looked like a Thanksgiving turkey in sunglasses, with a red shriveled neck.

'Help you?' he asked.

'No . . . no I'm good, thanks.'

'I'll be wanting to pull out of here in a couple of minutes.'

'Oh, really?'

'Well . . . you're kind of blocking me in here, aren't you?'

Jim took another deep breath. 'I'm having a brief think, OK? I don't recall anybody receiving a traffic citation for having a brief think. In fact more people ought to do more of it, what do *you* think?'

'I think I have to take my wife to the orthodontist and you're blocking my driveway.'

'I hear you. And when I'm good and ready, I'll go.'

The elderly man took a step back and looked at Jim's car. 'I've seen you before, haven't I, in this old junker? You live just up the road a ways, in Briar Cliff Apartments.'

'So?'

'So, if you want yourself a brief think, my friend, why don't you take your old junker up to your own driveway and have your brief think there?'

Jim stared at him. He couldn't remember when he had ever felt such contempt for anybody in his life. When he spoke, his voice was shaking with anger.

'How old are you, granpa?' he asked him.

'Eighty-one, not that it's any of your concern.'

'Eighty-one? Then for your information you have just exceeded the average life expectancy in Los Angeles County by seven months. I wouldn't take your wife to the orthodontist, old man. I'd visit your mortician and start making arrangements for Forest Lawn.'

'That's it!' the elderly man told him. 'I'm calling the cops on you! Nobody speaks to me like that, right in my own driveway! I used to be vice-president of Orange-Freeze!'

'Don't panic,' Jim told him. 'I'm going. You were just what I needed to remind me of something important.'

'Oh, yes? And what's that?'

'For some people, old man, death can't *ever* come too soon.'

With that, he swerved out of the elderly man's driveway and made his way two hundred yards further up the hill, to his own apartment block. He parked with a squeal of tires, and sat in his car for a further few minutes, with the engine and the air conditioning running. When he eventually climbed out he was still breathing hard, and the back of his shirt was clammy with sweat.

What the hell is the matter with you, Jim? You never shout at people for no reason. Mr Reasonable, that's you. Yet he was still so angry with that elderly man down the road that he could have walked back and punched him in the face, and broken his beak for him. Well, he looked like a fucking turkey.

He was climbing the steps to the first-story landing when the front door of Apartment 1 opened and Nadine stuck her head out, almost as if she had been waiting for him. She was wearing a droopy brown kaftan and smoking a cigarette in a very long holder.

'You're back early,' she told him.

Jim stopped in front of her, and shifted his eyes from side to side without actually looking at her directly, like a blind man. 'Oh yes. And?'

Nadine's forehead furrowed. 'And – you're back early, that's all. I was just wondering why. You know, neighborly nosiness. That's all.'

'If you must know there's been another homicide, pretty much identical to the first one. Some young man killed and whitewashed but nailed to a tree, this time, instead of a ceiling. He was surrounded by white Persian cats, eight of them, the same as before. You'll hear all about it on the news.'

'Oh my God. It's so *strange*. But it's so *magical*, too. Eight white cats! I can't imagine that this isn't magic. Why haven't my Tarot cards picked up on it? Usually, they're so sensitive to anything at all.'

'Because your Tarot cards are nothing but hocus-pocus, Nadine. You know that and I know that. I could sit down and draw my own deck of fortune-telling cards and they would be just as meaningful as the Tarot. Or not. The Rook Cards, think about it. I could be the Grumpy Teacher and you could be the Anorexic Hippie.'

Jim tried to make his way past her so that he could go up to his own apartment but Nadine caught his sleeve. 'Actually, no BS, Jim. It's Ricky.'

'What do you mean "it's Ricky"?'

'Well, you know how he kept on painting that same white face? Now he's stopped painting it, and he's painted somebody else. Please – come take a look, would you?'

Jim hesitated. He still felt fractious, and out of sorts, and he didn't want to discuss anything with anybody – especially that dopey nineteen-sixties throwback Ricky. But Nadine was looking at him so appealingly that he couldn't say no.

'OK,' he said. 'But I'm only coming in for a couple of minutes. I have a shitload of homework to mark.'

Of course he didn't have any homework to mark, but he desperately needed to lie down and close his eyes and try to get that woman's voice and that calliope music out of his head. At the moment he couldn't think about anything else. Even now he could still hear the seagulls crying, very faintly, as if somebody were calling him from very far away. '*Jim! Jim!*'

Nadine led him through to the living room. The drapes were drawn, so that the room was stuffy and almost in total darkness, apart from a single vertical band of sunlight which was shining in where the drapes didn't quite meet together. From what Jim could make out, the room appeared to be even more cluttered than usual. There seemed to be twice as many empty Raffallo's pizza boxes as he had seen in there before, and over by the window stood a half-dismantled moped, which he didn't remember seeing yesterday. The red parakeet was still sitting in its cage in the corner, noisily pecking at the bars and squawking from time to time, like some bad-tempered senior who was forced to stay in a sunset home.

The single band of sunlight fell directly down the center of Ricky's canvas. Ricky was hunched on the backless kitchen chair which he usually used when he was painting. He was still holding his palette, with his left thumb through it, and three or four brushes, all of which were still loaded with various shades of white and gray oil-paint. There were flecks of paint and rolling paper ash in his beard.

Jim negotiated his way between the pizza boxes and other assorted trash as if he were stepping through a minefield. As he approached, Ricky didn't take his attention away from his picture but sucked on the scrawniest of joints and said, 'Hi there, Jim. Glad to see you. You finished early today, didn't you?'

'Had some more trouble at college,' Jim told him. 'If you ask me, something very stupendous this way comes, and it won't be long in coming.'

'Well, I agree with you there, man. There's something in the air, all right. But I'm not so sure about stupendous. More like cata-fuckin'-strophic.'

He jabbed his brushes at the canvas.

'Take a look at this, man,' he said. 'Just take a look and tell me if you know who that is.'

In Ricky's freshly finished painting, The Storyteller was no longer the pale, watery, almost seraphic figure that he had been trying so hard not to paint before. Now it was dark, and shadowy, in an undulating cloak, just like the shadowy presence that Jim had almost run down in the smog, and which had appeared like a coil of black smoke on his balcony.

It had begun to appear more distinctly in his nightmare, sitting in his car with its eyes glittering deep inside its hood and its gray-gloved hand resting on the steering wheel. But now he could see clearly what it was – or *who* it was.

'Jesus Christ, Ricky,' Jim told him. 'That's amazing.'

'Amazin'? You think so? I think it's the scariest fuckin' thing I ever painted in the whole of my life – especially considerin' I was tryin' to paint this merry old fat guy.'

The shadowy figure's head was no longer covered by a hood. It was large, and gray-skinned, and bony, with an overhanging forehead and pronounced cheekbones and a lantern jaw. Its eyes glittered as they had in Jim's nightmare, but now they looked triumphant, rather than sly.

He was smiling, gray-lipped, but not in the knowing way that Simon Silence smiled. He was smiling at his own superiority.

Without knowing why, Jim felt exhilarated. Here was the power to end all powers. Here at last was a presence who was strong enough to take command of a world which was falling to pieces all around us.

He stood in front of the painting and slowly reached out to touch it with his left hand. The eyes were mesmerizing. They promised him everything. Glory, success, wealth, and rampant destruction. The fire to end all fires.

Yes, he knew who this was. There was no mistaking him. Out of his tangled black hair, two curved horns protruded – the unmistakable horns of the beast.

NINE

Nadine said, 'What does it mean, Jim? Is it the Devil? How can Ricky start to paint a cheery old storyteller and end up by painting Satan?'

Jim still couldn't take his eyes away. The portrait gave him a feeling of huge empowerment that he had never felt before in his life. What had Joe Chang called it? *Strempf.* Jim recalled his words: '*Nobody stand in our way. Nobody. They dreaded us, is why. They* dreaded *us!*'

Eventually, he patted Ricky's shoulder and said, 'Listen, Ricky, you shouldn't worry about it. It's a brilliant work of art, and you've painted it for a reason, even if you don't know what that reason is.'

'What are you saying to me, man? I didn't paint this. Well, I didn't *mean* to paint it, which is pretty much the same thing, ain't it?'

'Oh, you painted it all right. It was just that your talent got taken over by a force which wanted you to create a portrait of the Lord and Master.'

'The Lord and Master?' queried Nadine, blowing out a long stream of smoke. 'That's goddamn *Satan* we're looking at there. He sure ain't *my* Lord and Master.'

'I know,' said Jim. 'But that's how the spiritual force that influenced Ricky to paint him would have thought of him.'

Jim took two or three steps back, although he still couldn't take his eyes away from the portrait's triumphant eyes. *I am here. You can see me now. You can recognize me for who I am.*

Jim said, 'This kind of thing happens all the time in the spirit world. Not usually so *dramatic* as this, I'll grant you. But spirits can't pick up pencils and write messages, so they guide people's hands on Ouija boards. How many times have you seen that happen? Spirits can't speak, so they talk to their relatives through mediums. Spirits can't throw things, or hurt anybody, so they possess people and get them to do it for them.

'In this case, a spirit obviously wanted to create a portrait of Satan, for one reason or another, and it used Ricky's artistic ability to paint it.'

'Just like I was fuckin' hijacked,' Ricky complained, taking out a Zippo lighter and relighting his joint.

'If you like, yes. You were hijacked.'

'But what's the *point* of it?' asked Nadine.

Jim looked at Satan, with all of the little children gathered around him, telling them stories. He didn't fully understand the point of this portrait himself, but he was beginning to get an inkling of what was happening. A faint, faraway feeling like the feeling that came over him when he bit into one of Simon Silence's apples. Seagulls screaming, and the ocean washing on the shore, and the endless piping of a steam calliope.

'How about a cup of chamomile tea?' asked Nadine.

'No, thanks, Nadine. Like I said, I have a whole lot of homework to catch up on.'

'I'm supposed to hand this painting over to the library by Friday,' said Ricky. 'What the hell am I going to tell them? I can't show up with this, can I?'

'Can't you paint another one, from scratch? Maybe if you paint another one, it'll turn out the way you originally intended it.'

Ricky puffed out his cheeks. 'I don't know, Jim. Does anything in this fuckin' life ever turn out the way you originally intended it?'

'*Silence!*' screamed the red parakeet. '*Silence!*'

Jim went up to his apartment and let himself in. Tibbles was sitting up close to the sliding window that gave out on to the balcony, with his nose against the glass, but when Jim came into the living room he turned his head around as if he had been caught doing something he shouldn't. Jim approached the window and saw the Siamese Queen from next door curled up seductively on one of the plastic armchairs outside.

'Forget it, Tibs,' he told him. 'That lady is pure one hundred per cent pedigree. Way out of your league. And her owner never lets her out when she's on heat.'

Tibbles didn't turn back to look at the object of his desire. Instead, he continued to stare at Jim with his eyes wide, almost as if he didn't recognize him.

'You want something to eat, fatso?' Jim asked him. 'What's it to be today? Shrimp or chicken?'

Still Tibbles stared at him, and now his mottled gray fur began to rise, and his lip curled back, baring his teeth.

'I'm asking you a question here, Tibs. What's it to be? Or if you're not hungry, just say so, although I can't believe that for a moment. You're *always* hungry!'

Tibbles hissed, and began to sidle across the living room sideways, his head low and his back arched, and his claws sticking out so that they snagged on the carpet.

'What the hell is the matter with you, Tibs?' Jim demanded. He took a step toward him but Tibbles hissed even more viciously, and backed right up against the wall.

'Are you sick or something? What? Let me take a look at you.'

He knelt down in front of Tibbles to pick him up, but without any warning Tibbles spat and cackled at him and jumped straight into his face, biting and scratching at him in a blizzard of claws and gray fur. Jim lost his balance and toppled over backward, but Tibbles kept on ripping at his cheeks, and even seemed to be trying to claw out his eyes.

'*Get off, Tibs! Get the hell off me!*'

He felt Tibbles tear his right earlobe, and the sudden wetness of blood sliding down the side of his neck, into his collar. But then he managed to lever up his left elbow to shield his face, and with his right hand seize a handful of loose skin between Tibbles' shoulder blades. He swung Tibbles sharply to the right, and then flung him all the way across the room so that he hit the air-conditioning unit with a thump and a reverberating clang.

He climbed to his feet. Tibbles was lying on his side, his eyes open, clearly not dead, but with a look of intense resentment on his face.

Jim hunkered down beside him and tried to stroke him, but

Tibbles hissed at him again, and batted at him with his left paw.

'Tibs, what's wrong with you, dude? I've never seen you act so crazy.'

He tried again to stroke Tibbles, partly to calm him down and partly to make sure that none of his bones were broken. But Tibbles managed to roll himself sideways on to his feet, and shake himself, and then limp into the kitchen for a drink of water.

Jim wondered if he ought to take him to the Laurel Pet Hospital. Even if no bones were broken, he might have suffered some internal injury. And besides, why had he attacked Jim in such a frenzy? Maybe he had eaten or drunk something that had affected his brain – not that he was a very bright cat to begin with. Maybe he had developed a brain tumor.

Jim watched him for a while through the kitchen doorway, although Tibbles kept turning around and looking at him as if to make sure that he wasn't coming too close. Tibbles didn't appear to be hurt, or in pain, so Jim thought: *I'll just keep him under observation for a while. Pet care doesn't come cheap, after all. Even having your cat put down costs an arm and a leg these days. I could save myself a whole lot of money by digging a hole in the back yard and burying the stupid moggy alive.*

He looked across and suddenly saw his face in the mirror in the hallway, as if it were somebody else standing there. *Did I just think that? Was that* me?

He slowly approached the mirror and stared at his face. It *looked* like him. Tousled mid-brown hair, light brown eyes. The same stern frown that his mother always put on, when she was pretending to be angrier than she really was.

Jim? Was that you? Did you think that? Did you really think of burying Tibbles alive? Not only that – you pictured it, didn't you, in your mind's eye, tossing the dirt down on to him by the shovelful, and Tibbles shaking himself and panicking and trying to scrabble his way out of the hole?

The face in the mirror *looked* like him, but there was a quality in his eyes that wasn't quite him. A mischievous glint, a hint of cruelty, as if he would actually find it quite entertaining to bury Tibbles in the back yard. And pat the dirt down afterward – pat, pat, pat. And then bend down, with one hand mockingly cupped to his ear, as if he were listening for one last pleading mewl from under the ground.

He went back across the living room, opened the balcony door, and stepped outside. It was hot out here now, and he found it difficult to breathe. He grasped the balcony rail and looked down into the yard, where Santana had been digging up gopher holes. Santana wasn't there now, but he had left his long-handled shovel leaning up against the fence.

You see? It wouldn't be that difficult, would it? Santana's dug most of the hole for you already.

Are you nuts? What the hell are you thinking about? What do you think would happen to you if you did that? You think that nobody would see you doing it? You'd be arrested for cruelty to animals and you'd probably lose your job.

My job? Teaching English to morons who can't even speak Gibberish? Who cares? And anyhow, how long will it be before it's all over, and it's the end for all of us, and the only job that anybody *will have to do is serving the Lord and Master?*

Jim closed his eyes. *Calm*, he told himself. *You're losing it. Give yourself a break, for Christ's sake. You discover a girl's body nailed to the ceiling of your classroom, and then you find out that it was the daughter you never knew you had. Anybody would be shaken up by something like that, especially since you've seen a second body, nailed to the cypress tree. And the face of Satan, smiling at you.*

Calm. Om, or whatever.

After ten minutes or so, he went back inside and took a bottle of Fat Tire out of the fridge. There was no sign of Tibbles anywhere.

'Tibbles?' he coaxed him. 'Tibs? Do you think you and I could be friends again now?'

Wherever Tibbles was hiding himself, he stayed there. Under the bed in the spare room, probably, or behind the dishwasher.

He was on his way back to the balcony when his doorbell

rang. When he went to answer it he saw blonde hair and pink ribbons through the hammered-glass porthole.

'Summer!' he said, opening the door for her.

Summer was wearing a tight pink T-shirt, a tiny pair of white cotton safari shorts, and pink wedge-heeled sandals that were so high that she was teetering two inches taller than Jim. She was chewing bubblegum and flapping a sheet of paper as if the two actions were somehow coordinated. Flap, *chew*, flap, *chew*.

'Jimmy, I could really use your help.'

'OK, Summer. Help what with?'

'Is it OK if I come in?'

'Sure, yes. Come on in.'

'I'm not interrupting anything?' she said, peering into the kitchen.

'No, you're not interrupting anything. What do you want?'

'It's just that I'm applying for a job at Shine, you know the beauty parlor on Melrose? And they want me to write them a rezzamay or whatever it's called.'

Jim led the way into the living room. Summer followed him, still chewing and flapping her sheet of paper.

'So you want me to write a resumé for you? Is that it?'

'I've never been no use at all at writing, Jimmy. I can't even write my own name without spelling it wrong. I was hoping that maybe you could do it for me, you being an English teacher and all.'

'I know English, Summer, but I don't know anything about polishing nails, or plucking eyebrows, or waxing.'

'Yes, but that's the point. Neither do I, unless it's been done to me by somebody else. But I have to sound as if I do. You can do that for me, can't you?'

Jim turned around and looked at her. She may be ditzy, he thought, but she does have a really great body, doesn't she? And she smells wonderful, like fresh peaches. And she's very pretty, in a blonde, bouncy way, if you had a penchant for cocktail waitresses and pole dancers and *Playboy* centerfolds.

'OK, maybe I can help you out,' he told her. 'Not for nothing, though. I will expect something in return.'

Summer stopped chewing and flapping her sheet of paper. 'Come on, Jimmy, you know I'm flat busted. Otherwise I wouldn't be looking so hard for a job.'

'You don't have to pay me in money. There are plenty of other forms of recompense, aren't there?'

Summer frowned and said, 'I could bake you a Key Lime Pie.'

He came up close to her and gently tugged the sheet of paper out of her hand. 'There must be something else you have to offer.'

'Jimmy?' she said, batting her eyelashes. 'You don't mean what I think you mean, do you?'

'Why not, Summer? We're good friends, aren't we? What could be more natural?'

'You tell me. The first time we tried to get together, you had a problem with Mr Floppy, and the last time I suggested it, you said you had the bellyache. Not exactly flattering, for a girl who's trying her darnedest to show a guy how much she likes him.'

'Maybe I've changed my mind,' said Jim.

'Oh, come on, Jimmy. This isn't the moment.'

'So you say.'

'I do, Jimmy. I have to hand in my rezzamay by six p.m. otherwise I'll lose my chance of getting the job.'

Jim raised both hands and pushed her backward, toward the couch. She tried to retaliate, but he pushed her again, harder, and this time she lost her balance on her high wedge-heeled sandals and toppled over on to the cushions.

'What are you *doing*, Jimmy?'

'I'm collecting my resumé-writing fee, in advance,' he told her. With that, he clambered on top of her, on to the couch, so that he was kneeling astride her, and he started to wrestle with the golden buckle of her little white safari shorts.

'*Jimmy!*' she squealed, and pummeled him furiously with both fists.

It was then that he slapped her face, very hard. Immediately, her left cheek flared up scarlet and she stared at him in shock.

'You hit me! Jesus, Jimmy, you *hit* me!'

'Too right I hit you!' he barked back at her. 'And I'll hit

you again if you don't shut the fuck up! You want me to write your stupid resumé? This is what it's going to cost you, OK? You don't get anything in this world for nothing, sweetheart! Not even a job at some dumb beauty salon!'

'Jimmy – what's *wrong* with you? Jimmy – get off me, will you?'

Summer twisted and struggled, but Jim forced her down on to the couch with his left hand, while he wrestled off her safari shorts with his right. She was wearing only a tiny white lace thong underneath, and he pulled that off along with her shorts. He pried her knees apart so that her bare waxed vulva opened up, like two moist petals.

He unfastened his own belt buckle, and wrenched his chinos down below his knees. His penis was so hard he felt almost as if it might break off. He took hold of it in one hand and pushed it up inside Summer as hard and as deep as he could.

Immediately, she stopped struggling. Jim pushed again, and again, but she did nothing to resist him, and nothing to respond to him, either. She just lay there, completely inert. He pushed once more, and then he stopped pushing.

They looked at each other, nose to nose.

'Well, carry on,' said Summer. 'You've got what you wanted. Enjoy.'

Jim said, 'What the hell is the matter with you? You've been prick-teasing me for months.'

'What *I* was offering you was free, Jimmy. It didn't come with a price tag.'

They continued to stare into each other's eyes for a very long time. Jim gradually became aware of how red Summer's cheek was, where he had slapped her. She would be lucky not to have a black eye by the morning.

His penis began to soften, and he lifted himself off her. 'You've been asking for it ever since you moved in,' he told her. 'What did you expect?'

'I expected sex,' said Summer. 'You know, like normal consensitive sex, without being pushed around or slapped or nothing like that.'

Jim pulled up his chinos and buckled his belt. He had never forced himself on a woman like that before, and he had no clear idea of why he had done it now. All he knew was that he somehow felt entitled to have her, whenever he wanted her, whether she wanted him or not. His blood was pumping so loudly in his ears that he was almost deafened.

Summer stood up, too. She picked up her thong and her white safari shorts, but she didn't immediately put them on, almost as if she wanted to taunt Jim with what he could have enjoyed if only he hadn't been so aggressive.

'Oh, *Jimmy*,' she said.

Jim turned away. He couldn't think what to say to her.

'Listen,' she said, 'Forget about the rezzamay. There's no point me trying for that job anyhow, with my face all swelled up.'

Jim wanted to say that he was sorry, but somehow he couldn't. Even the thought of saying sorry made him feel as if his mouth were filled with grit.

At that moment the doorbell rang. Jim went to answer it while Summer hurried to pull on her shorts.

Detective Brennan and Detective Carroll were standing outside. They both looked grim-faced.

'Mr Rook? OK if we come in?'

'Oh, yes, sure.'

They followed him into the living room. Summer was quickly brushing her hair across the left side of her face, to hide her bruise.

Jim said, 'This is my downstairs neighbor, Detectives. She just came up to borrow some—'

'Coffee,' Summer put in. 'Yes – I was just leaving.'

With that, she went, and slammed the front door behind her. When she had gone, Detective Carroll turned around and said, 'She forgot her coffee.'

'Did she?' said Jim. 'So she did! She's so darn scatty, that girl.'

'Fights with her boyfriend, too, by the looks of it.'

'Oh, really?'

'Well . . . somebody just gave her a big fat bruise on the cheek, and she wasn't wearing a wedding band, so I kind of put two and two together.'

'Oh,' said Jim. 'Really? I wouldn't know.'

Detective Brennan paced around Jim's living room, taking in all of his bookshelves and all of his pictures and all of his trophies.

'I just thought you ought to know that we've identified the victim who was nailed to the cypress tree.'

'Oh, God. Don't tell me it's another of my students.'

'No . . . as a matter of fact, it's not. When the MEs had washed off the paint, they found a tattoo on his upper left arm: Los Primos.'

'Los Primos? That's an Hispanic street gang, isn't it?'

'Oh . . . you're quite the expert, Mr Rook.'

'I'm a college teacher, Detective. I teach remedial English. All of the street gangs have their own language. It's part of my job to know what the hell they're talking about.'

'Well, you're right, Clikos Los Primos are a small gang from East LA, pretty much exclusively Hispanic. We showed a picture of our vic to various members of the gang and they identified him right away.'

Detective Brennan produced a color scan of a young Hispanic man. He was quite handsome, although his eyes were closed and his cheeks were puffy and his skin was unnaturally gray.

'His name is Alvaro Esteban, more usually known as Santana. He works as a gardener, right here at Briar Cliff Apartments. He's your gardener, Mr Rook.'

TEN

Jim found it impossible to sleep that night. Every time he closed his eyes he saw that dark Satanic face that Ricky had painted, gradually materializing in the shadows. After three hours of twisting and turning and thumping his pillow he switched on his bedside lamp, climbed out of bed and went into the living room to watch *Brothers and Sisters*, even though he had no idea what the story was all about and what terrible secret Kitty was trying to keep from Tommy.

When the sun eventually began to fill his apartment, he took a long shower with his forehead pressed against the tiles, and then he made himself a mug of strong black Java coffee. He watched *Good Morning, America*, and even *Good Cookin' With Bruce Aidells*, but he was still ready to leave for college nearly an hour earlier than usual. Tibbles was still refusing to come out of hiding, but Jim filled up his bowl with tuna dinner and poured him a saucer of fresh milk.

'You want to sulk, you feline faggot, then sulk!' he called out, before he closed the front door. 'But just remember who started it – OK?'

On his way down the steps, he hesitated outside the door of Summer's apartment, wondering if he ought to knock and apologize for forcing himself on her yesterday evening. After a few moments, though, he decided against it. She was probably still in bed, and he still found it hard to think of saying sorry. Come on, she was always flaunting herself, wasn't she? She was always asking him if he thought that God had endowed her with big enough breasts, and did she need a boob job, and she would religiously tell him every time she went to Raya for a Brazilian. If that wasn't asking to be jumped on, he didn't know what was.

When he arrived at West Grove, the staff parking lot was almost deserted. He climbed out of his car and stood there for a moment, with the sun in his eyes and the early morning wind rattling in the yuccas all around him, and he was sure that he caught a snatch of that calliope music again. *In The Good Old Summertime*. Then one of the groundsmen started up his grass-cutter, and the moment was gone.

Inside, the college corridors were echoing and empty and smelled strongly of floor wax. As he opened the door of Art Studio Four, however, he was surprised to find that Simon Silence was already sitting in his place, with his spring-bound notebook and all of his felt-tip pens arranged neatly on the bench in front of him. He was listening to an iPod, with his eyes closed, nodding his head in time to some inaudible music. The sun was shining on him through the window, so that it looked as if he were being illuminated by a celestial ray from heaven.

Jim stood in the doorway for a moment, but Simon Silence showed no indication that he was aware of him standing there. He just kept on nodding in time to his iPod music.

Jim sat down and flopped his briefcase on to his desk. He had mended its handle with a wire coat hanger and duct tape. He opened it up and took out two poetry books and a red folder of questions on grammar and spelling.

Nearly a full minute went past. Then, without opening his eyes, Simon Silence said, 'Sorry about your gardener, Mr Rook.'

Jim looked up. 'Oh, yeah? How'd you know about that? I thought you never watched TV.'

'Our cleaner told me. She heard all about it on the local news channel.' Now Simon Silence opened his eyes and gave Jim one of his creepy, enigmatic smiles.

'Your *cleaner* told you?'

'That's right. She's a very bright young lady, our cleaner. She wants to be a paralegal, one day, and represent Mexican immigrants.'

'So what did she hear on the news?'

'Aha! Apparently, the police have been trying to work out why the victim was nailed up *here*, at West Grove College. So far, though, they've only managed to come up with one connection. The victim worked as a gardener at an apartment building in the Hollywood Hills. And who should happen to live in that apartment building but a certain English teacher from this very same college.'

'You're kidding me. They said that, on the news?'

'That's what my cleaner told me. I don't think they mentioned you by name, Mr Rook, but I couldn't help putting two and two together.'

He paused, and then he reached down into his gunny sack and said, 'Here – would you like an apple? I have plenty.'

Jim pushed back his chair and walked up the side of the classroom. 'Tell me something, Simon,' he said, 'what are you really here for? I mean here, in Special Class Two?'

'I don't know what you're driving at, Mr Rook.'

'First of all, you speak fluently and grammatically which means to me that you can probably *write* that way, too. Second of all, you have complete self-confidence, which is a quality that almost everybody who tips up in this Godforsaken class sorely seems to lack. You even took it upon yourself to set the rest of the class an essay when I wasn't here. You don't need remedial English, do you, Simon? I don't know what I can possibly have to offer you.'

'Ah, but that's where you're wrong, Mr Rook. You have more to offer me than you can imagine.'

'Like what, for instance?'

'You have a gift, sir. A very rare gift. In fact, it's unique. You can see the world as it really is. Not just *half* of it, like most people.'

'Meaning?'

'Meaning that you can see the dead as well as the living. You can see presences and shapes and apparitions. You can even see monstrosities that people don't believe in – or, at least that they don't *want* to believe in. Even the most pious of churchmen find it difficult to see monstrosities like that, if not impossible.'

Jim stared at Simon Silence for a long time before he said anything. What a speech. The sunlight that had first illuminated him had gradually inched away, leaving his face in shadow, and the expression in his eyes began to look darker and much more calculating.

'Who are you, really?' Jim asked him. 'How do you know all that about me?'

'I am Simon Silence, Mr Rook, that's all. The first and only son of the Reverend John Silence of the Church of the Divine Conquest. I am nobody, sir. You shouldn't be afraid of me.'

'Believe me, I'm *not*. But I still want to know exactly what it is you're doing here. You're having an effect on my class, Simon, and I'm not too sure that I like it. I'm even beginning to think that you're having some kind of an effect on *me*.'

Simon Silence said nothing, but kept on smiling, and with the fingertips of his left hand he traced a complicated pattern on top of the bench, around and around. A face? A pentacle? Circles within circles, like snakes that swallow their own tails?

'How about that essay on Paradise?' Jim asked him. 'Did you finish *yours* yet?'

'Of course,' said Simon Silence. He picked up his notebook and handed it over. Jim didn't read it in front of him – didn't even look at it until he had taken it back to his desk and sat down. Simon Silence returned his earphones to his ears, folded his arms and closed his eyes and started nodding again, as if he didn't care one way or the other what Jim thought of what he had written.

Simon Silence's handwriting was reasonably tidy, although it leaned backward and climbed uphill from left to right. It also had exaggerated loops on the descenders, like the g's and the p's and the y's.

Jim was no graphologist, but he had read enough scrawly and block-lettered English essays over the years to recognize some of the personality traits that were given away by a student's handwriting. A backward slope usually betrayed shyness and uncertainty, although it could also indicate a considerable attention to detail – what Jim called planespotters' handwriting. On the other hand, heavily emphasized descenders showed practicality and a matter-of-fact approach to life: auto-mechanics and builders and plumbers.

Jim glanced up at Simon Silence, and thought: *This hand-writing is deliberately meant to mislead me. He doesn't really write like this at all.*

If he had been asked to guess what Simon Silence's natural handwriting was like, he would have said sharply forward-sloping, with most of the emphasis on the ascenders like b, d, h, k and l. An aggressive, domineering personality, but with a strong spiritual element, almost fanatical.

He didn't know if the essay itself was intended to be misleading. It read: 'For me Paradise will come on the day when the Fires are lit all over the world from one horizon to another and are stoked with Those Who Never Should Have Been. Paradise will come when the Smoke has cleared and the Bones are Heaped High and the Great Blasphemy has at last been Atoned For.'

Jim read the essay a second time and then took out his red pen. Underneath the last line, he wrote, 'Very apocalyptic, Simon, but you need to explain yourself more fully. What, pray, is the Great Blasphemy? And who is it Who Never Should Have Been, when they're at home?'

As critical as he was about it, this essay confirmed his belief that Simon Silence had no place here in Special Class Two. It was a rambling, Old-Testament type rant, but it was fairly grammatical. There was no text speak in it, nor street slang, and he had actually spelled 'blasphemy' with a 'ph'. He doubted if anybody else in the class would have done that, even if they had known the word 'blasphemy' to begin with.

Jim was about to take Simon Silence's notebook back to him when the classroom door banged open and the rest of Special Class Two came barging in, chattering and laughing and pushing each other. Simon Silence opened his eyes again, and smiled at him.

You can see presences and shapes and apparition, Mr Rook. You can even see monstrosities that people don't believe in – or, at least, that they don't want *to believe in.*

Jim made his way to the back of the classroom, where Rebecca Teitelbaum was sitting. In contrast to the drab green dress in which she had showed up for class yesterday, she was dressed in a glaring scarlet-and-yellow blouse with a zigzag print on it, and she had used red-and-yellow beads to fasten her chaotic black hair into a topknot.

She was also wearing tight red jeans and yellow sandals. Everything she wore looked new, as if she had gone out shopping yesterday evening with the intention of changing her image entirely, from dutiful Jewish daughter to *X-Factor* wannabe rock chick.

Jim noticed that Nudnik, the grubby white teddy bear, was still sitting beside her. He, too, was sporting a necklace of red-and-yellow beads.

'Hey – I thought you were taking Nudnik off to be auctioned.'

'I was. But then I thought, no, he's *mine*. I've had him ever since I was little and he understands me more than anybody else does. Why should I give him to some stupid orphan kids at Lev LaLev who won't even realize how much he knows?'

'Oh, OK. I see. Well, he's your bear. Guess you can do what you like with him. But maybe he'd like to stay at home from now on. If I let *you* bring a mascot into class, everybody else will want to do it, and we don't want a remedial English group looking like the teddy bears' picnic, do we?'

'Nudnik isn't a *mascot*,' Rebecca Teitelbaum retorted. 'He's not a toy, either. He's my *confidant*. I tell him, like, *everything*.'

Jim looked at Nudnik and the bear stared back at him, glassy-eyed. Jim knew it was ridiculous, but today the bear looked quite sinister, as if it really did know all of Rebecca Teiltelbaum's secrets. What was more, it looked as if it could understand what they were talking about, even if it chose to stay silent.

'How about letting me see your essay on Paradise?' asked Jim.

Rebecca Teitelbaum handed him a torn-out sheet from her notebook. Her writing had unusual thick and thin strokes, almost as if she were writing in Hebrew characters rather than English. She had written *Paradise* as a heading, but underneath she had also written *Ganedyn*, which Jim assumed was the same word in Yiddish.

'My dream is to be most famous of all woman in the World. I step out of car and paperazi flash and flash with camera. I walk on to stage platform and thousands people stand up to ther feet and screem my name they love me so good. I am always on TV in movie and everybody beg me writ my name for them. All men say marry me marry me Rebecca you are most butiful of all woman in the World. Ever day I wear desiner cloths and diamon and everybody love me.'

'That's really your idea of Paradise?' Jim asked her.

Rebecca Teitelbaum nodded.

'Come on,' said Jim, 'you're a pretty good-looking girl already. Don't you think you might get a little tired of all that adulation?'

She shook her head. 'All my life nobody ever gave me any attention like that. And don't tell me that I'm good-looking. You're just saying that to make me feel better. I have horrible hair like wire and my nose is too big and I have to wear these really thick eyeglasses. No boy ever said to me come out on a date, let alone marry me.'

'Rebecca,' said Jim, 'everybody has beauty inside of them, and that includes you.'

He couldn't count the number of times he had said that to girls in Special Class Two who were lacking in confidence in their looks. '*Everybody has beauty inside of them, no matter how big their butts or how homely they are.*' He believed in it, too. At least, he *used* to believe in it. But looking at Rebecca Teitelbaum this morning, even in her new red-and-yellow outfit, he couldn't help thinking that – yes, her nose *was* kind of prominent, to put it politely, and her hair *was* frizzy. Not only that, her front teeth protruded like an indecisive beaver's and she had a large wart just in front of her right ear, and another one on her neck. In fact, he wasn't at all surprised that she had never been asked out on a date.

He handed back her essay. 'You've made a couple of bloopers with your spelling, Rebecca, and your grammar needs some fixing, here and there. But those are minor details that we can fix later. Otherwise – yes, you've given me a very interesting insight into what you want out of life. Fame, and adoration and huge popularity.'

None of which will ever come your way, gelibte. Not until hell freezes over, anyhow.

Next, he walked around to the chubby Hispanic boy who was sitting on the end of the third bench back, next to Simon Silence. His chair was tilted back and his legs were spread wide and he was softly drumming on his thighs. He had shiny jet-black hair tied back with a leather thong into a ponytail, and a round, cheerful face.

'Want to tell me your name?' Jim asked him.

'It's not there, my name, in the register?'

'Of course it is, *muchacho*. But I'd like to hear you say it first, so that when I get around to calling it out loud, I pronounce it properly. That's called "respect".'

'OK. Cool. My name is Javier Alejandro Alvarez. But it is cool if you call me Al. That is easy to say with respect, yes?'

'All right, Al. How about you show me your essay?'

Al Alvarez rocked his chair forward so that all four legs were on the floor, and then he said, 'I did not exactly write it.'

'I see. And why was that? Couldn't you imagine what Paradise might be like? All mariachi music and chocolate chimichangas and hot young señoritas? *Arriba! Arriba!*'

'You make fun of Mexican culture,' Al Alvarez pouted. 'That is not respect.'

'Well, since you haven't bothered to write anything down, maybe you'd like to *tell* me what you think Paradise might be like. Right now I'm thinking that you were simply too bone idle to put pen to paper, and that doesn't deserve too much respect, does it?'

Al Alvarez turned his head away. For a fleeting moment, Jim saw him catch Simon Silence's eye, and Simon Silence gave him a quick nod of his head which looked to Jim like encouragement – like, '*go on, don't be afraid – tell him!*'

Jim said, 'OK, Al. If you don't have any ideas about Paradise – or if you *do* have ideas but you don't want to tell me what they are, that's fine by me.'

He started to walk back toward the front of the class. 'You want to work, you don't want to work, that's entirely up to you. I'm only here to tell you guys the difference between a preposition, a proposition, and a sharp kick in the ass. The whole point of Special Class Two is that you're all here to help yourselves.'

But before Jim had reached his desk, Al Alvarez stood up. '*I tell you!*' he called out, and he sounded so shaken that Jim immediately turned around.

His nostrils were flaring and he was clenching both of his fists. 'I tell you about my Paradise!'

'Go on, then, Al,' Jim coaxed him. 'Let's hear it.'

'In my Paradise, I am surrounded by beautiful girls! So many beautiful girls I cannot count them! They take off all of their clothes and they dance around me! Then they kiss me and stroke me and take off all of my clothes, too!'

'Al,' Jim interrupted him. 'I'm not so sure this particular concept of Paradise is going to be suitable for a mixed class of remedial English students. Maybe you should tell me later, in private. You know, man to incorrigible lecher.'

But Al Alvarez wouldn't stop. 'I tell you what I do! I make love to them all, every one, in every way! Front, back, every way! And they are screaming with the pleasure! And they are all sweaty and shiny, and wriggle all around me like nest of snake!'

'Al,' said Jim. 'How about you put a sock in it, OK?'

'Then I take razor! Old-style razor! And every one of those beautiful girls, I slit their throat – *slit*! *slit*! *slit*! And we are all covered in blood! And I lift up my hands and my hands are all covered in blood, and I lick it with my tongue! This for me is Paradise!'

ELEVEN

Jim marched straight up to Al Alvarez and seized his upper arm.

'OK, you,' he told him, 'you're out of this classroom as of right now!'

Al Alvarez stared at him, as glassy-eyed as Nudnik the teddy bear. He was sweating and shivering, almost as if he were having a fit.

'You *axed* me!' he protested. 'You axed me what my Paradise was like!'

Jim locked his elbow so that his arm was rigid and started to march him toward the door. As he did so, however, Simon Silence called out, in the clearest of voices, '*H-R Four-Two-Four-Seven!*'

Jim stopped abruptly and turned around, although he still kept his grip on Al Alvarez's arm. 'H-R Four-Two-Four-Seven?'

'That's right, sir.'

'I know what H-R Four-Two-Four-Seven is, Simon. It's the act of Congress which was passed in two thousand nine to prevent the harmful restraint and seclusion of students, even though most of them heartily deserve it. However . . . Al here has been duly and properly cautioned about his disruptive conduct, and I am merely escorting him out of the classroom for his own safety and the general well-being of Special Class Two, most of whom didn't come hear to him babbling on about orgiastic massacres.'

Simon Silence was unfazed. 'He isn't breathing right, Mr Rook. H-R Four-Two-Four-Seven specifically says that a member of staff must not forcibly escort a student by restricting his or her breathing.'

Jim took three or four steps back toward Simon Silence, and Al Alvarez had to come stumbling behind him. 'Listen, Mr Silence. How about I restrict *your* breathing so that you keep your opinions to yourself?'

Simon Silence kept on smiling at him. 'You should chill, Mr Rook. There's too much at stake. You can't afford to lose your cool.'

'You think so? Well, OK, we'll have to see about that. Now, come on, Al, I want you out of here, now.'

He manhandled Al Alvarez into the corridor. When they were outside, and the classroom door was closed behind them, he released his grip on the boy's elbow, but he shoved him hard against the wall.

'What the *hell* did you think you were saying in there?' he demanded.

Al Alvarez shook his head. He was still perspiring and his nose was running, too. He sniffed and wiped his nose on the back of his sleeve.

'I don't know, sir.'

'You don't *know*? You don't *know*? All that stuff about having women every which way and then cutting their throats and licking their blood?'

'I swear I don't know, Mr Rook. It all just come into my head. It was like my brains was boiling. I never thought nothing like that before, never. If I said something like that at home, my momma would kill me.'

Jim stood close to Al Alvarez, saying nothing, while the boy gradually calmed down. After a while Jim laid his hand on his shoulder and said, 'How about a drink of water?'

'I'm OK, sir. Really. I don't know what happened in there.'

'You want to go back in, or do you want to go home? I don't mind if you want to call it a day.'

Al Alvarez leaned across and cautiously peered through the porthole in the studio door, as if he were afraid of what he might see. Most of the students were milling around between the benches – the boys throwing a baseball to each other, and the girls all trying to dance like Rihanna. Only Simon Silence had remained in his place, writing and sketching in his note-book and coloring in his drawings with his felt-tip pens. He looked up and saw Al Alvarez and Jim looking in through the porthole, and he smiled to himself and went back to his work.

'Tell me,' said Jim, 'what do you think of that guy?'

'Simon? He got something, sir. Don't know what it is exactly, but it's like he got *mojo*, only stronger than *mojo*. My grannie would have called it *brujeria.*'

'You feel that?' asked Jim. He knew what both of those words meant. *Mojo* meant self-confidence and personal magnetism and sex appeal. *Brujeria* meant serious magic, which would normally be cast by a *brujo*, or a worker of spells.

'Don't know what it is exactly,' Al Alvarez repeated. 'But, yes. I feel that.'

'So when you came out with all that orgy stuff, and slitting women's throats . . . do you think maybe that it was Simon who made you think of that?'

Al Alvarez glanced at Jim and Jim could tell that he was nervous. 'I don't know, sir. I wouldn't like to say nothing like that.'

'What are you afraid of?'

'I ain't afraid of nothing, Mr Rook. I don't want to cause no trouble, that's all.'

'Yesterday, Al, I would have picked you out as the joker of the class. So what's different today?'

Al Alvarez looked down at the floor and wouldn't catch Jim's eye. 'I don't want to cause no trouble, that's all.'

Jim hesitated for a moment, and then he opened the studio door and ushered Al Alvarez back into the classroom. Immediately, the boys stopped throwing their baseball around and the girls stopped swaying their hips and waving their arms in the air.

'OK, everybody,' said Jim. 'The situation is now settled and it's time to carry on with some work. I'm going to read you another poem and then I'm going to give you a half-hour to make some notes about what you think it means.'

He went across to his desk and picked up one of his poetry books. 'This is by a poet called John Lupo, and it's called *The Book of Years.*

'High on a windy hill
With a steel-gray lake glittering in the distance
I was reading The Book of Years
And the wind in the grass whispered footnotes to me
Explaining what each sentence really meant.

Codas, cadenzas.

I read about my childhood; and my father
And my brothers; and the days I went to school
It was all there, my childhood, in The Book of Years
And the wind in the grass kept on whispering to me
"This is what your teacher tried so hard to tell you
And – see – your father loved you, even if he never
    found the words."

Codas, cadenzas.

And then I turned a page and you appeared
Laughing and dancing, and the wind blew warm
I read about you dancing in The Book of Years
I read about your laughing and your tears.
But then I turned the page and all the grass could say,
Confused, was *"What? Where is she?"*
And the day grew dull; and the steel-gray lake no
    longer shone.

I closed The Book of Years, for you were gone.

Codas, cadenzas.'

'Hey, that's a tearjerker, man,' called out DaJon Johnson, from
the back of the class. 'Next time why don't you read us a
poem that make us all bust out laughing.'

Jim smiled and said, 'I will, don't worry.' He held up another
book, with a yellow cover. 'Ogden Nash, one of America's
most humorous poets. Next time I'll read you his poem *A Tale
of the Thirteenth Floor*. It's about a bum who goes to a hotel,
intent on murder, but Maxie, the elevator boy, takes him to
the thirteenth floor, where murderers have to shuffle around
and around together with their victims in a conga, for all
eternity.

'Here,' he said, and opened the book, and read a few
lines.

"'We are higher than twelve and below fourteen,"
Said Maxie to the bum,
"And the sickening draft that taints the shaft
Is a whiff of kingdom come.
The sickening draft that taints the shaft
Blows through the devil's door!'"

'That don't sound at all humorous to me!' DaJon Johnson
protested. 'That sounds real scary! The dead and the living,
dancing a frickin' conga together, for ever and ever? Hooo-*wee*!'

But it was Simon Silence that Jim was looking at. He wasn't
just smiling now, he was grinning, and showing all his teeth.
Jim could almost have sworn that his eyes lit up like two
quartz-halogen pinpricks.

'OK . . . I'll be back in a minute,' said Jim. 'Jot down some
of your thoughts about *The Book of Years*. Try to relate what
the poet is saying to your own lives. Did your parents make
a point of telling you that they loved you, or did they keep it
to themselves? Did you listen to your teachers, or did you
always think that you knew better? Did you ever lose anybody
that you really cared about? If you wrote a book about your
own life, what would you choose for a title?'

'*How Gorgeous Am I?*' suggested Jesmeka Watson.

'*Stupid And Fucked-Up But With Really Cool Hair, Part
One*,' said Rudy Cascarelli.

Jim left Art Studio Four and went downstairs to the main
corridor. He walked past the open door of his usual classroom,
Special Class Two, and saw that the decorators had nearly
finished replastering and redecorating the ceiling. The floor
was covered with white-spattered sheets and the air was filled
with a strong smell of emulsion paint.

As he passed Senior Spanish, Sheila Colefax came hurrying
out, with a clutch of plastic folders pressed against her bosom.

'Jim!' she said. 'How are you?'

Jim stood in front of her and lifted both his hands to stop
her. 'Wait a second, Sheila, let me get this right.' Very slowly
and carefully, he said, '*No debemos comer la carne como esto.*'

Sheila blinked at him. 'What are you trying to say to me,
Jim?'

'I'm trying to say, "We must stop meeting like this." It's only a joke, Sheila. You know how much I like you.'

'Well, all right. I understand it's a joke. But next time say, "*Debemos parar el encontarnos como esto.*" What *you* said was, "We must stop eating meat like this."'

'Oh, shoot, I'm sorry. Back to the phrase book. But you knew what I was getting at, didn't you?'

'No, to be truthful, I didn't. I'm a vegetarian.'

'Oh. OK. How were the Woodpeckers?'

'The Woolspinners. I didn't go.'

'Not because of me, I hope?'

'No. Yes, a little, maybe. I guess I wasn't in the mood.'

'Maybe some other time, huh? Things are kind of fraught at the moment.'

'I know. I'm surprised they haven't closed the college altogether.'

'If that last victim had been a student, I think they would have done.'

Sheila said, 'What's going on, Jim? Do you have any idea? I mean, you know quite a lot about those black magicky sorts of things, don't you?'

Jim thought about Ricky's Satanic painting, and the look on Simon Silence's face when he had quoted Ogden Nash's line about '*a whiff of kingdom come.*'

'Yeah, I guess I know a little about those black magicky sorts of things. But I have no idea at all what this particular ritual is all about – if it *is* a ritual. The white paint, and the eight white cats. I've never heard about anything like it, ever.'

Sheila touched Jim's arm. 'I have to go this way, to have these test papers copied. I'll see you later.'

Jim watched her go, in her high-necked white blouse and her black pencil skirt, and he thought he could detect a slight suggestion of sashay in the way she was walking. It occurred to him that maybe she liked him more than she had previously let on. In fact, maybe, in her own suppressed way, she was flirting with him. Pity this wasn't the time for it.

He knocked on the door of Dr Ehrlichman's office. Dr Ehrlichman was smooth-talking someone on the phone, and repeatedly smoothing his bald head with his hand as he did so.

When Jim stepped into his office he mouthed 'sit down' and pointed to the chair in front of his desk. Jim waved his hand to indicate that he would prefer to stand. He knew from experience how low down that chair was.

'Well, that's so generous of you,' said Dr Ehrlichman, on the phone. 'That really is so generous. We'll be seeing you at Thanksgiving, I very much trust?'

He hung up and then he steepled his hands and raised both eyebrows and said, 'Jim? And what can I do for you?'

'I want that kid out of my class,' Jim told him.

'I'm sorry. Which kid?'

'You know what kid I'm talking about. Simon Silence. Only son of the Reverend John Silence of the Church of the Holy Outburst, or whatever it's called.'

Dr Ehrlichman gave an exaggerated double-take. 'Simon Silence? I talked to him myself, when the Reverend Silence brought him here. I thought he was unusually polite, and articulate, and eager to learn.'

'Exactly. Everything that my usual students are *not*.'

'I thought you would be delighted to have a student like that in your class. Somebody to set a level of excellence to which all of his fellow students could aspire.'

'Walter – Special Class Two does not have levels of excellence. Special Class Two exceeds my expectations if they make any kind of sense at all. These are kids who don't know how to make letters into words, let alone words into sentences, and most of the time they speak in riddles. Like, what the dilly yo?'

'Excuse me?'

'What's going on, Walter?'

'I still don't understand why you should want Simon Silence out of your class. He can only improve your end-of-year average.'

'The reason why I want him out is nothing to do with his academic ability. The reason I want him out is because he's creepy, and he's having a very bad influence on all of the rest of Special Class Two, and he's even having a bad influence on *me*. I have never been so bad tempered and erratic in my behavior in my life.'

Dr Ehrlichman tugged a Kleenex out of a box on his desk and made an elaborate performance of blowing his nose. 'Ragweed,' he said. 'It always gives me post-nasal drip.'

'I want him out,' Jim insisted. 'I want him out today. You can put him into any other class you like, but not mine.'

At the same time, strangely, he thought about Simon Silence's offer of an apple. He could picture what it would have looked like, pink and green, and what it would have tasted like. That sweetness, that sudden burst of acidity. And that calliope playing, far, far away.

Here – would you like an apple? I have plenty.

Dr Ehrlichman carefully folded up his tissue and tossed it into his wastebasket. Then he gave a grimace and said, 'I'm sorry, Jim. No can do.'

'Of course you can. You principal, he student. You tell him, "Go to other class, student," he have to go. End of smoke signal.'

'Well, in this particular case it's a little trickier than that. Without beating around the bush, the Reverend Silence specifically requested that Simon be enrolled in Special Class Two.'

'That's insane. He doesn't need remedial English. All he needs is somebody to sort out his face. Goddamn kid keeps smiling all the time, like he thinks something's funny.'

'Jim, this is beginning to sound very much like personal dislike.'

'Walter – no wonder they made you principal! You have such a keen understanding of human nature!'

Dr Ehrlichman jabbed his finger at Jim and said, in a bunged-up voice, 'Don't you get sarcastic with me, Jim. The Reverend Silence believes that Simon needs to learn more street slang in order to spread the word of God into the ghettoes and among the gangs. The way he speaks now, they won't listen to what he says for a moment.'

'So he's joined Special Class Two not to improve his English but to dumb it down. You know something, Walter, I don't think there's an antonym for "remedial English". Maybe West Grove should invent one. We could call it "stupedial English."'

'That's enough, Jim. I'm very sorry that you're not interacting constructively with Simon Silence, but the plain fact is that the Reverend Silence donated a very substantial sum of money toward the upgrade of our sports facilities.'

Jim said, 'What? Say it isn't so.'

'The pool, as you know, is in a serious state of disrepair. It urgently needs a new filtration plant, and new pumps, and new tiling. The Reverend Silence has agreed to give us three-point-five million toward it.'

'Three-point-five million dollars? He wants his son to speak like a wanksta and he's prepared to pay three-point-five million dollars for it?'

Dr Ehrlichman shrugged. 'You should be proud of yourself, Jim. Your reputation has obviously spread far and wide. The Reverend Silence insisted that Simon be tutored by you, and you alone. You've done this college a very great service.'

Jim slowly shook his head. 'I think you'll find that I've done exactly the opposite, Walter. Is your nose still blocked up?'

'Well, yes. It's the ragweed.'

'If your nose is still blocked up, that's why you can't detect the sickening whiff of kingdom come.'

Jim stalked back along the main corridor, fuming. As he reached the foot of the stairs the math teacher, Roger Ball, came squelching past in his thick-soled sneakers, with his unkempt brown beard and his brown check shirt and his brown corduroy pants.

'Jim! Where have you been? How was your vacation? Laura and me, we went to Cancun! What a time we had there! We had one of those bottles of tequila with an agave worm in it, and Laura – goddamnit, you're not going to believe this – Laura swallowed the damn thing! She *swallowed* it!'

'What?' said Jim, staring at him as if he didn't recognize him.

'We had one of those bottles of tequila with an agave worm in it,' said Roger Ball, less certainly this time.

'Yes? And?'

'Laura . . . swallowed it.'

Jim kept staring at him. He was so angry that he didn't trust himself to say any more. He knew that it wasn't Roger Ball's fault that he had to keep Simon Silence in Special Class Two, but the way he felt at the moment he would have yelled at anybody, even the janitor.

He turned his back on Roger Ball and started to climb the stairs.

'Maybe we could have a drink one night?' Roger Ball called after him. 'I could ask Henry and Ricardo to come along. Maybe we could go for burgers, too?'

Jim didn't answer. He was only halfway up the stairs, however, when a young girl came breezing past the top of the staircase. She was slim, and wearing a clinging gray jersey dress. Her hair was light brown and long and flowing as if she were walking in a wind.

High on a windy hill . . .

As Jim went up the next three stairs, the girl turned her head and looked down at him. He recognized her at once from her photograph. She was beautiful, even more beautiful than her mother had been. Those hazel eyes, and those feline cheekbones, and that slightly pouting smile.

I read about you dancing in The Book of Years . . .

Jim's entire skin felt as if it were shrinking. He gripped the handrail tightly, and for a split second he thought he was going to lose his balance and fall backward. As it was he stumbled and struck his left knee on the riser in front of him.

'Jim!' shouted Roger Ball. 'Jim, are you OK up there?'

But now Jim was clambering up the stairs, as fast as he could. By the time he reached the top, the girl was already halfway along the corridor.

'*Bethany!*' he shouted. '*Bethany!*'

TWELVE

Before she reached the end of the corridor, she turned around. She was lit up by the sunlight that came through the second-to-last window in the same way that Simon Silence had been illuminated when he had first walked into the classroom that morning. A celestial ray from heaven.

'Bethany!' he panted. He was running now, with all his loose change chunking in his pants pockets.

He knew that Bethany was dead. He wasn't deluding himself that she had somehow mysteriously come to life again, or that Jane had made a mistake when she had identified her body. But ever since he was seven years old he had been able to see dead people, and talk to them – especially if they *wanted* him to see them, and to talk to them – and if the dead daughter that he had never known about wanted to talk to him now, this was an opportunity he wasn't going to miss.

He slowed down as he approached her. He was panting. The sunlight that surrounded her was dazzling, and swarming with golden specks of dust. She looked so bright that he could barely see her face, and her light brown hair waved all around her in that unfelt wind.

'Bethany,' he said. 'What are you doing here?'

'I came to see *you*, Daddy.' Her voice was very muted, as if she were speaking to him from inside a closet, with the door closed. 'I came to tell you something.'

'I never knew about you, sweetheart,' said Jim. 'Your mommy never told me about you. I never even knew that you were born.'

'I want to come back, Daddy.'

Jim had tears in his eyes, but he had to shake his head. 'You can't come back, sweetheart. There's no way that you can come back.'

'You can do it, Daddy. I know you can.'

'I can't, baby. If only.'

'Think of all the things we could do together, Daddy. We could go for picnics. We could walk on the seashore. We could read a book together, on a windy hill. We could talk and talk and talk and never stop.'

Jim reached out his hand for her, but he knew that even if he touched her, he would feel nothing at all. This was Bethany's spirit, that was all, not her body. As Ogden Nash had written, in his poem about the Thirteenth Floor, '*The clean souls fly to their home in the sky.*'

Bethany said, 'Please, Daddy. Please find a way. Simon will help you.'

'Simon? You mean Simon *Silence*?'

Bethany nodded. 'Simon will help you. You only have to ask him.'

'How do you know Simon? Bethany – *how do you know Simon*?'

'Daddy, don't be angry with me.'

'I'm not angry, sweetheart, but I need to understand what the . . . what the connection is. How can *Simon* help me to bring you back? You're gone, and I wish so much that I had gotten to know you before you went, but there's no way for you to come back. I'm sorry. I'm so very sorry, but that's the way it is.'

'I *can* come back, Daddy. We can *all* come back. Simon will help you.'

'Bethany—'

'We could walk on the seashore, Daddy. You remember the seashore. We could ride on the horses on the carousel.'

In The Good Old Summertime . . .

Jim felt as if an earth tremor had rippled through the floor underneath his feet. 'What do you know about that?' he asked her.

'We could read a book on a windy hill. We could talk and talk and talk and never stop.'

'What do you know about the seashore?'

But now Bethany turned away, and the sunlight shone brighter, until it was dazzling, and she simply melted out of sight in front of him.

He stayed where he was, with tears sliding down his cheeks.

The sunlight faded again, and then a cloud passed over the sun.

'Mr Rook?' said a voice, and it was a voice that he recognized.

'What is it, Simon?' he asked, keeping his back to him.

'I was just making sure that you were all right, Mr Rook.'

Jim dry-washed his face with his hands. 'Any reason why I shouldn't be?'

'Well . . . it's always very stressful, when you lose somebody you love. Especially if you never had the chance to get to know them.'

Jim turned around and walked back toward Art Studio Four. The door was open and the usual noise was coming from inside – the boys throwing their baseball around and drumming dubstep rhythms on the benches, the girls laughing and chattering and singing.

Simon Silence was standing outside the door in his loose white linen shirt and his loose white pants. He wasn't smiling, though, and in some subtle way his face seemed to have altered. His nose looked flatter and his eyes appeared to slant more than they had before. He looked *older*, too, although Jim couldn't work out why.

He held up an apple – pink, and green, and shiny. 'I polished it for you already,' he said.

Jim hesitated, and then he took it. 'What kind of a game are you playing here, Simon? What's going on?'

'No game, Mr Rook. You saw her for yourself, didn't you?'

'Don't tell me that you saw her, too?'

Simon Silence shook his head. 'I can't do that. I don't have that facility, unlike you. But I heard you calling out her name, and I heard you talking to her.'

'Then you'll have guessed what she said.'

'Yes.'

There was a long silence between them. Then Jim said, 'Let's get back to this class, shall we? Let's see if the rest of them can all aspire to be as good at English as you are. And let's see if *you* can learn some more street speak.'

'I'm koolin' it.'

'Don't you try to mock me, Simon. I mean it. You and I, we need to sit down at recess and we need to talk.'

'Of course we do, sir,' said Simon Silence, and returned to his place.

Jim stood in front of the class and held up his hand for silence. 'Let's hear from somebody who hasn't spoken out before.' He looked from one disinterested face to the next, until he stopped at the baby-pretty girl with the scraggly blonde curls. Today she was wearing a tight white T-shirt with the slogan I BEAT ANOREXIA on her breasts, in shiny scarlet letters. She was chewing gum and staring into the middle distance.

'You,' said Jim. 'What's your name?'

'You talking to me?' she said, in a squeaky voice, pointing at herself like Robert De Niro in *Taxi Driver*.

'Yes, I'm talking to you. Do you want to tell us your name?'

'Oh – OK, it's Hunni. It's spelled the same way as "funny", but with an "i" instead of a "y". Hunni Robards.'

'OK, Hunni, what feelings did you get when I read you *The Book of Years*?'

'What feelings did I get? I felt sorry for myself. That's how I felt.'

'Why is that, Hunni?'

'I felt sorry for myself because it's, like, obviously *me* who's laughing and dancing and like lighting up the whole world and making the wind feel warm, and then I'm kind of like written out of it. It's a bit like being the best character in a daytime soap, you know like *Days Of Our Lives,* and then you get some fatal illness or knocked down by a truck and you can't even come back in a later episode unless it's a dream.'

'So you really thought that poem was all about you.'

'For definite,' said Hunni, chewing her gum even more emphatically. 'Absolutely and for definite.'

Jim pointed at Kyle Baxter, sitting in the front row. 'How about you, Kyle? What did it mean to you?'

'I felt very strongly that it was written about me. The wind whispering in the grass, explaining how to put words together so that you can understand what they mean. And then that chorus of *coda*, which means the conclusion or closing part of a statement, and *cadenza*, which means a virtuoso solo passage in a piece of music, typically near the end.'

'Hey, I'm glad you explain that, man,' put in DaJon Johnson. 'I thought *coda cadenza* was some kind of a drug, like, you know, codeine, like the dude who wrote the poem was whacked out of his brain.'

Jim paced from one side of the classroom to the other. He felt that he was beginning to detect a pattern here. It wasn't unusual for his students to see the world only from their own point of view. Many of them had lived all their lives within the same twenty-block neighborhood, and had rarely ventured further than the bodega on the corner. In the past, he had known students had never even been to the beach, even though it was less than twenty minutes away, and who had never seen the ocean.

But almost all of the responses that this class had been giving him this morning had been selfish almost to the point of absurdity. Both Jesmeka Watson and Rebecca Teitelbaum had wanted to be celebrities – 'mega famus' in Jesmeka's words – and adored by thousands. Joe Chang had wanted to be a member of a gang that inspired fear wherever they went. Even Kyle Baxter the Dictionary Dude had wanted everybody in the whole world to know that he was smarter than they were.

It had been the same with the poem, *The Book of Years*. Every student seemed to think that the poet had written it especially for them, as if he had known them personally.

Jim was always aware that one of the most important aspects of his job as a teacher of remedial English was to develop his students' sensitivity to other people's needs – particularly when it came to a potential employer, who was assessing their suitability for a job. Yet in only two days, this class were beginning to show signs that they were oblivious to everybody's needs except their own.

Or maybe I'm just being hypersensitive, thought Jim. *They're only kids, after all, and kids are selfish by definition. Maybe I'm just being grouchy.*

He went up to the boy with the red hair and the raging red

acne, who was sitting directly behind Joe Chang. Today he was wearing a black T-shirt with showers of dandruff on his shoulders.

'So, what's *your* name, son?' he asked him.

'Tomas – well, Tommy. Tommy Makovicka.'

'Makovicka? That's unusual. What kind of a name is that?'

'It's Czech, sir. My great-grandfather came from Kladno, that's a city near Prague.'

'OK. That's interesting. Does it mean anything, "Makovicka"? I know that most Czech names have a meaning. Like "Rybar" is a fisherman, and "Novak" means somebody who's new in town.'

Tommy Makovicka flushed redder than ever. 'It does mean something, yes, sir. It means "Poppyhead".'

With the exception of Simon Silence, everybody in Special Class Two burst out laughing. Jim immediately lifted his hand for them to quieten down.

'OK, OK. Don't tempt me to go around the class and tell you what all of your surnames really mean. Some of you would be laughing on the other side of your face, believe me.'

He turned back to Tommy Makovicka and said, 'All right, Tommy, what did *The Book of Years* mean to you – if it meant anything?'

'Some of it's true and some of it isn't.'

'Excuse me? You want to explain that?'

'When it says my dad loved me even if he never said so, that's not true. He never said so because he never did. He only loved my sister, Khrista. He was always telling her how clever she was and how beautiful she was and he was always telling me how stupid and ugly I was.'

'Can't blame the dude for tellin' the truth!' sang out DaJon Johnson.

Jim turned around to DaJon Johnson and made a zipper gesture across his lips. Then he said, 'OK, Tommy – what part of the poem do you think is true?'

'Khrista was always laughing and dancing like it says in the poem. She was always flirting and going out with these really evil guys, just because they had money and fancy cars. "Laughter and tears," that's what it says in the poem and that was true, because these guys always used to treat her so bad, but she still kept on going back for more.

'One day she didn't come home and they found her in Selma Park, and she was dead. One of those guys must have given her too much smack and then dumped her when she OD'd. So that's the true part of the poem. You give somebody too much, more than they deserve, and you end up killing them. They're gone.'

'Well, that's a very sad story, Tommy, even though I'm not too sure that the poem really says that, and I'm not too clear what your point is.'

'The point is, I was so glad when she died,' said Tommy, his face flushing even redder. 'It was like I finally got my revenge on my dad, right? It was better than sticking a knife in him, because he had lost his beautiful, clever Khrista for ever, and he was stuck with stupid, ugly me, and it was *his* fault. Like, *yessss*!'

The classroom was silent. Jim saw that one or two students were staring at Tommy, and they were obviously shocked. But most of them looked as if they understood how he felt, and some of them were actually nodding in approval.

He turned to Simon Silence, to see if he was smiling, and of course he was. But it was not the sloping, self-satisfied smile that he usually smiled. It was a smile of quiet acknow-ledgement, as if everything was working out just the way he wanted it.

'All right,' said Jim, 'I think that's enough about *The Book of Years*. The poet who wrote it, John Lupo, said himself that it was all about memory, and how our lives seem to be so different when we look back at them. Why the hell didn't we see some of the things that were going on right under our noses? Why didn't we realize what was about to happen to us, before it was too late?

'Anyhow – now I'm going to hand out some papers which have ten sentences on them. Some of these sentences have words that are spelled incorrectly, or very bad mistakes in grammar.'

'*Grammar*?' frowned DaJon Johnson. 'Like, a grammar coke?'

'Grammar like in the English language, DaJon. I think even you know that.'

He started to walk slowly down the side of the classroom, giving four papers to the students sitting at the end of the benches, so that they could pass them down. He had just handed four papers to Tommy Makovicka when his attention was caught by one of the scores of pictures on the wall beside him.

Pinned up among the garish landscapes and lopsided vases of orchids and misshapen animals was a small, dark portrait of a smiling man. One of the reasons Jim noticed it was because its surface was shining in the morning sunlight, as if it had been freshly painted. Not only that, it looked much more professional than all of the other pictures.

He went across to study it more closely. As he approached it he experienced that same shrinking-skin sensation as he had when Bethany had appeared at the top of the stairs. The portrait was a scaled-down version of the last Storyteller that Ricky had been attempting to paint, with his gray skin and his knobbly horns and his triumphant grin. Six or seven small children were gathered around him with expectant expressions on their faces as if they were waiting for him to tell them how bombastic God was, and how effete Jesus had been, and how the Bible was nothing but lies and riddles and fairy stories.

Again, without any warning, Jim felt that deep surge of empowerment, as if this Satanic creature could give him the strength to do anything he wanted. So far, he had used his gift of seeing spirits and demons only to protect himself and his friends and the students of Special Class Two, and to give peace to some poor bewildered souls who hadn't understood that they had passed over. But now, when he looked at this picture, he felt that he could not only talk to the dead, if they appeared, but that he could *summon* them. He could call them, as many as he wanted, and once he had called them he could command them.

He stepped back. He was aware that Simon Silence was watching him. He could see him out of the corner of his eye, but he didn't turn around. Instead, he handed four test papers to Al Alvarez, and then went on to give four more to DaJon Johnson.

'How long we got for this, Mr Rook?' DaJon Johnson asked him. 'Like, I'm kind of a slow reader, innit? I have to savor every word like a fine wine, like.'

Jim didn't answer him. He was staring out of the windows at the back of Art Studio Four, down to the grassy slope and the eucalyptus grove. Standing on the slope were more than seventy or eighty people, all of them looking up at him. They were perfectly motionless, all of them, and they were all pale-faced. Even the African-Americans and the Asians among them had a gray, ashy appearance.

Some of them were dressed in dusty-looking suits, or faded sweats, in gray and maroon. Others wore yellowed nightgowns or crumpled pajamas. The morning breeze lifted their hair and made their clothes flap, but apart from that, none of them moved.

Jim stood and stared at them for nearly a minute. After a while he became conscious that Simon Silence was standing very close behind him.

'I think you're forgetting that you have a test paper to complete,' he said, although he knew that he didn't sound very authoritative.

'What can you see, Mr Rook?' asked Simon, quietly. 'What are you looking at, out there on the grass? There's nothing there that *I* can see, Mr Rook.'

'I think you know exactly what I'm looking at,' Jim told him. 'The point is, what are they all doing here?'

Simon Silence didn't answer at first, so Jim turned around to face him. There was no doubt that Simon Silence's features had altered, and that his forehead seemed to be much more pronounced, as if he were permanently frowning.

'You were the one who called them, Mr Rook. They heard you, and they came. It won't be long now, and you will have the power to call all of them – *all* of them, and they will come through from the other side in their hundreds of thousands. In their *millions*.'

'But why the hell would I *want* to call them? Tell me that.'

Simon Silence reverted to that sly, self-satisfied smile. 'You will call them, Mr Rook, because you are the only one who can, and because it will make you feel greater than any man on Earth, or in Heaven. It will make you feel even greater than the Lord God Not-So-Very-Almighty, amen.'

THIRTEEN

J im stared down for another few seconds at the people standing motionless on the grassy slope, and then he said to Simon Silence, 'Back to your seat, OK? Get on with your work.'

'Aren't you going to go outside to welcome your flock?' asked Simon Silence, in mock surprise. 'They're waiting for you.'

'You said yourself that you can't see them,' Jim retorted. 'How do you even know that there's anybody there?'

'Oh, they're there all right, Mr Rook. I can feel them. My father says that you can always tell when the dead are close by. It feels as if the wind has changed around, and the barometer's falling.'

'Just sit down and finish your test, Simon.'

'Whatever you say, Mr Rook. I just hope your flock won't be too disappointed.'

Jim said nothing but returned to his desk. He was strongly tempted to go down to the grassy slope and tell the spirits who were gathered there that he had nothing to offer them, and that they would be better off returning to the other side. They were dead, and so far as he was aware there was no way that he could bring them back to life, even if Simon Silence said that he could.

He spent most of the afternoon teaching Special Class Two how to spell awkward words like 'necessary' and 'argument' and 'geography.'

'You just have to learn a little phrase, that's all. It's called a mnemonic, not that you have to remember that. Take the word "necessary" . . . just say to yourself "not every cat eats sardines – some are really yummy". Or, "geography" . . . "General Eisenhower's oldest granddaughter rode a pony home yesterday". Or, "argument" . . . "a rude girl undresses, my eyes need taping".

'I'll tell you something else . . . when two vowels go walking, it's the first one does the talking . . . like "beach" or "coat" or "rain" . . . words like that.'

'So how come "bitch" is always pronounced "be-atch"?' asked DaJon Johnson.

'I'm going to ignore that comment,' Jim told him. 'I don't care how you speak out on the street. But in here, in this classroom, you're going to learn to speak and spell so that you can hold your own against anybody – a potential employer, a teacher, a cop, a store manager, a waiter in a restaurant – *anybody* – no matter what situation you happen to find yourselves in. Knowing how to speak grammatically and spell well, that's the greatest power that you can ever have.'

To finish up the day, he read them a passage from *Go Tell It On The Mountain*, James Baldwin's novel about a Pentecostal Church in Harlem called the Temple of the Fire Baptized. DaJon Johnson closed his eyes and nodded off while he was reading but Jim let him sleep. He wasn't snoring too loudly and Jim was mainly reading this for Simon Silence, nobody else.

In the last scenes of the novel, the hero, John, has a dream-like vision of heaven and hell, and believes that he has found Jesus. But the Reverend Gabriel, the leader of the church which has inspired him, is a moral hypocrite, and has a sordid past of womanizing and drunkenness and adultery.

'So what did we learn from this little story?' said Jim, as he closed the book and dropped it with a bang on to his desk, so that DaJon Johnson woke up with a jolt. Before anybody in the class could answer, he said, 'What we learn is that sometimes those people who set themselves up as messengers of God are not all that they pretend to be. Sometimes they exploit people's weaknesses and vulnerabilities to further their own ends. To make money, or to satisfy their sexual urges, or simply because they love to dominate other people – even to the point of deciding if they live or die. Think of Jonestown.

'That's one of the reasons you need to be very good at English . . . so that you can tell when somebody's flim-flamming you. They might be a salesman or a card player or a priest, it doesn't matter. It's important for you to be able to tell the difference between somebody who's sincere, and somebody who's a huckster.'

Simon Silence put up his hand. 'You really are very cynical, Mr Rook. What about faith? If all of his disciples had suspected that Jesus was a fraud, there never would have been a Christian religion, would there?'

Jim said, 'Maybe. But if everybody had been able to see that Satan was an out-and-out swindler, there wouldn't have been any call for a Christian religion. You don't need saving if you know how to save yourself.'

All afternoon, he resisted the temptation to go to the window to see if the dead people were still standing on the grassy slope outside. Eventually, as the last stragglers pushed their way out of the door, he went to the back of the classroom and looked out.

There was nobody there, only two girls from the West Grove Athletics Team, jogging together, one blonde and one brunette.

He stayed there for a while, but the dead had definitely gone back to the world beyond – for now, anyhow. He didn't know if he felt sorry for them or not. They were probably better off where they were.

He fastened his briefcase, closed the door of Art Studio Four behind him, and went home.

As he climbed the steps to his apartment, Summer's apartment door suddenly opened and Summer stepped out. Her hair was wrapped up in a towel and she was wearing a pink halter top and a short pink denim skirt with an appliqué picture of a smiling cartoon cat on it. She still had a purplish-yellowish bruise on her left cheek where he had slapped her.

'Summer!' said Jim. 'I was going to call on you later. I think I owe you an abject apology, to say the least.'

Summer slowly shook her head from side to side. 'You don't have to apologize, Jimmy. It was just as much my fault as it was yours.'

'Summer, for Christ's sake. I practically raped you.'

'Only 'cause I wasn't in the mood for it. I would have willingly particified, else.'

'Excuse me?'

'I really, really like you, Jim. I'd love us to do the wild thing together. But like *equals*, right? Not you jumping on top of me or me jumping on top of you. Or taking it in turns, at least.'

Jim said, 'I hit you. How can you forgive me for that?'

'Well, that's easy,' she said. She turned away slightly and then she swung her arm and slapped him across the face, so stunningly hard that he almost lost his balance and fell backward over the railing.

'Jesus!' he said. 'Shit!'

He pressed his hand against his cheek and said, 'Shit, Summer – that really, really hurt!'

Summer smiled at him and said, 'There – you're forgiven! Is that OK?'

Jim touched his cheek again. 'Shit.' Then he went up to her, wrapped his arms around her and kissed her full on the lips. She had just applied pink shiny lip gloss which tasted strongly of synthetic strawberries, but he didn't mind that – in fact he found its cheapness arousing. She put her arms around him, too, and they stood on the landing kissing for over a minute, their tongues fighting each other like two argumentative seals.

Summer gripped Jim through his pants and said, 'I want you, Jimmy Rook. Don't ever think that I don't. But it has to be, like, *Paradise.*'

Jim stopped kissing her and frowned at her, although she was so close that her face was out of focus.

'What do you mean, Paradise?'

'Just you and me, Jimmy. Nobody else. Like the Garden of Eden.'

'I'm not too sure I follow what you're saying.'

Summer gave him a second hard squeeze and kissed him. 'You will when it comes, Jimmy. When kingdom comes. When *we* come, you and me. When we're naked and we know it and we couldn't care less what God thinks about it.'

She kissed him again, and again, and again. 'I'm going to go fix my hair, and pretty myself up, and maybe we can meet up later. How about that?'

Jim didn't quite know what to say. Of course he wanted her, but her talk about the Garden of Eden and God had distinctly unsettled him. She sounded almost like Simon Silence, with his strange quasi-religious comments and his talk of God-Not-So-Very-Almighty.

'Well, sure, fine,' he said. 'Maybe you'd like to come up for a drink. Say around nine, nine thirty?'

She leaned forward and whispered in his ear, and her breath was like hot thunder. 'I'll suck it for you.'

Jim found himself smiling like an idiot. He thought: *How else am I supposed to react? Say, 'Great, I look forward to it, but do you mind if we have a little less of the Old Testament talk?'*

Summer gave him a little finger-wave and disappeared back into her apartment. Jim stood there for a few seconds, his cheek still singing with pain. Inside, he could hear Kenny Rogers singing *You Picked A Fine Time To Leave Me, Lucille.* ('. . . *with four hungry children and a crop in the field* . . .') He had never felt so detached from reality in his life. This simply wasn't the way that things worked. You didn't see seventy or eighty dead souls standing outside your window and then come home and have a pole dancer-cum-beautician slap you across the face and tell you that, as far as she was concerned, the wrath of God amounted to a hill of beans.

He trudged up the last flight of steps and opened his own front door. Tibbles had emerged from his hiding place and was sitting on the kitchen table, where he knew that he wasn't allowed to sit. Normally he jumped off it as soon as Jim came home, but this evening he stayed where he was, narrowing his eyes, as if he were defying Jim to throw him off.

'Well, how are you, fatso?' Jim asked him. 'Gotten over the sulks, have you? Just remember that you belong to me, and not the other way about. Me owner, you pet, and you don't go all spitty and scratchy on me because if you do you'll get the same treatment again, only more so.'

He went through to the living room and switched on the TV, although he muted the sound. Outside, the sun was beginning to go down behind the yuccas, so that the sky looked like the grating of a huge furnace. He couldn't help thinking about what Simon Silence had written in his essay about Paradise. *Paradise will come on the day when the Fires are lit all over the world from one horizon to another.*

He went back into the kitchen and opened up the fridge. He had defrosted a pork chop yesterday so he supposed he ought to cook it and eat it today, although he didn't feel like it now. His tastes varied so much from one day to the next. What he really felt like this evening was chicken fajitas, with a hellishly hot chili sauce.

He opened his briefcase. The handle that he had attempted to mend was coming apart already and he thought that he would probably have to try repairing it again, or even buy a new briefcase. As he opened it, the pink-and-green Paradise apple that Simon Silence had given him came rolling out halfway across the kitchen table.

Tibbles sniffed it, and then immediately sprang off the table on to the floor.

'What's the matter with you?' Jim asked him, picking up the apple and holding it toward him. 'You don't like fruit? Well, no, of course you don't, you're a cat. I have to admit I never saw a cat eating a banana.'

Tibbles hissed at him and retreated into the living room, sway-backed. Jim felt a rush of annoyance, and had the strongest urge to pick him up and throw him out on to the balcony, or even throw him right off the balcony into the back yard. However, Tibbles turned around and fled into the bedroom, as if he could read Jim's mind.

Jim rinsed the apple under the kitchen faucet and bit into it. He wondered if he ought to have accepted it, considering how much he disliked and distrusted Simon Silence, yet he hadn't been able to resist it. It was so much more than an apple, as sweet and crisp as it was. It was almost like another installment in a continuing story – a story which was gradually making more and more sense with each Paradise apple that he ate. He needed to know how the story ended, even if it meant compromising his principles.

He went back to the living room to see what was on television. *Wheel of Fortune,* or *Mirror, Mirror*, or the news. He bit into the apple again, and this time he was flooded almost at once with a feeling of sadness and nostalgia, but bewilderment, too. He chewed it very slowly, and as he did so he could feel that warm wind blowing again, and the weary shushing of the ocean, and hear that faraway calliope music, *In The Good Old Summertime.*

He suddenly thought: *I know where this is. I remember. I know where this is and I know that something terrible happened. I have to go there. I have to go there now.*

He switched off the television and went through to the hallway. He lifted his khaki cotton jacket from the peg and left his apartment without calling out goodbye to Tibbles. As far as he was concerned, Tibbles could stay in hiding for the rest of his life and starve to death. One day he would drag his body out from under the bed, all mangy gray fur and bones.

With his apple clamped between his teeth, he hurried down the steps and climbed into his car. He swerved out backward into Briarcliff Road, narrowly missing a primrose-yellow Volkswagen Beetle being driven up the hill by a middle-aged woman in a matching primrose-yellow headscarf.

'Watch where you're going, asshole!' she screamed at him.

'Oh, *bésa mis nalgas!*'

Jim sped down Briarcliff on squittering tires and then headed west on Franklin, toward the ocean. Traffic along Sunset was crawling all the way, and he drummed his fingers impatiently on the steering wheel. As he drove, he finished his apple, and even sucked the core, then laid it carefully down on the seat beside him. The sweet-and-sour taste of it had at last brought everything back. The wind, the ocean, the seashore. The weeping of seagulls and the faraway music from the carousel.

It was almost dark by the time he reached Santa Monica Beach, with only a hazy streak of purple in the sky. He parked his car and walked across to the fine gray sand. He stood there for a long time, feeling the ocean breeze blowing in his face, and listening to the endless sound of the surf. About three-quarters of a mile to the south, he could see the candy-colored lights of Pacific Park, on Santa Monica Pier, with its Ferris wheel turning and its roller-coaster rattling, and he could hear people screaming as they went round and round and up and down on all of the rides.

It was here that it had happened, that terrible thing. It was right here, at this very place where he was standing on Santa Monica Beach, thirty-three years ago. Jim remembered it now, he remembered it all, and he remembered it so vividly that he found it difficult to believe that he had ever forgotten it. Or buried it, rather.

He was still standing there when – out of the darkness – a tall figure in white came walking toward him, from the direction of the ocean. When he was less than a hundred feet away, Jim recognized him. It was the Reverend John Silence, in his loose white shirt and his gold chains and his white flappy pants. He was wearing a straw skimmer with a black hatband around it, and he was carrying a black staff with a gold knob on top of it. He looked more like some strange kind carnival entertainer than a pastor.

'Well, well, Mr Rook!' he called out, as he approached. 'You made it! And much sooner than I thought you would! Congratulations!'

He came closer and held out his hand, but Jim didn't take it.

'Reverend Silence. Do you want to explain to me what you're doing here, exactly?' Jim demanded.

The Reverend Silence shrugged. 'Probably the same thing that *you're* doing here, Mr Rook. Reliving the past.'

'This is a past I never wanted to remember, for Christ's sake. Like, *ever.* And this is a past which I had successfully managed to blot out of my mind, until you and your son started feeding me those apples. It *is* the apples that do it, isn't it?'

'Yes, the apples! But you didn't have to take them, Mr Rook. And once you *had* taken them, you still didn't have to eat them. You could have thrown them in the trash. Or let them rot.'

'So what do you spike them with?' Jim asked him. 'Do you inject them with some kind of drug? Like scopolamine, maybe, or temazepam, or something like that?'

'Of course not. The Paradise apple is the purest of apples. That is why it brings back all of your memories with such clarity. The Paradise apple is the fruit of the tree of knowledge, Mr Rook. That is why we call it the Paradise apple. You eat the apple, and you see *everything*. Why do you think God drove

Adam and Eve out of Eden? They ate the apple and they could suddenly see everything. More than anything else they could suddenly see the many shortcomings of God.'

'Aren't you supposed to be a pastor?' said Jim. 'I thought pastors were supposed to exalt God, not go around telling everybody how fallible He is.'

'Truth is what is important in this world, Mr Rook. Truth, not reputation. And something else is just as important, and that is for everybody to have a second chance. God never gives us second chances, Mr Rook. If you sin – or what counts for sinning in His eyes – then you are damned for all eternity. If you die, you stay dead for ever. At least you do if God has anything to do with it.'

He paused, and then he said, 'What happened on this beach, Mr Rook, thirty-three years ago? Tell me, in your own words.'

Jim had thought that he would be able to talk about this easily, but without any warning at all he found that his throat had tightened up, and that it was difficult for him to get the words out.

'Come on, Mr Rook. It will do you good. You have had it all wrapped up for so long, it's time to unwrap it, and remember it.'

Jim took a deep breath, and then he said, in a choked-up voice, 'It was – *ahem!* – it was my dad.'

'Go on. What did he do, your dad?'

'He brought me here, to this beach. I was seven years old. He bought me a little shovel and a bucket and I sat right here and I tried to make a sandcastle, although the sand was much too dry.'

'And then what, Mr Rook?'

'He walked off. I didn't know then that my mom had told him that morning that she was going to leave him, and take me with her. Well, how could I? As far as I know he wasn't an easy man to get on with. Something like me, I guess. Anyhow, I found out years later that she had fallen in love with somebody else.'

Jim's eyes were crowded with tears. He took another deep breath and cleared his throat, and then he said, 'I sat right here trying to build a sandcastle and my dad just walked off toward the ocean. He was fully dressed – coat, shirt, pants, even a necktie. I watched him as he went, and he just kept on walking. Into the surf to start with, but he kept on going. The water came right up to his shoulders, and then all I could see was his head, and then I couldn't even see that.

'I remember standing up to see what had happened to him. I thought that he was going to turn around and come walking back, all wet . . . like this was one of his practical jokes. He was always playing practical jokes, like filling the sugar bowl with salt, and sometimes he used to kid people that he had a really bad stammer. But I waited and I waited and he never did come back.'

'Didn't you *tell* anybody? Didn't you run to the lifeguard and ask for help?'

Jim shook his head.

'But why on earth not? You had just seen your father walk fully dressed into the ocean, but you didn't say a word?'

'I thought he was going to come back,' Jim said, miserably. 'Whenever he left us before he always came back. How was I to know that this time was going to be any different? I was only just seven years old.'

'So what did you do?'

'I waited for him until it grew dark, and then I lay down on the sand and I must have fallen asleep. The next thing I knew it was early morning, and the sun was coming up, and some guy walking a dog was asking me if I was OK.'

'A sad story, Mr Rook,' said the Reverend Silence. 'A very sad story indeed.'

'That's why I wanted to forget it. Now I'm going to have to forget it all over again, thanks to you and your son and your goddamned apples, and believe me that's not going to be easy. In fact it's probably going to be impossible. So thanks a lot, Reverend. I really needed some more pain in my life.'

For over half a minute, the Reverend Silence stood facing the ocean breeze with his eyes half closed, saying nothing. Then he took off his skimmer and pressed it against his chest, as if he were man paying his respects to a passing funeral. 'It was that night, wasn't it – the night that your father walked into the ocean – when you contracted the pneumonia that almost killed you?'

'How the hell do you know that?'

'I am in touch with all things spiritual, Mr Rook, as well as all things temporal. You nearly died, but when you nearly died, you were given a very rare gift, so in a way your father did you a favor. You can see so much, Mr Rook. You can see so much! You don't know how much I envy you! And there are many others, much greater than I, and they envy you, too!'

'What others? Who are you talking about?'

The Reverend Silence turned and smiled at him. 'You saw your daughter today, didn't you, Mr Rook? How would you like to see your father?'

'What?' said Jim. 'I don't have to listen to this crap! I don't know why you're playing me like this, but I'm not taking it any more! You understand me? I'm going, and so goodnight, and I'd appreciate it if you'd take that creepy son of yours out of my class, OK? The sooner the better.'

He turned to go, but the Reverend Silence caught his sleeve. 'Wait just one moment, Mr Rook – please!'

Jim yanked his arm free, and took two or three steps back. As he did so, however, he saw that somebody was walking across the beach toward them, as quickly as the soft sand would allow. A thirtyish-looking man, wearing a light-brown coat with a white shirt and a dark brown necktie. As he came nearer, another person materialized out of the darkness behind him, also walking toward them, but staying some way behind. This person was much taller and darker, and appeared to be wearing a hooded cloak. Either that, or it wasn't a person at all, but a swirl of thick gray smoke, like the swirl of smoke which had appeared on Jim's balcony.

The man in the brown coat was only fifty feet away now. He waved his right arm and whooped out, 'Jim! *Jim!*'

'Oh, no,' said Jim, under his breath. 'Oh, no. Oh, Jesus. It can't be him. Please don't let it be him.'

FOURTEEN

When he had last seen him, Jim had been only seven years old, so his father looked much shorter than he remembered him, and narrow-chested, but he also looked startlingly young.

Jim realized, though, that William 'Billy' Rook had been no more than thirty-six when he had walked into the ocean, which was nearly four years younger than Jim was now.

He was soaking wet, drenched. Seawater was pouring from his sleeves and his thinning dark brown hair was plastered down on either side of his head. All the same, he was smiling, and he was holding out his arms, like a man who has just completed a record-breaking swim – which, in a spiritual way, he had. He had been swimming continuously for thirty-three years – or drowning, rather.

He looked so much like Jim's grandfather, with his sharp pointed nose and his heart-shaped face and his little clipped moustache. Jim's mother had always wanted him to shave off his moustache because she said it made him look like a card sharp or a door-to-door salesman, but Jim's father had insisted on keeping it, because Rook men had worn moustaches for generations. Jim was the first Rook who hadn't grown a moustache since the mid-1900s, when Los Angeles was nothing more than a single main street and a cluster of wooden oil derricks.

'Jim!' he said, in that familiar croaky voice. 'Jim – are you OK? It's so good to see you!'

'Dad, you shouldn't have let them bring you here. You really shouldn't.'

'Look at you, Jim – shoot! How you've grown up! Here – give me a hug, will you? It's been so long. It's been so darn confusing.'

He came right up to Jim with both of his arms still held wide. Jim looked over his shoulder at the tall, smoky figure behind him. It was the same figure that had appeared on his balcony, and it was the same figure that had visited him in his nightmare, and it was the same figure who had appeared in Ricky's painting of The Storyteller.

'What's the matter with you, Jim?' his father asked him, and he began to look uncertain. 'Can't you give your old man a hug?'

Jim looked across at the Reverend Silence. 'You don't see him, do you?' he challenged him. 'You don't hear him, either?'

The Reverend Silence nodded. 'You're quite right, Mr Rook, I don't. But I'm aware that he's here, and I can guess what he's saying to you.'

'You can't see this other person, either, this one standing right behind him, whoever he is?'

'He has a name, Mr Rook. In fact he has a multitude of names.'

'But you don't see him like I do?'

'No, I regret to say that I don't. If only I shared your wonderful gift, Mr Rook.'

'*Jim!*' begged his father. 'What's wrong, Jim?'

'Nothing's wrong, Dad, except that I can't hug you.'

'What? Why not? I swear to God I didn't mean to leave you all alone on the beach like that. I thought you'd just find your way home. You had some bus fare. I left you some bus fare in that paper bag along with the Oreos.'

'Dad, it's not that I blame you. The reason I can't hug you is because you're not physically here. Of course it's *you*, Dad, but it's only your spirit.'

'My spirit? You mean like a ghost? How can I be a ghost? That doesn't make any kind of sense at all!'

Behind Jim's father, the tall twisting figure began to come closer, until Jim could look up into the dark recesses of its hood, and see its eyes glittering, just as they had in his nightmare. The figure raised its left hand, and Jim saw that ring again, with the snakes entwined on it.

'*What?*' Jim said. 'What do you want?'

At first he heard only the sound of the surf, and the wind fluffing in his ears, but then the figure's voice suddenly boomed and reverberated inside his head like a giant church bell.

'*Time is blowing away, Mr Rook*! *Time is blowing away like the sands on the beach*! *You should make up your mind what you want, and very soon*!'

'Jim?' said his father. He was looking more distressed by the second. 'What's happening, Jim? I don't understand.'

'You're dead, Dad. You're gone. Thirty-three years ago. Drowned. The coastguard searched for a week but they never found your body. Christ, Dad, we had nothing to bury.'

'I don't get it. I can *see* you, Jim. I can talk to you!'

'That's not because of *you*, Dad, that's because of *me*. That's why these people have brought you back here. It's *me* they want.'

'But why can't you even give me a hug?'

Jim held out his hand. He hated to do this. There was nothing more devastating for spirits than to discover what they really were – nothing but memories, and reflections, and echoes. Nothing but the faint disturbances that a living person had once created as they walked through the physical world.

'Take my hand, Dad,' he said. He was choking up again, and he had to pucker his lips to control himself.

'What?'

'Just do as I say, OK, and take my hand.'

Billy Rook reached out and tried to hold Jim's hand. He tried once, he tried twice, he tried a third time. Each time his fingers passed clear through Jim's hand as if they were nothing more than an image of fingers on a movie screen. Light, color, shadow, but no substance.

He stared at his own hand with an expression of utter shock. 'I can feel *your* hand,' he said, hoarsely. 'Why can't I feel mine?'

'I told you, Dad. You're dead. You're a spirit.'

'*But I'm here*!' he protested, and he was starting to panic. '*I can see you*! *I can see the beach*! *I can feel the sand*! *I can talk to you*! *I'm real*!'

'I'm sorry, Dad. I'm so sorry.'

The Reverend Silence interrupted them. 'You *could* bring him back, you know.'

'No,' said Jim. 'It's impossible.'

'Which law says so? The laws of biology? The laws of physics? I don't think so.'

'What about God's law?' said Jim.

The Reverend Silence grinned, almost wolfishly. 'I believe I know more about God's law than you do, Mr Rook. A great deal more. But of course there are other laws, apart from God's law. Equally powerful. Equally earth-shattering.'

Jim looked back at his father. The expression of despair on Billy Rook's face was heart-wrenching. Jim would have done anything to be able to hug him, or even lay his hand on his shoulder or take hold of his hand, but he was no more substantial than the wind.

Without a word, Jim turned around and started to walk back across the parking lot, leaving his father and the Reverend Silence standing on the beach. He didn't look back to see if they were still standing there, because he knew that his father and the hooded figure would probably have melted away as soon as he made it clear that he was leaving. In fact, they probably would have vanished as soon as he stopped looking at them. And if the Reverend Silence's magical disappearing act at Barney's Beanery was anything to go by, *he* would have vanished, too. *Abracadabra.*

Jim sat in his car with his head bowed. The thought of going back to his apartment and being jumped on by Summer and spat at by Tibbles was more than he could take. After a while he started up the engine and drove back along Hollywood Boulevard until he reached the Cat'n'Fiddle English Bar. He stopped outside for a moment with his engine running and then he backed up and swerved into the parking lot.

He had talked to his long-drowned father. He had been forced to tell him that he was nothing more than a ghost, and that he couldn't bring him back to the world of the living. That had hurt, badly. What he needed now wasn't confrontation, of any kind. What he needed now was a bottle of Fat Tire beer or three and some irritating Dixieland jazz and a couple of hours of flirtatious banter with one of the young girls who perched around the bar looking for a pick-up.

*   *   *

It was nearly midnight by the time he climbed the steps back to his apartment, and he had to hold on to the handrail to keep his balance. Three Fat Tires had turned into five, and he had exchanged phone numbers with an absurdly young girl with hefty thighs and a purple tube top.

He was lurching past Ricky Kaminsky's apartment when the door opened and Nadine came out, wearing a loosely woven black poncho and baggy brown satin loons.

She was smoking a cigarette without her usual holder. 'Jim!' she said. 'Have you seen Ricky?' she said.

Jim blinked at her as if he had never seen her before in his life. 'Ricky?'

'I thought him and you might have gone out together for a few brewskis.'

'I went for a drink, yes. But I didn't see Ricky.'

Nadine blew smoke out of her nostrils and bit her lip. 'This is not like him at all. He *always* calls me when he's out late. Mostly because he's so drunk that he doesn't know where he is, and wants me to come find him.'

'Well, I was at the Cat'n'Fiddle, and he wasn't in there. There was a guy at the bar who looked just like him, but it wasn't him.'

'Jim, that is so un-useful. These days he drinks in The Stone Bar mostly because the drinks are strong and there's an alley out back where he can smoke.'

'I'm sorry, Nadine. I haven't seen him. I promise. He'll show up when the Wild Turkey wears off.'

'I don't know. For some reason I have a very bad feeling about this. Things have been so weird for Ricky lately. All those Storyteller paintings going wrong.'

'I don't understand that painting thing either, Nadine, to be honest with you. Maybe it's like that automatic writing – you know, when people find that some dead author like John Steinbeck is pushing their pen for them.'

'But Ricky's been talking in his sleep, Jim, which he never did before. I mean, he always *snores*, yes. He cuts down a whole frickin' rainforest every single night. But up until now he never said anything coherent. These nights, he keeps banging on about three white angels. Over and over. "The three . . . white . . . angels," he says, in this real hollow voice. "The three . . . white . . . angels . . . who open the door." I mean, what the hell is that all about?'

Jim had to shake his head. 'Search me, Nadine. Maybe Ricky's been smoking a little too much of that prime Peruvian pot.'

'Yeah, maybe you're right,' Nadine agreed. 'But I think I'll wait up for him a little longer. What a goddamn waste of space that man can be.'

Jim managed to reel past Summer's apartment without her coming out to ambush him. She was probably asleep by now, anyhow. He negotiated the last flight of steps up to his own landing mostly on his hands and knees, and he had to jab his key six or seven times into the door before he located the keyhole.

He stumbled into the hallway and closed the door behind him, standing with his back to it for almost a minute with his eyes closed, thanking Bacchus for bringing him home safely.

Then he tilted his way into the kitchen, opened the fridge and took out a can of Mountain Dew Throwback, the one with real sugar in it. He popped the top and drank almost half of it without taking a breath. Afterward, he sat down at the kitchen table and let out a long, ripping belch.

He didn't know why he felt so drunk. He didn't normally drink as many as five beers, but even so the floor seemed to be tilting underneath him and he found it hard to focus.

He was still sitting there when Tibbles stalked into the kitchen. Tibbles came up close to Jim and looked up at him, sniffing suspiciously.

'It's all right, Tibs. I don't have any more of those apples, thank God. And I don't have the energy to throw you around the room.'

Tibbles mewed at him.

'You hungry?' Jim asked him. 'I gave you plenty this morning, fatso. If you've scoffed it all, that's your fault. You'll have to wait until tomorrow before you I give you any more. Overfeeding is just as cruel as starving.'

But Tibbles mewed again, and this time Jim realized that

it wasn't his hungry mew. It was more of a yowl, as if he were trying to warn Jim about something.

'What's the matter, Tibs? Don't tell me we have roof rats again. I'm too smashed to go rat-catching in the attic. I still have that exterminator's number from last time. I'll call him tomorrow.'

But Tibbles mewed again, and again, and then quite suddenly he rolled over on to his back and lay on the floor with his legs wide apart, his eyes staring at nothing at all.

'Tibbles? Tibs – are you OK?'

Jim leaned forward and shook him, but Tibbles remained inert and floppy.

'Tibbles?'

He shook him again, but there was still no response. Jesus, he thought, Tibbles has just died on me. Maybe he's had a heart attack, or a stroke. Do cats have heart attacks? Or maybe I hurt him more than I realized when I threw him across the living room and he's been bleeding internally, or his spleen was ruptured. Do cats have spleens?

He knelt down next to Tibbles and stared into his open, unblinking eyes. He certainly *looked* dead. In a way Jim hoped that he *was* dead because he didn't want to have to give him the kiss of life. It took only a single hair to get caught in Jim's mouth to make him retch, and even if Tibbles had stopped breathing, his breath was still rank with this morning's shrimp.

'Oh, Tibs, I'm sorry,' he said. 'When you think how long we've been together . . .'

But as soon as he had said that, Tibbles yowled and rolled over again and stood up. He gave himself a quick shake, and let out another yowl.

'What the hell was all *that* about?' Jim snapped at him. 'Cats don't play dead! Only dogs play dead, when they're acting in movies! Or possums!'

Tibbles yowled yet again, and then rolled over a second time, lying on his back like before, spreadeagled.

Jim frowned at him. 'Are you trying to tell me something, Tibs?' He had known Tibbles to be highly sensitive to some of the spirits that he had conjured up, and openly terrified of some of the demons, even though nobody else but Jim had been able to see them. Nobody human, anyhow. So if Tibbles were trying to give him a warning, he was anxious to find out what it was. Tibbles had no reason to like him at the moment, not at all, so whatever he was warning him about, it had to be pretty goddamned serious.

'You're dead, and then you're not dead, and then you're dead again. OK . . . what does that mean?'

Tibbles shook himself a third time, rolled over and stood up.

'You're dead twice, and then you're alive again twice? I still don't quite get it.'

Tibbles rolled over on to his back and lay still. After a few moments, he stood up again. He repeated this over and over until Jim had counted that he had done it eight times. Then he yowled at Jim again, and came up close to sniff at the back of his hand.

'OK . . . so you're dead eight times. Is that it? Now what?'

Without any warning, Tibbles scratched the back of his hand. Only lightly, almost playfully, but it still made Jim whip his hand away.

'Hey, cat, that stung!'

Cat, he thought. *Is Tibbles trying to emphasize that he's a cat? I know he's a goddamned cat. He's been a cat ever since I first adopted him, and it's highly unlikely that he's ever going to change.*

But a cat who had died eight times. What did that mean, if it meant anything at all?

A cat who had died eight times. *Or maybe eight cats who had all died once.*

Jim suddenly pictured Bethany, nailed naked and white-washed to the ceiling of his classroom; and Santana, naked and whitewashed, too, nailed high up among the branches of the cypress tree.

Each of them surrounded by eight dead cats, pinned in the same position that Tibbles had adopted on the kitchen floor, with his legs spread apart.

Jim gripped the edge of the table and levered himself to his feet. He was rapidly beginning to sober up. The floor had stopped tilting and the walls had stopped rotating and everything was coming back into focus, like the old railroad clock on the wall. Its hands were pointing to a quarter after midnight.

'Tibbles,' said Jim. 'What are you trying to say to me, boy? Come on, give me a clue, will you? Are you trying to tell me that somebody else has been nailed up someplace? Is that it?'

Tibbles ran out of the kitchen into the hallway. '*Great*,' said Jim, waving his scratched hand dismissively. 'Just when I thought we were beginning to communicate, man and moggy, the greatest zoological breakthrough since Doctor Dolittle.'

But almost immediately Tibbles came running back into the kitchen, and let out another yowl.

'Jesus, Tibs. You go out, you come back in. What?'

Tibbles ran out into the hallway again. This time, he stayed out there, yowling softly and persistently. Jim waited for a moment, steadying himself, and then he followed him.

'Come on, Tibs. I'm drunk and I'm tired. I don't have the time for any of this.'

Tibbles kept on yowling, and purring, too. Not that soft, satisfied purr that he usually gave when Jim was watching football on the TV and absent-mindedly stroking him. This was more of a death-rattle.

At the same time, Tibbles was looking directly up at the single oil painting which hung between the coat pegs and the main bedroom door. It was only a small painting, about ten inches wide by eight inches deep. It showed a group of people having a picnic under a tree, in leaf-dappled sunlight, a conscious imitation of *Dejeuner sur l'Herbe*, by Manet, except that the women had clothes on.

Jim stared at the painting for a long time before he began to understand what Tibbles was telling him, but when he did, he felt the back of his neck prickling with dread.

It had been painted in the grounds of West Grove Community College, three summers ago, when Ricky and Nadine and Jim and some other friends had gathered together for lunch *al fresco* under the trees. Ricky had made three or four sketches when he was there, and then finished the painting later. He had given it to Jim as a souvenir.

Eight dead cats, thought Jim. *The grounds of West Grove Community College. And Ricky, who was now missing.*

He slammed his apartment door behind him and vaulted down the two flights of steps to Nadine's apartment. He rang the bell and shouted out, 'Nadine! It's Jim! Nadine!'

Nadine opened the door and stared at him frowzily. She was wearing green satin pajamas now and had obviously decided to try and get some sleep.

'Is Ricky back yet?'

'Is he hell. I'm not waiting up any longer. This is the last time, I can tell you.'

Jim hurry-stumbled down the last flight of steps and climbed into his car. He knew that he shouldn't be driving, but how long would he have to wait for a taxi? Besides, he felt stone-cold sober now, even if he was about four times over the legal limit.

He drove westward as fast as he could, keeping an eye open for police cars. At this time of the morning, it took him less than fifteen minutes to reach the college entrance, and he sped up the driveway at nearly fifty miles an hour, slewing to a stop right outside the main entrance.

The main revolving door was locked, but the left-hand side door was open, so that the cleaners and the security staff could get in and out. Most of the lights were on, too. Jim walked quickly along the corridor to the staircase. Off to his right, he saw the silhouette of a lone cleaner, mopping the floor. She didn't even look up as Jim hurried past.

He leapt up the stairs two at a time, and almost ran along the corridor to Art Studio Four. Inside, the lights were on, because he could see them shining through the porthole in the door. He burst in, and came to a dead stop.

All of Special Class Two were gathered in the classroom – Kyle Baxter and Jesmeka Watson and DaJon Johnson and Joe Chang and Hunni Robards and Jordy Brown and all of the rest of them. They were sitting in a circle – some of them straddling chairs, others perched on top of the benches. When Jim cannoned in through the door, they all turned around and stared at him.

So did Simon Silence, who was standing in the center of the circle, holding up a large book bound in white leather. Maybe it was the overhead lighting, but Jim thought that his face looked even flatter than before, and his eyes even more slanted.

His smile was just the same, though: sly and knowing and self-satisfied.

'Mr Rook!' he said. 'I didn't expect you so soon!'

Jim slowly approached him, stiff-legged with anger. 'What the hell are you doing here, Simon? It's the middle of the night!'

'Yes, Mr Rook, I know. But it's very much later than you think. In fact, it's almost time.'

'Time for what, exactly?'

'Paradise, Mr Rook. Time to go back to the very beginning!'

FIFTEEN

Jim said, 'You need to leave, all of you. I don't know how you managed to get in here without alerting college security, but you're not permitted to enter the building after hours. Apart from that, class starts at nine and what kind of state are you guys going to be in, if you've been up all night?'

'We have very nearly finished, Mr Rook,' said Simon Silence. 'Then we shall go.'

'I don't think so, Simon. You're going now.'

'I'm afraid that Doctor Ehrlichman will not be very pleased.'

'What does Doctor Ehrlichman have to do with it?'

'It was Doctor Ehrlichman who gave us special permission to meet here tonight. It had to be tonight.'

'Doctor Ehrlichman gave you special permission? I don't believe it.'

'My father asked him as a favor. Today is September the twenty-seventh, which is the Day of Divine Conquest.'

'Meaning precisely *what*, exactly?'

'Today is the anniversary of the day on which Lilith was expelled from Paradise. Today is the day when my father's church renews its determination that the world shall be restored to the way that it was originally intended to be.'

'What the hell are you talking about, Simon?' Jim snapped at him, making no attempt to disguise his irritation. He was very tired, and still badly shaken from having encountered the spirit of his father, and still quite drunk, too.

'You've got it in one, Mr Rook. *Hell*, that's what I'm talking about.' Simon Silence held out the book from which he had been reading. 'Here . . . you are a man of learning. You should acquaint yourself with this. The Book of Paradise, which was excluded from the Old Testament in the fourth century because it tells the truth about the Garden of Eden. It explains what was meant to happen there, and how mankind was betrayed by its own Creator, because of His jealousy of the very thing that He had created.'

As Simon Silence was speaking, Jim was looking around the classroom, first at the students of Special Class Two – who were all listening to Simon with rapt expressions on their faces – and then at the paintings on the walls, and the sculptures, and the pottery.

Instead of landscapes and ships and nudes and horses, every single picture was a portrait of the gray-faced Satanic figure that Ricky Kaminsky had painted, when he was trying so desperately to paint a jolly, child-friendly Storyteller.

Every sculpture, too, was an interpretation of the same devilish creature, with his leering smile and his horns, even though some of the sculptures were almost abstract, and two or three of them were only maquettes – the rough wire models that were twisted together to carry the finished clay figurine.

Every vase and plaque was glazed in shiny metallic gray, and every one of them carried either a likeness of the demon, or a symbol which looked like a man with his arms and legs spread wide, inside a circle of stars.

Jim thought: *Shit, I'm hallucinating. Too much to drink. Or if I'm not hallucinating, then something seriously wrong is happening here.*

He turned back to face Simon and raised his hand to stop him talking. 'Can it, Simon. That's enough. I don't want to hear any more. If you really think you have to, you can explain it to me tomorrow, during recess. This is a remedial English class, not some wacky Bible group. *My* remedial English class, remember?'

'But, Mr Rook, we have one last prayer to finish.'

'You're leaving, Simon, all of you. Like, now.'

Simon took a very deep breath. 'Very well, Mr Rook. But I can't say what the consequences will be. This is the Day of Divine Conquest, and my father is not going to be happy unless all of the prayers are spoken according to the sacrament.'

'Simon, I honestly don't care if your father is dancing his ass off with delight or weeping into his sacrificial wine. No, I tell a lie. I *do* care, as a matter of fact, because ever since he bribed Doctor Ehrlichman into admitting you into this class, all of us here have been behaving as if each one of us is the center of the universe, and nobody else on the planet counts for squat.'

'It's only one last prayer, Mr Rook. That's not so much to ask, is it? After that, we will all go quietly, I promise you.'

'Look at these goddamn pictures!' Jim retorted. 'Look at all of these pictures, and all of these sculptures, and all of these pots! It's like an art gallery straight out of hell!'

Simon looked around, and so did Jim, but all of the portraits of the gray-faced Satan had vanished, just like the Reverend Silence had vanished from the bar at Barney's Beanery. Now the walls were covered with the same pictures that had been hanging there before – the same amateurish landscapes and misshapen horses and lopsided vases of flowers. The same crude, brightly colored pottery.

All of the students of Special Class Two looked around, too, frowning in bewilderment.

'What's going down, Mr Rook?' asked DaJon Johnson. 'Simon here promised us a real special night, like we was going to get everything we ever axe for. Like each one of us was going to get our own personal paradise.'

'Oh, really?' said Jim. But at the same time he couldn't stop himself from thinking about Bethany, standing in the radiant sunlight at the end of the corridor, and about his father, walking toward him out of the darkness on Santa Monica Beach. *I can come back, Daddy. We can all come back. Simon will help you.*

Tommy Makovicka stood up and said, haltingly, 'Excuse me, sir, but you said it yourself, that none of us ever got much of a break out of life. OK, maybe it was our own stupid fault, some of us, for thinking that we knew everything and never paying attention. But that's all that Simon promised us. Just a break.'

'All's we want the chance to make our mark, Mr Rook,' put in Jesmeka Watson. 'You know – so that people like recognize who we are, and stuff, and we're not just nobody.'

Joe Chang joined in. 'You can call us selfish, sir, but tell us who isn't? These days one dog eats the other dog. If we don't try to find our own personal paradise, nobody else is going to help us, are they? And if we don't, what was the point of us being born? We might as well walk into the ocean and drown ourselves.'

Jim stared at him and said, '*What* did you just say?'

'I'm not saying nothing, sir, except that we won't never amount to nothing at all unless we help ourselves, and Simon can help us. Nobody else never offered to do that before.'

I can come back, Daddy.

Jim stood in front of his students for a long time, not speaking.

We can all come back. Simon will help you.

Simon Silence filled Jim with uncertainty, more than any student he had ever had in his class before. In fact it was much deeper than uncertainty, it came very close to dread.

In almost every college year, Jim had to deal with at least one cocky, self-assured young man who tried to undermine his authority and dominate the classroom, but he had years of teaching experience and he invariably knew how to put them in their place. Not by losing his temper, or trying to make them look small, but actually by bolstering their self-esteem, which was what most of his students sorely lacked, no matter how aggressively they behaved.

But Simon Silence was something altogether different. Simon Silence was calm and sarcastic and completely confident. Jim was sure that his father had enrolled him into West Grove Community College with a very specific agenda. He had come here to seduce the students of Special Class Two into becoming supporters of the Church of Divine Conquest – and not just the students, either. Quite openly and unashamedly, he had been tempting Jim to support him, too. That was why he made Jim feel so uncertain, and almost to dread him.

As he stood in front of his class, Jim was thinking: *This is seriously scary. This young man is doing something much more frightening than undermining my authority. He's tempting me. He's offering me something that I dearly and desperately want, and because I can call up the dead I know I could probably have it. But it can't be right, can it? And what the hell will the consequences be, if I give in to him?*

'So, what do you say, Mr Rook?' asked Simon Silence.

'One last prayer? Doctor Ehrlichman has agreed to us holding this little get-together, after all, and what harm can it do?'

'I'm damned if I know the answer to that, Simon,' said Jim. But he looked around at all the faces of Special Class Two and every one of them was appealing to him to say yes.

If I say no, will I be letting them down? Maybe Simon is offering them Paradise, and if he is, who am I to deny it to them? And what if Bethany does come back to me, and I can make up for all of those missing years? And what if my dad comes back, too? Is that really so wrong?

He checked his watch. 'OK,' he heard himself saying. 'You have five minutes and then you have to be out of here.'

There was a collective '*yesss!*' of relief, and some of the class applauded and banged on the tops of the benches. Simon Silence smiled and said, 'A very wise and generous gesture, Mr Rook. You will not regret it, I promise you.'

With that, he lifted up the large white book and opened it. On the front cover, embossed in silver, Jim could see the word πειρασμός – the same Greek letters that were scrawled on his desk, underneath the doodle of the naked woman with the green snake wound around her.

'*Paradise,*' said Simon Silence, as if he could read Jim's mind. 'That's what it means. This is the book that was excised from the Bible by the unbelievers. Only one copy of it exists in English . . . this one, which belongs to the Church of the Divine Conquest. You should read it some day.'

Jim turned and walked out of the room, closing the door behind him. He didn't want to hear Simon Silence's prayer. He felt guilty enough as it was. All the same, he stood with his back against the door for a moment and closed his eyes and whispered, '*Bethany.*'

He was in a strangely mixed mood as he drove back home. He was nagged by doubts about the decision he had just taken, but he was also elated. Ever since he had first discovered that he could see spirits and ghosts and demons, and talk to them, too, he had tried to use his ability to help people. He had protected his family and his friends and those around him from supernatural harm, especially his students.

He had also given peace of mind to the dead by helping them to understand that they really *were* dead, and that they could never come back.

Now it seemed as if the Reverend Silence and his son were about to give him the power to change all of that, and to recall the dead to the land of the living. The feeling it gave him was almost like being high. He knew it was wrong. It had to be wrong. People always die for a reason, and there are no second chances. But how much happiness could he give to their loved ones, if he could bring them back from the spirit world?

Most of all, he could show his father that life can go on, even when you feel that you've lost everything you care about. And he could redeem himself with Bethany.

Everybody else in Special Class Two was going to be given their own personal Paradise – why shouldn't he have his?

It was a quarter of four by the time he turned into the sharply sloping driveway outside Briar Cliff Apartments. It was still dark, but the sky was gradually beginning to lighten toward the east. There was a cool early morning breeze blowing, and the yuccas were whispering all around him as if they knew that something momentous was about to happen.

He paused outside Ricky Kaminsky's apartment, but decided against knocking. Knowing Ricky as well as he did, he was pretty sure that he would have found his way home by now, and that he wouldn't appreciate being woken out of a dead-drunk snoring slumber.

He climbed up the next flight of steps until he reached Summer's door. He was about to continue up to his own apartment when he thought: *Why not*? Summer easily qualifies as part of my personal paradise, and what had she said to him, only a few hours ago?

Just you and me, Jimmy. Nobody else. Like the Garden of Eden.

He pressed her doorbell and waited. There was no answer, so he pressed it again and this time he kept his thumb on it for almost fifteen seconds.

Eventually, he heard a door opening somewhere inside Summer's apartment, and the light was switched on in the hallway.

'Who is it?' Summer demanded, in a thick, throaty voice. 'What *time* is it, for Christ's sake?'

'It's me,' said Jim. 'I'm sorry if I've left it kind of late, but I was wondering if you still wanted to join me for that drink.'

'Jimmy! It's the middle of the night!'

'I know, Summer. But I couldn't sleep. And I couldn't stop thinking about you, sweetheart.'

There was a long pause, and then Jim heard the locks turn and the safety chain drawn back. The door opened and there was Summer wearing a yellow sleeveless T-shirt and a white lace thong. Her blonde hair was all twisted up in yellow ribbons, so that it looked like snakes.

'Where have you *been*, Jimmy? I was expecting you hours ago!'

'I'm sorry, Summer. Something came up.'

'You don't say? Any chance of it coming up again?'

'It's nearly – what – four a.m. I guess it's too late for that drink. Or maybe it's too early. I don't know which.'

Summer shrugged. 'I could manage a middle-of-the-night nightcap, if you could. You know me.'

'OK. I have some prosecco in the fridge if you fancy that.'

'Hey, I'm not too sure I could eat anything.'

'Prosecco is like champagne, only it's Italian.'

'In that case, what are we waiting for? I just *love* champagne, and I adore *anything* Italian, especially the men. Al Pacino, *mmm-mmmh*! When he was younger, anyhow, and not so wrinkly! Just let me get my keys.'

Summer went back inside and reappeared a few seconds later with a short white satin robe wrapped around her, jingling her door keys on her finger. She climbed the steps in her tippety-tappety high-heeled slippers, and Jim ushered her along to his apartment.

'Just you and me, Jimmy,' she said, as he unlocked the door, and she kissed her fingertip and touched it against his lips. 'Just like the Garden of Eden. Adam and that other girl.'

'Eve.'

'No, not *Eve*. Eve was only a rib, wasn't she? I mean that really sexy girl who liked it cowboy style.'

'I don't think they had cowboys in those days, Summer. I don't even think they had cows.'

Jim opened the door and switched on the lights. 'Tibs!' he called out, as he led Summer through to the kitchen. 'Where are you, Tibs?

He opened the fridge and took out the bottle of prosecco. 'That cat, he's been acting so weird lately. Sometimes I think he's possessed.'

'Well, cats – they're magical, aren't they?' said Summer, sitting on a kitchen stool and crossing her legs. 'That's why witches always have them. Black cats, anyhow.'

'What about dirty gray cats?'

'I guess they're for people who can't make up their mind whether to be good or evil. Like, they'll give money to charity, but if a storekeeper gives them too much change, they'll just pocket it and won't say a word.'

'*My* cat is dirty gray, thanks,' said Jim, popping the cork from the prosecco bottle. 'So that's me you're talking about.'

Summer blew him another fingertip kiss. 'I always knew you had a flawed character. Whenever you talk to me, you can never take your eyes off my boobies.'

Jim poured out two glasses of sparkling prosecco, and then said, 'How about we take them through to the bedroom? It's more comfortable in there. Less vertical, more horizontal.'

'I love it when you talk like a teacher. Go on, then. The bedroom it is.'

They went back into the hallway, but when they did so they found Tibbles waiting for them in front of the bedroom door, almost as if he were guarding it. He was sitting bolt upright, his eyes slitted, his ears folded back flat on his head.

'So there you are, you mangy animal,' said Jim. 'I'm still not sure what you were trying to tell me with all of that playing-dead performance, but I'm still glad you did it. Otherwise I wouldn't have found out what my creepy little friend Simon Silence was up to, in the dead of night.'

Summer said, 'Hunh? What's all *that* about?'

'Nothing,' Jim told her. 'Nothing that needs to spoil tonight, anyhow, or what's left of it. Come on, Tibs. Clear the way, cat.'

But Tibbles stayed where he was, right in the middle of the doorway, and slitted his eyes even more, as if to show Jim that he had absolutely no intention of budging an inch. Jim handed his glass of prosecco to Summer and bent down to pick him up, but Tibbles immediately hissed and lashed out at him with his claws, scratching the back of his hand.

'There,' said Jim, sucking blood from his knuckle. 'I told you he's been acting weird.'

Jim stood up, and made as if he were turning away, but then he suddenly swung around and grabbed Tibbles with both hands, flinging him along the hallway so that he collided with a dull thump with the bathroom door.

'Mademoiselle,' he said to Summer, opening up the bedroom door and bowing.

'I should report you to the ASPCA,' said Summer. 'Poor defenseless pussy.'

'I don't know what the hell is wrong with him,' said Jim. 'Maybe I should take him to a cat psychiatrist. First of all he was pretending to drop down dead. Eight times he did that. Then he was trying to show me this picture that Ricky Kaminsky painted for me. Now he's sitting in the bedroom doorway trying to stop us from going in.'

Summer had started to take off her wrap, baring one shoulder, when she stopped and said, '*Jimmy.*'

Jim was walking across to his nightstand in order to switch on his bedside lamp.

'Jimmy,' Summer repeated. 'The *ceiling*, Jimmy.'

Jim switched on the lamp and looked up. Immediately, he sat down on the side of the bed in shock.

Nailed to the ceiling, naked and thickly coated in white paint, was Ricky, with his arms and legs stretched out wide apart. His ponytail had been untied and his paint-stiffened hair radiated from the top of his head like the spokes of a wheel. All around him, eight white furry cats had been nailed in a circle.

Summer dropped her glass of prosecco on to the carpet and said, 'Oh my God, Jimmy. Oh my God. Oh my God I can't believe it!'

Jim managed to stand up again, a little unsteadily. 'Go through to the living room,' he told her. 'Dial nine-one-one.'

Summer continued to stare up at the ceiling with her mouth open so Jim shouted at her, '*Summer! Go through to the living room and call the police! Do it now!*'

Summer stumbled out of the bedroom. Jim walked across the carpet until he was standing directly underneath Ricky's spreadeagled body. He could see now that blood was speckled all over the pale-beige carpet and the white woven bedcover. There was even a curved spray of blood across the drapes. It looked as if Ricky might have violently flapped one arm while he was being nailed up.

Jim had no idea what to think of this. It was so elaborate, so sadistic, so ritualistic, and yet he couldn't even begin to imagine what kind of a ritual it could be. In all of the research that he had ever done into mystical religions and sacrificial cults and demon-worship, he had never come across anything like this before.

He was still standing there looking up at the ceiling when a warm drop of blood splashed on to his cheek. Ricky opened his eyes and stared down at him as if he couldn't understand where he was or why he was in so much pain.

'Jim,' he croaked, and more blood dripped out of the side of his mouth. 'Jim, help me. I'm dying, Jim. Help me.'

SIXTEEN

'Summer!' Jim shouted. 'Tell them we need paramedics, too! And firefighters!'

Summer came back into the bedroom, wide-eyed with panic, holding up the phone. 'Is there a fire?'

'Ricky's still alive! We need somebody who can get him down from there!'

'Still alive? My *God*! OK, sure. *Jesus*! Paramedics. Yes, OK.' She was still on the line to the emergency operator so she told her in a gabbly voice that they also needed the fire department to send an ambulance and a rescue team.

'Hold on, Ricky!' Jim told him. 'Hold on, man, we have help on the way!'

He climbed on to the bed and tramped across the mattress, raising his left arm so that he could steady himself against the ceiling. Ricky was breathing thick and slow, and blood was still sliding out of the corner of his mouth. His face was completely caked in white paint and his eyes were bloodshot, so that he looked as if he were wearing an Aboriginal mask.

Jim tried to get a grip on the nail that had been driven through the palm of Ricky's right hand, but it was slippery with blood and it had been hammered in far too hard for him to be able to pull it out manually.

Not only that, all of the nails that had been driven through his hands and knees and ankles were L-shaped, so that it would have been impossible to lift him down without prying them out first.

'You won't be able to do it, Jim,' Ricky whispered. 'They pinned me up here hard and fast, believe me.'

'We'll get you down, I promise,' said Jim. 'Just stay with me, that's all. Keep your eyes open and keep breathing.'

'Bastards grabbed me just as soon as I stepped out of my front door,' said Ricky. 'I was high. Drunk. Nothing I could do to stop them.'

'Just take it easy, Ricky. Save your strength.'

But Ricky twisted his head around and stared at Jim fiercely with his bloodshot eyes. 'They stripped me bare-ass naked, Jim, and then they beat the living shit out of me. I could feel things bursting inside of me. I could hear my bones breaking. I played dead, but it didn't make no fuckin' difference.'

He coughed more blood, and spat, but then he said, 'They painted me all over and they carried me up here and did this to me. Hammer and nails. And all these cats, too. And they was screeching, these cats, like all hell let loose.'

'Who did it, Ricky?' Jim asked him. 'How in God's name did they get you up here?'

'Two guys in white. That's who they were. Two guys all dressed in white. Older one, and a younger one. Two guys in white.'

Jim's mouth went dry. *The Reverend John Silence, and Simon Silence. Who else could it have been? Two men dressed in white? Especially since Ricky had somehow found it impossible to paint anybody but that gray-faced Satanic figure, who appeared wherever the Silences appeared.*

'Did they say anything, these two guys in white?' Jim asked him. 'Did they call each other by name?'

Ricky shook his head, and more drops of blood were spattered on to the bedcover.

'Come on, Ricky, stay with me. You have to. Don't give up on me now. How did they do it, Ricky? How the hell did they manage to nail you up here?'

Ricky's eyes closed and he let out a bubbly, snorting noise. Jim felt like shaking him awake but he thought that he would only cause him more pain, and he must already be suffering more than Jim could imagine possible. He couldn't help thinking of that Easter hymn: *We may not know, we cannot tell, what pains he had to bear.*

'Ricky,' he repeated. 'Come on, Ricky. It won't be long now.'

Even as he said that, he heard the scribbling sound of an ambulance siren in the distance, accompanied by the deep blaring horn of a fire truck.

Ricky opened his eyes again, staring down at the bed as if he had forgotten where he was.

'Ricky, the paramedics will be here in a minute, and the firefighters to get you down.'

'Firefighters?' Ricky frowned, and the dry white paint on his forehead cracked into furrows.

'Just hold on, Ricky. Think about Nadine. What would Nadine do without you?'

Ricky turned his head again, and blinked at him. '*They flew*,' he said, in his clogged-up whisper.

'What? Who did? What are you talking about?'

'The two guys in white. That's how they nailed me up here.'

'What? I still don't understand.'

'They flew, Jim. They fuckin' *flew*.'

He continued to blink at Jim for a few more seconds, with metronomic regularity – *blink, blink, blink* – but then he stopped blinking and his eyes glazed over. His head dropped forward and his lungs let out a long, congested wheeze.

'Ricky!' Jim shouted at him. 'Ricky! The paramedics are here! Ricky! Don't give up on me now!'

Summer came back into the bedroom, followed by two paramedics, a man and a woman, both of them African-Americans. The woman stopped as soon as she came through the door and stared up at the ceiling with her mouth open, wide-eyed in disbelief. The man slowly lowered his shoulder bag to the floor and said, 'Hol-*eee* sh*ee*-it!'

Detective Brennan came into the interview room carrying a cup of coffee and a donut with sprinkles on it.

'Breakfast,' he said, holding them up. 'Or maybe lunch.'

Jim was sitting at the plain wooden table in his shirtsleeves. His eyes were swollen from drinking and lack of sleep. He was unshaven and his hair was all messed up.

The interview room was painted pale green, with windows that were covered with security mesh. Through the mesh Jim could see a small sunlit courtyard, where three uniformed police officers were talking and laughing, and a Korean woman was sitting by herself, reading a book and eating a sandwich.

Detective Brennan dragged over a chair and sat down on the opposite side of the table. He was wearing a creased brown shirt and a yellow necktie with catsup stains on it, and crumpled khaki pants.

'So what's the connection?' he asked, taking the lid off his coffee and blowing on it.

'I don't know what you mean. What's *what* connection?'

'Three people get whitewashed and crucified, along with eight white Persian cats each, and every one of those people is connected to you. Your long-lost daughter, your gardener, and now your painter buddy from the same apartment block. Your daughter is discovered in your classroom, your gardener is discovered in the grounds of your college, and your painter buddy is found on the ceiling of your own bedroom.'

'I had nothing to do with any of those killings. Nothing at all. I've been telling you that for three hours solid.'

'Well, to be fair, that's what our CSIs said about the first two homicides, your daughter and your gardener. First of all, there was no forensic evidence of any kind to suggest that you might have been involved in either of them. No fingerprints, no footprints, no blood, no fibers, no DNA. Second of all, that you couldn't have nailed them up like that, either of them, without some kind of mechanical assistance like a hydraulic lifting platform, and even then you couldn't have managed it on your own.'

'This third homicide, Mr Kaminsky . . . it's still too early to say anything for sure. But there's always the possibility that you were copying the other two homicides in order to make it look as if you had nothing to do with killing him, either.'

Jim slowly shook his head from side to side. 'What possible motive could I have had for nailing Ricky Kaminsky to my bedroom ceiling, especially when I was intending to bring a girl in there?'

Detective Brennan took a large bite of donut and when he spoke his left cheek was bulging. 'OK – even if *you* didn't have a motive, maybe you can think of somebody else who might have? Maybe it's somebody with a weird kind of a grudge against you – killing your daughter, and then your gardener, and then this artist guy who lived downstairs from you.'

'That doesn't make any sense at all,' said Jim. 'I didn't

even know I *had* a daughter until Bethany was murdered. I
didn't know the gardener personally, not at all, except to
say "*buenos dias*" to. And Ricky – sure, I liked him, and we
sometimes went out and had a few beers together, but we weren't
close friends.'

'Well, your stories check out. You were drinking at the
Cat'n'Fiddle like you say you were, and you went back to
West Grove College around two a.m. to collect your cellphone,
even though you shouldn't have been driving after so much
drinking. Then you came back and asked Ms Summer Parks
to come up to your apartment with you.' He paused, and then
he added, 'For whatever reason.'

Jim said nothing. He had lied to Detective Brennan about
accidentally leaving his cellphone in his desk, and going back
to the college to retrieve it. But he hadn't wanted to say
anything about the Silences until he had found out much more
about the Church of the Divine Conquest, and their promise
to bring back Paradise. In *his* Paradise, Bethany and his father
would both come back to life, and he didn't want to jeopardize
the possibility of that happening, not before he understood
how the Silences were going to do it and what it was going
to cost.

Not only that, he hadn't told Detective Brennan that Ricky
had described 'two guys in white'. Nor, especially, that
Ricky had claimed that they could fly. He doubted very much
that Detective Brennan would treat either claim as anything
except the hallucinations of a dying man. Especially a man who
had not only been dying but drunk, and high on Peruvian grass.

'Who else has access to your apartment, other than you?'
Detective Brennan asked him. 'Anybody else hold a key? Old
girlfriend, maybe?'

'Only the rental agency. Maybe the maintenance guy.
Nobody else that I know of.'

'There was no indication of forced entry, Mr Rook. There
were no signs of a struggle. And there were no indentations
in the carpet which might have indicated that a stepladder or
some kind of framework was set up in order to nail the victim
and all of those cats to the ceiling.

Detective Brennan pushed the last piece of donut into his

mouth and then sat back, fixing Jim distrustfully with those glittery near-together eyes.

'Let me put it this way, Mr Rook. I'm not a great one for hunches. I'm not like that goddamned *Mentalist* on the TV. But in your case I have this very, very strong feeling that you know a darn sight more about what this all means than you're telling me.'

He stuck up four fingers and then bent one of them back down again. 'Three ritual homicides. Well, we're assuming that they're ritual homicides but we don't have the first idea what kind of a ritual we're talking about here. People nailed to the ceiling and halfway up trees? Each of them surrounded by eight white cats? I've Googled it, and come up with zilch, except a couple of people who have multiple white moggies to find a home for, because their owner has kicked the bucket.

'But I'm thinking that maybe *you* have an inkling. After all, you're into all of this supernatural malarkey, aren't you? Lieutenant Harris used to say that you make John Edward look like he wouldn't know a spirit if it gave him a smart kick up the rear end.'

Jim said, 'I swear to you, Detective, if I had the slightest clue what this nailing up was all about, I'd tell you. I've Googled it, too, and I have dozens of books on magic and religious rituals. But I'm still as baffled as you are.'

'OK, Mr Rook, let's leave it at that for now. The CSIs tell me they're going to need your apartment for another forty-eight hours at least. Where are you going to stay in the meantime?'

'Well, Ms Parks has generously offered to let me sleep on her couch for the next couple of days.'

'I see. Her couch. Very generous. Just make sure you don't go back into your own apartment and contaminate the crime scene. And – Mr Rook . . .'

Jim was already opening the door. He stopped and said, 'Yes, Detective?'

'No more DUI, got it? I think we have enough dead people to deal with as it is, without you adding to the sum total.'

Jim arrived at college a few minutes after two p.m. He could hear the noise that Special Class Two were making from the opposite end of the corridor – laughing and shouting and scuffling and singing. He recognized Jesmeka Watson and Rebecca Teitelbaum singing a Rihanna song in screechy harmony; and he could hear Tommy Makovicka honking with laughter like a walrus, while DaJon Johnson was slapping out some grime rhythm on the bench in front of him.

Jim came in through the door and immediately the class quietened down, although there was still a lot of shuffling and whispering and giggling. He went to his desk and put down his briefcase and then he turned to face them. The first thing he noticed was the absence of Simon Silence.

'OK,' he said, 'I guess you all know what's happened – why I'm late.'

'A guy got crucified in your apartment,' volunteered DaJon Johnson. 'I seen it on the news this morning. That's some freaky shit, man. I mean, sir.'

'That's right,' said Jim. 'I found a neighbor of mine nailed up on my bedroom ceiling when I came home early this morning – the same way that unfortunate girl was nailed up in my classroom and my gardener was found nailed up in the cypress tree outside.'

'That is *so* gross,' said Hunni Robards. 'You must have barfed.'

'Do they know who done it?' asked Rudy Cascarelli. 'Must be like some serial psycho.'

Jim said, 'The police are looking into it, obviously, but right now I don't know any more about it than anything that you've seen on the TV. Less, probably.'

'It seems to me like you are having a run of very bad luck, Mr Rook,' said Joe Chang. 'But not such bad luck as some of the people close to you.'

'Let's change the subject, if you don't mind,' said Jim. 'I wouldn't have come into college at all today if I hadn't needed urgently to talk to you about *this*.'

He went to the blackboard, picked up a stub of red chalk, and wrote, in large letters, PARADISE. Then he turned back to his class, smacking his hands together.

He didn't say anything for nearly fifteen seconds. Gradually, his students began to settle. Kyle Baxter loudly blew his nose but nobody laughed or made any ribald comments like they usually would have done.

Jim looked from one student to the next, and said, 'You were all here in the middle of the night last night, with Simon. Ever since Simon joined this class, there's been a lot of talk about Paradise, and everybody getting what they want for themselves.

'I'm not sure if getting everything you want for yourself is a great thing, or a good thing, or a bad thing. It could turn out to be a truly evil thing. Maybe you've heard that saying that "power corrupts, and absolute power corrupts absolutely." From the way you guys have been talking, I'm beginning to think that you could say the same thing for Paradise.'

'But how can it be evil, sir, to get everything you ever dreamed of?' said Jesmeka Watson, with the colored beads shaking in her hair.

'I don't know, Jesmeka,' Jim told her. 'I'm just opening this up for discussion. But I'd like you to tell me what happened here last night, and what you expect to happen next.'

Rebecca Teitelbaum put up her hand, from the back row. Nudnik the bear was still sitting next to her, with a mournful expression on his face.

'Simon said that it was no secret, sir, and that we should tell you all about it if you asked.'

'I see. Go on, then. Please. Tell me.'

In her usual monotonous gabble, Rebecca said, 'Today is September twenty-seventh which is the anniversary of the day when God told Adam's first partner Lilith to get out of the Garden of Eden and never come back. God was angry with her because she believed that she was equal to Adam, and not just put on this Earth to have Adam's children and do whatever Adam told her to do. Lilith also believed that she and Adam should be able to know everything there was to know, so that they could choose for themselves how they wanted to live their lives, and so that they could make their own decisions instead of God making all the decisions for them.'

'And what do you think about that?' asked Jim.

'I think good for her,' put in Hunni Robards, shifting her chewing gum from one side of her mouth to the other. 'Even if wimpy Adam didn't stand up for himself, at least Lilith had the stones to do it.'

'And you, Rudy, what's your opinion?'

Rudy Cascarelli gave a one-shouldered shrug. 'It's OK by me, women being treated equal and everything. At least you can let them *think* they are. Where's the harm in that? They still got to do the cooking and the cleaning and have all the babies, don't they?'

'Booo!' said Rebecca Teitelbaum.

Rudy Cascarelli shook his head and laughed. 'Boo all you like, darling. Do you know any guys who can get themselves knocked up? Because I sure don't!'

Jim said, 'You all said some prayers last night, right?'

'That's right, sir, yes,' said Al Alvarez. 'There was three prayers altogether. One about God, and one about Jesus, and one about the Holy Ghost. Simon read them line by line out of that book of his, and we had to say something back to him at the end of each line.'

'You mean like responses? Like the priest says in church, "*the Lord be with you*" and everybody says "*and also with you*".'

'I guess so, yes. He said something like, "God took two handfuls of mud and squished them into, like, people." Well, not exactly that but something that meant that. And we all had to say "OK" and a few other words in, like, Greek or something.'

'Go on.'

'That was about everything. He said the prayers would help his dad to change the world back the way it should have been, because his dad could raise up this special power.'

'And when is this supposed to happen?'

'Before the end of today, that's what he told us. He said it was all explained in that book of his, what's going to happen.'

'The Book of Paradise?'

'That's right.'

Jim looked around the classroom. 'So where is Simon now?'

'He was here in class this morning, Mr Rook,' said Kyle Baxter. 'But he said he had to take the book back to his dad's church because it's unique and it's the sole copy and it's the only one there is.'

'He told you that his dad is going to change the world back to what it should have been, sometime before the end of today, but he didn't tell you exactly how his dad is proposing to do that?'

'He said one thing,' Joe Chang put in. 'He said we would know when it was starting to happen because everything would go real dark, like an eclipse, you know? But after a while everything would come back light again.'

'That sounds pretty apocalyptic, don't you think? Aren't any of you *scared*?'

'Not if it's going to be Paradise, sir,' said Jesmeka Watson.

'So you do believe that it's actually going to happen?'

'Why not? We'll soon see, won't we? If it doesn't, it doesn't, and we'll be stuck with the same old crap lives like always.'

'But even if it does happen – when it gets light again – do you think it really *will* be Paradise?'

'If we all get what we want, Mr Rook, then for sure.'

Jim thought: *Somehow, Simon Silence has convinced all of these kids that from sometime today the rest of their lives are going to be blissful. And they all believe him. Just like I believe in my heart of hearts that the Reverend John Silence can give me the power to bring Bethany and my father back to life. It's madness. It should be impossible. But I believe it.*

Sometime today, September twenty-seventh, everything was going to lock into place, like the mechanism of a giant clock. Bethany's death, Santana's death, Ricky's death. His dead father appearing on the seashore, drowned and bewildered. The dark hooded figure, smoky at first, but appearing more and more solid every time that it appeared. The Reverend John Silence, vanishing from his bar stool. Simon Silence, always smiling, but whose face gradually appeared to be changing into something strange and cold.

All of these different parts were coming together, and they were coming together sometime today.

They flew, Jim. They fuckin' flew.

Jim checked his watch. Then he said, 'I'm sorry, class. I have to be someplace. I'm going to hand out some worksheets on plurals. Once you've answered them, you can go.'

'Oh, no, sir,' said Jesmeka Watson. 'We're all going to stay here till Paradise comes.'

'Right, OK, do whatever you like,' Jim told her. 'Let's hope it doesn't come too late, and you have to wait up for it.'

He tugged a sheaf of test papers out of his briefcase and gave them to Kyle Baxter to distribute around the class. Then he hurried away along the corridor, down the stairs, and out of the front entrance.

He nearly collided with Sheila Colefax, who was coming up the steps.

'Jim!' she exclaimed. 'I heard what happened!'

But Jim said, breathlessly, 'Can't stop!' and jogged across the parking lot until he reached his car. He opened the door, flung his briefcase into the passenger seat, climbed in, and started up the engine.

He pulled down the sun visor and stared at his face in the mirror. He looked wild and unkempt and he still hadn't shaved. But there was no time for that. He swerved out of the parking lot, down the driveway, and hung a howling left on to Sunset, provoking a barrage of protesting car horns.

He just hoped that he could make it to Lookout Mountain Avenue, and the Church of the Divine Conquest, before it grew prematurely dark, and it was time for the arrival of Paradise.

SEVENTEEN

T raffic on Sunset was down to its usual crawl, so by the time he had reached the intersection with Laurel Canyon Boulevard and driven the two miles up to Lookout Mountain Avenue, it was only five minutes shy of four p.m.

Lookout Mountain Avenue was narrow and bright and dusty, with some ramshackle houses and rickety home-built car shelters and overgrown front yards. Jim drove slowly, trying to pick out house numbers.

He was feeling calmer now, but even more determined to find out what the Silences were doing. More to the point, he wanted to find out who they were, or *what* they were. Had it really been them who had nailed Ricky to the ceiling, and how could they possibly fly? Or had Ricky simply been delirious?

As creepy as they were, Jim had been forced to recognize that both of the Silences exerted a strong personal magnetism. Father and son seemed to be able to draw people toward them – not only because they offered them everything that they wanted most. The two of them had some other allure, too – an allure that was quite indefinable, like the sweet-and-sour taste of their Paradise apples.

Jim knew that he was very close to giving in to them. *You can bring back Bethany, and your father, and they can live out the rest of their lives as if nothing has happened to them. Who can it hurt?*

But he was still nagged by his natural skepticism, and his principles, and his logic. His common sense told him that there can never be such a thing as a Paradise for all, because one person's Paradise always turns out to be another person's Hell. That was why he needed to ask the Silences one burning question before the darkness descended. What was this all going to cost, and who would be paying for it? Morally, spiritually, and every other way?

He came to a long, high wall on the right-hand side of the road. It was rendered with maroon-painted cement and over-grown with creepers. Halfway along the wall there was a pointed archway, with a cast-iron gate. Over the gate, raised yellow lettering said *Church of the Divine Conquest.*

He parked his car on the rough, weedy verge on the opposite side of the road, and climbed out. There was nobody in sight, and the only sounds were the ceaseless murmur of traffic, the *flacker-flacker-flacker* of a distant helicopter, and the chirruping of cicadas.

The cast-iron gate gave a groan of protest as he opened it. Once inside, Jim found himself in a brick-paved garden. It was quiet, and shady, but it was badly neglected. The urns and planters contained only shriveled-up weeds, and although there was an ornamental stone fountain of a nymph, dancing, the fountain was dry and the nymph herself was covered all over with scabs of yellow-and-black lichen.

He walked through the garden until he came to the church building itself. It was a pale, sun-faded pink, and looked as if it had once been the home of a minor movie star, or a moder-ately successful director. It was built in the Spanish style, with pantiled rooftops and shady colonnades all around it. The only sign of life was a cluster of quail, sitting on the ridge of the main building and occasionally letting out their squeaky-toy mating calls.

Jim went down a short flight of steps and then walked around the colonnades until he came to a pair of carved-oak doors, one of which was half open. He peered inside and saw a wide reception hall, with glossy brown floor tiles, and a curving staircase that led up to a galleried landing. An elaborate crystal chandelier hung down from the ceiling like a giant spider's web. He could faintly smell sandalwood incense.

On the far side of the hall there was another pair of doors, and both of these were wide open. Beyond was a bright, sunlit room, although the sunlight made it too blurry for Jim to be able to see if there was anybody inside it.

'Hallo!' he called out. 'Reverend Silence! Simon! Anybody home?'

He waited, but there was no response, so he called out again.

'Reverend Silence! It's Jim Rook! I need to talk to you, sir!'

Still no response. He waited a little longer, and then he pushed the open door a little wider and stepped inside.

'Reverend Silence!'

He walked across the hallway and into the room beyond. This was obviously the main room where the members of the Church of Divine Conquest congregated, because it was filled with at least ten rows of plain white chairs, with an aisle in between them. The room was so bright because three walls were floor-to-ceiling windows, covered in nothing but thin white muslin drapes. Facing the chairs was an altar, covered in a blood-red cloth. On top of the altar stood two blood-red candles, in silver candleholders, and in between them was a small silver figure of a man with his arms and his legs outstretched, inside a hoop, like Leonardo Da Vinci's Vitruvian Man.

In front of this figure lay an open book, and as Jim approached the altar he saw that it was the same book from which Simon Silence had been reading to the students of Special Class Two in the middle of the night – the white-bound Book of Paradise.

'*You should read it some day.*'

Jim went right up to the altar. The Book of Paradise was quite slim. It looked as if it was probably no longer than Genesis or Numbers or Leviticus, or any of the other books in the Bible. The pages where it had been left open were marked with two blood-red strips of silk, embroidered with circular symbols like the silver figure of the outstretched man.

Jim looked around. The Church of the Divine Conquest was uncannily silent. He couldn't even hear the quail whistling on the roof. He leaned forward a little and started to read.

'And The Lord God created Lilith out of the dust of the earth to be given to Adam as his wife. Her hair was long and red like a rose, her cheeks were white and red. Her mouth was set like a narrow door comely in its decor, her words were smooth like oil. Her lips were also red like a rose and sweetened by all the sweetness of the world.

'She was naked but from her ears hung six ornaments, and

cords and ornaments hung from her nape and she was adorned with forty ornaments less one.

'But because she was fashioned from the same earth as Adam, Lilith would not acknowledge him as her master and become his servant. She left him and The Lord God was angered and exiled her from Paradise. She made the deserts and all the desolate places her home, and vowed vengeance for the unjust treatment that she had received.

'Before he created for Adam another wife, The Lord God sent three angels to seek out Lilith and return her to Paradise. And the angels' names were Samvi, Sansavi and Semangelaf. But Lilith spurned the entreaties of the three angels and refused to return to Paradise if it meant that she had to accept Adam as her master.

'When she refused to return, The Lord God put a curse on Lilith, that one hundred of her offspring should die every day, for ever, and that when they died, all should be condemned to Gehenna. In retaliation, Lilith became the mistress of Sammael, the uncircumcised arch demon, known also as the Angel of Death, and thus she became a queen of demons.

'Sammael and Lilith bore a son, Saklas. And when Saklas had grown, Lilith sent him in the guise of a serpent into Paradise. Saklas tempted Eve to eat of the fruit of the tree of knowledge, and The Lord God cast Adam and Eve out of Paradise for their disobedience. So it was that Lilith had her revenge.'

Jim was still reading when a voice quite close to him said, 'You *came*, Mr Rook! Good! We were expecting you.'

Jim said, '*Jesus!*' and took a quick step back from the altar.

The Reverend John Silence was standing only ten feet away from him, in his loose white shirt and his baggy white pants, smiling. Simon Silence was sitting on one of the plain white chairs, two rows from the back, although he was looking more serious, and his face appeared flatter than ever, as if he were pressing it up against a storefront window.

'We must apologize for not having explained ourselves more clearly,' said the Reverend Silence. 'But you must know from your experience as a teacher that the only sure way to ensure that your students do exactly what you want them to do is to make them believe that they are doing exactly the opposite.'

Jim said, 'Ricky Kaminsky.'

The Reverend Silence continued to smile, unabashed. 'Yes, Mr Rook. Ricky Kaminsky. What about him?'

'He was still alive when I found him. He said that he was nailed to the ceiling by two men in white.'

'He was still alive? That's incredible. What a resilient man he must have been.'

'Did *you* kill him? Did *you* nail him up there?'

'Yes.'

Jim opened and closed his mouth, but he was so shocked by the Reverend Silence's immediate confession that his lungs were emptied of air and no words came out.

'Before you ask,' said the Reverend Silence, 'we also nailed up Bethany Edwards and Alvaro Esteban.'

'*What?*'

'We needed people close to you – or people you knew, at the very least. We could have picked Sheila Colefax or Summer Parks, but as fate would have it, those three were the easiest for us to get to.'

'You murdered my daughter,' said Jim. His felt as if he were choking on a ball of thorns, and he couldn't stop his eyes from filling up with tears. 'That was my daughter, and you *knew* she was my daughter even before I found out that she existed, and you murdered her, *and you nailed her to the fucking ceiling*! You're a psychopath! You and your psycho son! You're both psychopaths!'

'Mr Rook, please.'

The Reverend Silence raised both his hands in a gesture of appeasement. He took a step closer, but Jim backed away and said, 'Don't you come anywhere near me, you murdering psychopath! I'm calling the cops and I'm calling them now!'

'I think you should listen first,' said the Reverend Silence.

'Listen? Listen to what? To some screwball psychopathic murderous Old Testament hogwash? Your son writes essays about the world on fire, and people who never should have been, and heaps of smoking bones! You're both of you crazy! I'm calling the cops!'

Jim fumbled in his pocket for his cell, and punched out 911, but the Reverend Silence simply shook his head. 'You won't get a signal here, Mr Rook. The Church of Divine Conquest is a dead zone, to coin a phrase.'

'OK. In that case, I'll make the call from outside. See you later, psychopath.'

'Please, Mr Rook – wait! If you walk out on this now, you will never be able to bring your Bethany back to life, nor your father, nor Alvaro Esteban, nor Ricky Kaminsky, for that matter.

'I admit it, yes, we killed two birds with one stone. We needed to make three human sacrifices before we could bring back Paradise, and it was my decision to sacrifice three people who were quite close to you. People you knew, anyhow.'

Jim smeared the tears away from his eyes with the back of his hand. He couldn't believe what he was hearing.

The Reverend Silence slowly paced backward and forward, while Simon Silence remained where he was at the back of the room, hunched forward in his chair, looking sullen.

'We never thought that this day would ever be possible,' said the Reverend Silence. 'The world is crowded with psychics and mediums and sensitives and people who claim that they can talk to the dead. There are countless people who have had a near-death experience like yours, Mr Rook, and some of them even say that it gave them the gift of second sight.

'The truth is, though, that not a single one of those psychics and mediums and sensitives is genuine. Not one of them, on the entire planet. Some of them genuinely believe that they can communicate with those who have gone beyond, and to be fair to them they probably *do* hear voices. But they're deluding themselves.'

The Reverend Silence stopped circling, and came right up to look Jim directly in the eyes. *If I had a gun*, thought Jim, *I would blow your fucking head off, right here and now*. But he knew that he had to listen. He had to find out how everything fitted together. Otherwise there would be no hope of putting any of this right.

'This may surprise you, Mr Rook,' said the Reverend Silence, 'but you are the only person in the world who can actually see the dead and talk to the dead and see spirits and demons and other wraiths, too. Nobody else can, no matter how much they pretend. Nobody. Not one.

'I have no idea why. What happened to you when you had that near-death experience when you were a boy – who knows? Maybe it wasn't that at all. Maybe you were born with that ability but it was only when you nearly died that you became aware of it.

'As it was, I found out about it purely by chance. It was Margaret Keaton, remember? That grade school teacher from Santa Monica who shot her husband because his cancer was causing him so much pain, and then shot herself? She didn't believe she was dead, did she? Not until she talked to you. But you took her walking through Woodlawn Cemetery, and you showed her the grave where she was interred, and then she believed it. But *I* was there, that afternoon, Mr Rook, and I saw you talking to that dead woman, and it was then that I realized that after centuries of searching, we had at last found the person we had only been able to pray for.'

Jim was beginning to feel light-headed, almost as if he were going to faint. 'I think I need to sit down,' he said. 'No – don't help me. I don't want your help. Don't come anywhere near me.'

He went across to the front row of chairs and sat down. The Reverend Silence followed him but stayed at a respectful distance.

'Would you like a glass of water, Mr Rook? Simon can bring one for you.'

'No, thanks. I'd rather die of thirst.'

'Very well. I can fully understand why you're angry. But I had to make sure that you would help us to bring about Paradise, and that you wouldn't change your mind.'

'By murdering my daughter?'

'Yes, by murdering your daughter. Because only by helping us to bring about Paradise will you be able to bring her back to life.'

'Jesus. I've heard of blackmail, but this beats everything. You and your son, you're way beyond sick.'

The Reverend Silence raised an eyebrow. 'Over six hundred people are murdered in this city every year, Mr Rook. Over six hundred – and for what? Nothing, except to make life more dangerous and more unpleasant. But the meaningful sacrifice of these three people will change everything for everybody. It will bring Paradise.'

'You beat somebody to death and cover them with white paint and nail them to the ceiling surrounded by dead cats. What kind of sacrifice is that?'

'It's the ritual sacrifice performed by the followers of Ba'al.'

'Ba'al? You mean like the King of Hell? You're even crazier than I thought.'

'You saw the figure made of smoke. You saw the face in Ricky Kaminsky's painting. You saw who was standing behind your father, on the seashore. You can't deny it.'

'You're trying to tell me that was Ba'al?'

The Reverend Silence nodded indulgently, like a teacher encouraging a very slow learner. 'The ritual for summoning Ba'al is this: three blameless people have to be taken out and punished for their blamelessness. Then they are painted white to show that they have committed no sin. They are nailed up high in a mockery of Calvary, to show that Jesus was not unique in being wrongfully crucified for being good, and that the Son of God doesn't have the exclusive rights to pointless martyrdom.'

'I can't believe I'm hearing this. What about the cats? Where do the cats come into it?'

'White cats symbolize purity and good fortune. The followers of Ba'al would nail a live white cat to the gatepost of anybody who had done them wrong, in order to make sure that their luck ran out, and that they were visited by poverty and sickness.'

'And for this lunacy, you murdered my daughter?'

'Oh, it's far from lunacy, Mr Rook,' said the Reverend Silence. 'Each of those three sacrifices unlocks one more door for Ba'al, and allows him to exercise his power in the world of men. And women, I might add.

'The first sacrifice unlocks the sanction of the Holy Spirit. The second sacrifice unlocks the sanction of the Son of God. The third sacrifice unlocks the sanction of the Lord God Himself.

'Ba'al is now free, Mr Rook, for the first time since the crucifixion of Jesus Christ. And with *your* help, he is going to set this earth to rights.'

Jim stood up. He glanced over at Simon Silence and then turned back to his father. 'Do you know what I think?' he said. 'I think you're nuts. And I think I'm just as nuts for listening to all of this BS.'

The Reverend Silence smiled indulgently. 'How can you say that, Mr Rook? You saw the great Ba'al for yourself.'

'I was tired. I was stressed. I was hallucinating. Too many beers, not enough sleep.'

'How do you think we nailed all those people to the ceiling, and up that tree?'

'I don't know, and I'm not sure that I want to know.'

'We did it like *this*, Mr Rook,' said the Reverend Silence. With that, he spread his arms wide, closed his eyes for a moment, and then rose up into the air, until he was floating more than six feet off the floor.

EIGHTEEN

J im took three or four clumsy steps backward, colliding with the chairs behind him. He had seen spirits levitate before now, and witnessed out-of-body experiences, when somebody's soul had risen out of their sleeping body and floated out through an open window.

But he had never seen a living human being lift himself up off the floor by sheer willpower, the way that the Reverend John Silence was doing, right in front of him. He was shocked and frightened, but at the same time he found it strangely enthralling.

'How the hell do you do that?' he said.

'Don't be alarmed, Mr Rook,' said the Reverend Silence, in the same soothing voice. 'My son and I are not what we appear to be.'

'Then what are you?'

'You will find out very soon, when we gather for the Great Atonement.'

'You still think I'm going to help you?'

'Of course, Mr Rook. You really have no alternative. You want your loved ones back, don't you? And you don't want any harm to come to your class. Well . . . no more harm than is strictly necessary.'

'My class? You mean Special Class Two? What about them? I swear to God, if you hurt any of them—'

'Please don't swear to God,' said the Reverend Silence. As he said this, he was gradually sinking back down to the floor, and after a few seconds his sandaled feet came softly into contact with the polished-oak parquet. 'In all momentous times, sacrifices have to be made, and your class will have to make sacrifices, like many others.'

'What do you mean, sacrifices? You're not going to start nailing them to the ceiling?'

'You will find out very soon, Mr Rook. Don't you see how dark it's growing?'

Jim looked around. The Reverend Silence was right. The sunlight had faded and the room was becoming gloomy. A soft, cold draft had begun to blow through the building, and the muslin drapes rose and fell as if they were breathing. Simon Silence was still hunched at the back of the room, and his face looked even more reptilian than it had before. He gave Jim a sloping, triumphant smile.

'Time to go now,' said the Reverend Silence. 'You don't have any objection to driving us, do you?'

'*Driving* you? Where to?'

'Back to your college, of course. That is where your disciples will be waiting for you. That is where our congregation will assemble. That is where you will assist Ba'al to make the Great Atonement.'

Jim felt as if his brain was being physically ripped apart. He was being asked to betray everything that he had ever believed in, and compromise every principle that made him who he was. Up until now, he had always retaliated against people who threatened him, no matter what natural or supernatural powers they possessed. But what alternative did he have? If he didn't bring Bethany and Santana and Ricky back from the dead, when he had the ability to do it, he would be just as guilty of killing them as the Silences were.

The room grew darker and darker, and the draft blew even more strongly, until the red altar cloth began to flap.

'OK,' said Jim. 'But I want you to know that I'm not doing this willingly.'

'Of course you're not,' smiled the Reverend Silence. 'Hardly any of the men and women who have made the most momentous contributions to the history of the world have done so *willingly*. They have done so because it was *necessary*. And now that your unique and wonderful gift has given us the opportunity to do so, it is necessary to right the wrongs that God has done to us, ever since Eden.'

'Let's just go, shall we?' said Jim. 'I don't need a sermon.'

Simon Silence stood up and waited for Jim and his father to walk up the aisle to the back of the room and join him.

The three of them left the church building and went Indian file through the derelict garden. Jim looked up. The sky was thunderously dark, and sheet lightning was flashing behind the clouds. As they stepped out of the front gate, the wind was blowing up dust and dried yucca leaves, which were scuttling across the road with a sound like rattlesnakes.

Jim unlocked his car, and opened up the nearside rear door.

'Go on,' he said, indicating with a nod of his head that both of the Silences should sit in back. 'I don't want to have either of you next to me, thanks.'

'You should not be so *aggrieved*, Mr Rook,' said the Reverend Silence, as he climbed in after his son. 'After today, I promise you, you will be a celebrity.'

Jim said nothing, but slammed the door and then climbed into the car himself.

The journey back to West Grove Community College was uneventful, even though the sky was now so dark that every vehicle was driving with its full headlights on, and it began to rain. None of them spoke.

After a few minutes Jim switched on the radio to hear if any of the news stations were carrying reports about the sudden mid-afternoon gloom, but all he could pick up was the endless hissing of white noise, punctuated by occasional spits and crackles.

They turned in through the college gates. As they made their way slowly up the driveway, Jim saw to his growing amazement that the entire forecourt and all of the slopes surrounding the main building were crowded with students – thousands of them. West Grove had enrolled more than eight thousand five hundred students for the new academic year, and at a guess he would have said that almost all of them were assembled here.

Although it was now thundering loudly, and rain was sweeping across the seventy-acre campus, the students all stood motionless, and drenched, although some of them were holding open books or folders or sodden magazines over their heads.

Jim slowed down as he reached the outskirts of the crowd,

and then stopped. A few students turned around to frown at his car, but none of them registered much interest in his arrival, and immediately turned back to face in the opposite direction.

Jim looked at the Reverend Silence in his rear-view mirror. 'So what are they all doing here? This must be every student in the whole darn college, and the extension, too.'

'You're right, Mr Rook. Every student who isn't away on some course or out of the country or home sick in bed. Why don't you park your car here, and we can get out.'

Jim steered over toward the curb and stopped. The Silences climbed out of the back seat and stood beside the car waiting for him to join them. Jim waited for a moment behind the wheel, wondering if he should back up fast and get the hell out of there, but then the Reverend Silence beckoned to him and pointed at his wristwatch, and Jim could see that he was miming, '*Come along, Mr Rook! We're wasting time!*'

He got out of the car and into the rain. Together, he and the Silences pushed their way through the crowds. Some of the students had to be given a sharp second nudge before they would move aside, but none of them seemed to resent it. They were obviously fixated with whatever was going on in the center of the forecourt.

As he elbowed his way to the front of the crowd, Jim saw at last what they were all staring at. It was the hooded figure, sitting cross-legged on the asphalt in its gray, rain-soaked robes. Even when it was sitting down, it was almost as tall as the students who were gathered around it. Its head was bent forward so that its face was completely hidden in the dark interior of its hood. Its shoulders were stooped and its robes were tucked underneath it, so that the only visible part of it was its grayish left hand, which was resting loosely on its knee. Jim recognized its ring at once, with its convoluted snakes.

It had arrived. It was here, in the real world, in the rain, and now it was visible not just to Jim but to everybody – all of these thousands of students. The Holy Trinity had kept it quarantined in limbo for thousands of years, but now the Reverend Silence and his three false crucifixions had released it. It had arrived, and it was ready for the Great Atonement – the reversal of everything that God had ordained since the creation of Adam.

Although he had been expecting the hooded figure to appear, and he had been reassuring himself all the way from the Church of the Divine Conquest that he would be able to cope with it, Jim felt a deep, cold sensation of dread – especially when the figure stirred slightly, underneath its robes, as if knew that he had arrived.

What really disturbed him, though, was the students of Special Class Two. They were here, all thirteen of them, standing in a semicircle behind the hooded figure, their arms by their sides, damp and dripping, but with patient expressions on their faces, as if they were prepared to wait for ever, if they had to.

'Mr Rook!' called out DaJon Johnson. 'We was beginning to think you wouldn't show!'

Jim circled cautiously around the hooded figure to join them. 'What are you all doing here?' he asked them. 'Kyle – Joe – Jesmeka?'

At that moment, Dr Ehrlichman came through the crowd. His bald head was spotted with rain and the shoulders of his khaki linen coat were dark with damp. He held out his hand and said, 'Jim! We've been waiting for you!'

'What's going on here, Walter?' Jim demanded. 'What are my class doing here?'

Dr Ehrlichman opened out his arms and spun slowly around. 'What a turnout! Look at them all! Our acolytes! Our faithful acolytes!'

'Walter, these aren't our acolytes. These are our students! These are just college kids!'

But now the Reverend Silence stepped forward, closely followed by Simon Silence. Their wet, white linen shirts were rippling in the breeze. 'The Great Atonement requires a congregation, Mr Rook, and what congregation could be more appropriate than the students of your own college? Doctor Ehrlichman has been most cooperative in assembling them all here. He has promised every one of them that they will find their own personal Paradise.'

'Come on, Mr Rook!' said Al Alvarez. 'It's going to be amazing! Think about it! Everything we ever always wanted!'

The Reverend Silence cocked his head to one side, and said, 'He's right, Mr Rook. In a few minutes, your Bethany could be standing here, holding your hand. Your father could be here, too. Ba'al will give you the power you need, and all you have to do is call them. Your disciples will help you.'

'My disciples? These are my class, not my disciples. I'm not Jesus, for Christ's sake.'

'Ah – but what you will be doing here today will be like the feeding of the five thousand. But it will be a much greater achievement, because there are so many thousands more – and instead of giving them loaves and fishes, you will be giving them their heart's desire!'

Jim couldn't stop himself from thinking: *blasphemy*. But he looked around at the huge crowd of students, and then back to his own class, and Dr Ehrlichman, and the rest of the faculty. He could see Sheila Colefax and she was smiling at him, and so was Roger Ball, the math teacher, and Heston Greene, who taught social sciences, and Cato Philips, the football coach, was nodding at him furiously and giving him a double thumb's-up.

The Reverend Silence tried to lay his hand on Jim's shoulder. Jim raised his arm to fend him off, but the Reverend Silence leaned towards him and said, in a low, cajoling voice, 'You cannot let all of these people down now, Mr Rook. Look at them! Look at their faces! They are all depending on you – every one of them! They have gathered here today expecting Paradise, and you are the only person who can give it to them! Here – take hold of your disciples' hands, and stand in a circle around Ba'al, and let the calling of the dead begin!'

Dr Ehrlichman called out, 'Come on, Jim! For the sake of West Grove! Think how great morale is going to be, when every student has everything they ever wanted! Think how high our reputation will rise! Think of our accreditation! And don't forget how much money the Reverend Silence is going to give us for our sports facilities!'

The Reverend Silence leaned even closer and added, in his

seductive tone, 'Think how *you* will feel, Mr Rook, when you get what *you* want!'

Jim thought: *This is madness. Here we are, all of us, over eight thousand students and their teachers, standing in a thunderstorm around a dark, gray demon, expecting to be given happiness.*

But then he thought: *Why not? When has God ever given us happiness? When has God ever given us anything but pain, and suffering, and tragic loss? Since Adam and Eve were expelled from the Garden of Eden, what have men and women ever had but toil, and doubt, and cruelty, and betrayal?*

He turned to DaJon Johnson and held out his hand. 'Come on, DaJon, let's do it. The rest of you, form a circle, OK? All hold hands around our hooded friend here.'

'You will never regret this, Mr Rook,' said the Reverend Silence. 'Your name will live for ever more.'

Jim didn't answer, but offered his right hand to DaJon Johnson, and his left hand to Rebecca Teitelbaum. Soon, Jim and the thirteen students of Special Class Two were standing in a ring around the hooded figure seated on the ground, all holding hands, shuffling their feet and looking self-conscious. Jesmeka Watson tossed her head to shake off the raindrops and the beads in her cornrows rattled.

'Are we all ready for this?' said Jim.

'If we ain't ready now we ain't never going to be ready!' said Rudy Cascarelli. 'Hey – I feel like some kind of a faggot here, holding two guys' hands!'

Directly above their heads there was an ear-splitting burst of thunder. Then, when the thunder had echoed and re-echoed across the hills, and grumbled into silence, it was followed by a low murmur that went through the crowds of students all around them, a rising tsunami of sound that eventually seemed to overwhelm the whole campus.

Jim understood what it was, that wave of sound. It was the sound of hope, and excitement. Almost every student had enrolled at West Grove because he or she had realized that they urgently needed to better themselves. This afternoon, in the rain, they were being offered success and happiness without any coursework, or study, or exams. All they had to do was show their devotion to Ba'al.

The Reverend Silence walked around the ring into which Special Class Two had formed themselves, and then came up and stood close behind Jim, Simon following in his footsteps. Jim could smell his breath and it was slightly garlicky. He raised his hands and sang in a high, tremulous pitch, 'The Lord God took in each hand the earth from the ground and shaped each handful into a human being, one male and one female. And they were equal. But did the Lord God regard them as equal?'

Jim was startled when all of Special Class Two shouted out in unison, '*OK!*' This must have been the response that Simon Silence had taught them when he had taken them for prayers in the middle of the night. But it suddenly occurred to him that 'OK!' didn't mean 'yes!'. He knew that the first use of 'OK' meaning 'all right' had not been recorded until the late eighteenth century. This response must be the Greek word *óxi*, which sounded like 'OK' but actually meant 'no'. Every response to what God was supposed to have done when He had created Paradise was '*no!*'

The Reverend Silence sang, 'The Lord God cast Lilith out of Paradise, but when He realized that Adam would need a wife in order to propagate the human race, He sent angels to bring her back. But what did Lilith say to the angels?'

'*Óxi!*' chanted the class.

'And did not the Lord God curse the offspring of Lilith for ever, that one hundred should die every day. And was this just? And was it merciful?'

'*Óxi!*'

'But we have found a savior, and today the offspring of Lilith shall reclaim the Paradise that they were denied by the Lord God, and by Jesus Christ, and by the Holy Ghost. And the great Ba'al shall rise again, and have dominion over the world which is rightfully his. At last we shall see the Divine Conquest, for which we have waited with such endurance for so many thousands of years.

'All hail to the great Ba'al!'

The wave of sound from the crowd grew louder and louder.

It was more of a reverberation than the sound of human voices, and Jim felt as if his teeth were buzzing.

Very slowly and jerkily, like some kind of mechanical automaton, the hooded figure started to unfold, and to climb to its feet. Underneath its wet gray robes it appeared to be skeletally thin, but when it had reached its full height it was nearly fifteen feet tall, and it towered over all of them.

It turned its hooded head slowly from side to side, as if it were relishing every moment of its reincarnation, and the huge crowd that had assembled to greet it. What impressed Jim more than anything else was that none of the crowd appeared to be frightened. Instead, they were all staring up at the figure with something approaching adoration.

The Reverend Silence sang, 'O great Ba'al! I am your servant and – here! – I have brought you the only man who can call back the children of Lilith from the realm of death.'

The hooded figure looked down at Jim, who was still holding hands in a circle with Special Class Two. Jim could just make out its eyes, glittering inside its hood. It seemed to stare at him for ever, not moving, not speaking, but then it reached out its gray, bony left hand toward him, with the silver snake ring shining on its ring finger.

'Take it,' the Reverend Silence coaxed him. 'Take the master's hand, and all of the power that you need will be yours.'

Jim released his hold on DaJon Johnson and Rebecca Teitelbaum. He knew that this was the critical moment. If he refused to take the hooded figure's hand, then all of this huge assembly would have to disperse without the gift of Paradise they so desperately wanted. The Reverend Silence and Simon Silence would have to return to their church and pray that they could find somebody else in the world who could really call spirits from the other side, like he could, and who could guess how many years that might take?

But if he refused to take the hooded figure's hand, the three sacrifices of Bethany, Santana and Ricky would have been nothing more than pointless butchery, and how could he live with that?

The Reverend Silence came up very close behind him and

murmured, 'Go ahead, Mr Rook. Remember what Khalil Gibran said. *"Death most resembles a prophet who is without honor in his own land or a poet who is a stranger among his people."* Take the hand of Ba'al, and you will defeat death.'

NINETEEN

J im took Ba'al's hand. It was surprisingly dry, like snakeskin, but it was intensely cold, and he could feel every bone in its finger joints. Unlike his father's hand, on the beach, it was real, and solid.

He thought to himself: *I can hardly believe this. I'm holding hands with one of the legendary kings of hell. This is almost like holding hands with Satan.*

The students kept up their low, resonant humming; and the sheet lightning flashed again and again, giving the clouds the appearance of a cheap stage-set.

From inside its hood, in a deep, muffled voice, Ba'al said, *'You are indeed the one. The only one. I never believed the day would come. I can see through your eyes. I can see so many of the dead, waiting to return.'*

'Just wait up,' Jim challenged it, although his throat was constricted with fear and he was so breathless that he could hardly speak. 'The Reverend Silence made me a promise.'

'The Reverend Silence? Ha! That is a most ironic name for one who has never been revered, and who is rarely silent.'

'Maybe. But I'm not going to help you until you give me back the three people who were sacrificed to set you free. You know – nailed to the ceiling, with the cats. I want those three back first. And my father, too. That was the deal.'

'Then call them,' said Ba'al. *'Call them, summon them, and I will give you the power that you need to bring them back to life.'*

Jim tried to steady his breathing. His heart was thumping hard against his ribcage. He thought of Bethany, standing at the end of the corridor, in a blur of sunlight.

'Think of all the things we could do together, Daddy. We could go for picnics. We could walk on the seashore. We could read a book together, on a windy hill. We could talk and talk and talk and never stop.'

He thought of Santana, looking up at him from his gopher-hole digging in the back yard at Briar Cliff Apartments.

'*Hola, Señor Rook!*'

He thought of Ricky, sitting in front of his easel, trying to paint The Storyteller.

'*I used to think the sixties were weird. Then I thought the seventies were weird. But today . . . whoa. The whole fuckin' world is weird.*'

Finally, he thought of his father, standing on Santa Monica Beach, still wet after thirty-three years of drowning.

'*How can I be a ghost? That doesn't make any kind of sense at all!*'

As he thought about them, he felt a soft, cold, rushing sensation up his arm. It was like being given a blood transfusion, except with blood that had been taken straight out of the fridge. It flooded up his arm and across his back and down his other arm, and then it quickly filled up his whole body, so that he shivered uncontrollably.

He looked up into the shadows of Ba'al's hood, and he could see that its eyes were glittering even more intensely than ever.

'*Do you feel it?*' said Ba'al. '*Do you feel the power? This is the power to defy death. This is the power of immortality. The Lord God thought that* He *was the master of life and death, but He forgot that we used to be angels, too, and that we used to execute sinners and idolaters at his command.*

'*Together with your gift, we can bring back all of those who died so unjustly, and we can sweep away all of those who should never have been.*'

Jim was about to ask Ba'al what it meant by that, when he heard a voice calling, 'Daddy! Daddy!'

He turned around, although Ba'al kept a painfully tight grip on his hand, so that he couldn't tug himself free. Hurrying toward him through the crowds of students was Bethany, her light-brown hair tied up with a ribbon, wearing the same gray dress in which she had appeared to him before, in college. Her face was bright with delight.

Even before she reached him, Jim saw Ricky and Santana coming through the crowds, too; and not far behind, he saw his father, William 'Billy' Rook. This time, his father was not wearing the suit in which he had drowned, but his favorite brown corduroy bomber jacket, and his khaki drill pants.

Bethany came running right up to him, her arms outstretched, but then she saw that he was holding Ba'al's hand, and she immediately came to a stop.

'Oh, OK,' she said, trying to peer inside its hood. 'You haven't finished the summoning yet? It's incredible.' She didn't seem to be at all unnerved.

'You know what this is?' Jim asked her. 'It doesn't *scare* you, even a little bit?'

'It's Ba'al,' she said. 'I used to belong to the Church of the Divine Conquest, too. They were always talking about Ba'al and setting it free and what it was going to look like and how they were going to take us all back to Paradise.'

'The Church of the Divine Conquest killed you,' said Jim. 'They beat you and killed you and that's what they did to set it free.'

Bethany glanced across at the Reverend Silence and Simon Silence. 'They said I had to make a sacrifice. They said that you would bring me back. They promised and I believed them. And – look – you have. And I'm alive again. And I feel perfectly fine now. And I love you.'

Ricky was shaking his head and holding up his hands so that he could show Jim that the nail-holes had all closed over. 'I don't know how the fuck you did that, man, but I feel OK too. Not that I forgive these Silence bastards. You just wait, you two. One of these days when you least expect it I'm going to catch up with you, and I'm going to beat the living crap out of the both of youse, and you won't be so silent then.'

Santana put his arm around Ricky's shoulders and said, '*Sostendré capa, señor, me creo* – I will hold your coat, sir, believe me.'

Billy Rook came up and stood beside Bethany. He didn't yet realize that he was her grandfather. '*There*, Jim!' he said, and there was a note of triumph in his voice. 'I told you I wasn't a ghost, didn't I?'

Jim looked down at Ba'al's hand, still tightly gripping his. The snakes on its silver ring had come to life, and were twisting

and writhing as if they were in agony. He raised his head and
looked up into Ba'al's eyes. Ba'al stared back at him for a
moment and then lifted its free hand and drew back its hood.
Its gray, sharply sculptured features were exactly like Ricky's
painting, including the two knobbly horns that protruded from
its hair. Haughty, aristocratic, with a hooked nose and very
thin lips, and a chin as sharp as a chisel.

'*You*,' said Ricky. 'It was *you* who was messin' with my
paints, then? And messin' with my mind, too? It wasn't that
Peruvian shit after all. Look at you. What the fuck *are* you?
Half a man and half a goddamned *goat*?'

Ba'al ignored him, but Jim said, 'Cool it, Ricky. Please.
This isn't the time.'

'Half a goddamned goat and half a long streak of piss, that's
what he is,' grumbled Ricky, but under his breath this time.

Ba'al spoke directly to Jim. '*Now that I have fulfilled my
part of our bargain, you must fulfill yours,*' it said. The expression on its face was triumphant, but its voice had lowered to
a menacing whisper.

'All right,' said Jim. 'What do you want me to do?'

The Reverend Silence approached him. He dipped his hand
inside his shirt and pulled out the large gold medallion with
the woman's face embossed on it. He dangled it in front of
Jim's face so that Jim could inspect it more closely. The woman
had a finely boned face, and she could have been beautiful if
she hadn't been glaring straight ahead of her as if she were
seething with rage.

'This is Lilith,' said the Reverend Silence. 'When the Lord
God cursed Lilith's progeny for all eternity, she had this medallion made. It was fashioned out of the rings which God had
given her to prove that she was Adam's wife and servant and
to decorate her naked body for Adam's pleasure.

'She said that as the centuries went by, this medallion would
be invested with the souls of every one of her descendants
whom God had cursed and condemned to die. Like an ancient
version of a solid-state memory, I suppose.'

'So . . . *what*, exactly?' said Jim. He was becoming aware
that the sky was growing lighter, and the thunderstorm was
already rolling away to the east. It had stopped raining, too.

The crowds of students were beginning to grow restless, and their hopeful humming was becoming more ragged.

'Press this medallion *hard* between your finger and your thumb,' explained the Reverend Silence. 'When you do so, you will summon out of it every one of the millions of Lilith's children who was cursed by God. With your ability, you should see them as a great multitude; and with Ba'al's unlimited power, you should be able to call all of them back to the world of the living.'

'Excuse me, you're talking about *millions*?'

'If you had the opportunity to resurrect every one of the millions who were killed in two world wars, would you not do so?'

'Jesus . . . how can you expect me to answer a question like that?'

'Because it's very similar to what you're going to be doing now, Mr Rook. And – if you don't mind – don't use the J word like that.'

'Daddy, *please*,' begged Bethany. Jim looked at her. He couldn't quite come to terms with how calmly she was taking all of this – her death, her resurrection, the appearance of Ba'al. But like so many young people who become seduced by religious sects, she had been brainwashed by the Silences to the point where she had allowed herself to be taken as a sacrifice, and he couldn't blame her for that. She was still a believer.

If only I'd known about it, Jim thought. *I would have gotten her out of there so fast*. But how could he feel guilty? He hadn't even been aware of her existence. Now, however, he did, and he couldn't allow her to die twice.

'Please, Mr Rook!' said Hunni Robards. 'I so want that Paradise!'

'We *all* do, sir,' Joe Chang put in. 'You say no to doing this, what do we have to look forward to then? No future. Nothing. Staying down the bottom of the shit heap, forever.'

'It's true, Mr Rook,' said Rebecca Teitelbaum. 'And it's not only us in Special Class Two . . . it's *all* of these students. You're a mentor to every one of them. You know what it says in the Talmud . . . *"Every blade of grass has an angel bending over it saying 'grow, grow'!"*'

To add to all of these entreaties, Dr Ehrlichman called out, in what he obviously thought was his most authoritative voice, 'Come on now, Jim! Let's get this show on the road, shall we?'

Jim hesitated, and while he did so the sun came out. He looked around, at more than eight thousand faces, all of them shining, all of them pleading with him to bring them Paradise.

He nodded, and the Reverend Silence lifted the Lilith medallion from around his neck and gave it to him. Jim held it in his left hand, smoothing the ball of his thumb over the raised features of Lilith's face.

'Now, squeeze it very tight,' said the Reverend Silence. 'Feel the souls inside it. Feel all of the people who have fallen, over the centuries. In tombs, in caskets, in cemeteries. Feel them, call them! They are slumbering now, but you can wake them up again!'

Jim pressed the medallion as hard as he could between finger and thumb. At the same time, Ba'al gripped his right hand even more forcefully, and again he began to feel that chilly infusion of power rising up his arm. This time, though, it was very much stronger and very much colder – so cold that it made him shake.

The crowd of students started to sing, in a strange high harmony, part devotional and part despair, as if a choir of thousands were falling together from hundreds of feet in the air. Jim thought: *that was what it must have sounded like, when God dismissed all of the angels who had displeased Him, and they fell from heaven.*

In his mind's eye, he suddenly saw a man's face – a swarthy, Middle-Eastern-looking face, unshaven, turning toward him as if he had disturbed him out of his sleep. Then another face, and then another. Then a whole flickering array of faces, men and women and children, all of them looking as if they had just been woken up. The flickering became faster and faster, until the faces were nothing but a blur.

The students' singing rose higher and higher, up to a piercing, sustained scream. Special Class Two had joined in the singing, although Bethany and Santana and Jim's father were standing silent. All the same, their faces were raised toward Ba'al, and their eyes were glistening with gratitude. Ba'al had given them their lives back, after all.

Only Ricky looked at all resentful, and he kept glancing at Jim as if to say, *What are you doing, man? Are you sure you know what you're doing? This goat-person might have brought me back to life, but then I shouldn't have been killed in the first place.*

The flickering of faces abruptly stopped, as if a film had run through its spool, and was simply going *flap, flap, flap*, while the screen remained blank.

Ba'al released Jim's hand, and said, '*It is done. The curse of centuries has been lifted. The dead have been returned to us.*'

The Reverend Silence laid his hand on Jim's shoulder. 'You have done very well, Mr Rook. Now – if I may have my medallion back?'

Jim turned around, and said, '*Jesus!*'

The Reverend Silence was still dressed in white, but his face had changed dramatically. His skull had narrowed, his eyes had become slanted, and his nose was curved and beak-like. Two long fangs curved out from underneath his upper lip, and from in between these fangs a forked tongue-tip flicked out.

'Did you not guess who I really am – not once?' he asked. His voice hadn't altered, although now he sounded even more mocking.

'You're a *demon*,' said Jim. 'I don't have any idea which one.'

'Of course, only *you* can see me in this shape,' said the Reverend Silence. 'Oh – and my lord and master, Ba'al. I am Sammael, Lilith's lover. Why do you think I have devoted myself for so many centuries to reversing the curse that God put on her? She defied God and chose to stay with me, as an equal, and the mother of so many of my children, rather than return to Adam as a servant.'

'Sammael? The Angel of Death?'

'Well, that is what the Jews called me. I was once God's executioner. But I refused to carry out God's curse on Lilith, and kill my own children.'

Jim could faintly hear shouting in the distance, on the far side of the campus. Bethany came up to him and linked her arm through his.

'It's all over, Daddy. You did it. We should go.'

The Reverend Silence grinned at her, and his forked tongue licked his lips. 'You have a wise daughter, Mr Rook.'

Jim turned around. The shouting was growing louder, and he was sure that he could hear screaming, too. A ripple went through the crowds of students, and then a moan, as if they were all beginning to realize that something was wrong.

'What's happening?' he demanded. 'I thought we were giving these kids everything they wanted!'

'*Perhaps we were deceiving you,*' said a deep voice, close behind him. It was Ba'al. '*Perhaps you should have studied your scriptures more attentively. Sammael is the Angel of Death, but Ba'al – Ba'al is the Master of Lies.*'

It laughed, a harsh, humorless laugh, and then it dragged its hood back over its head, so that its face was hidden.

'What have you done?' Jim shouted at it. 'What the *hell* have you done?'

'*Hell is the right word,*' Ba'al replied. '*But I have done nothing. It needed you to do this. If man has a worse enemy than God, it is man himself.*'

With that, gray smoke began to pour out of it, and blow away eastward on the wind.

'Stop!' Jim screamed. '*Stop!*' But within a few seconds, Ba'al had turned completely to smoke, and twisted off into the sky.

The shouting and screaming was much louder now, and suddenly the students all around them began to run, like a herd of cattle that gets spooked by wild dogs. Most of them ran across the forecourt toward the back of the college buildings, but some of them zigzagged across the parking lot and ran down the hill toward the tennis courts, and the road beyond.

Jim turned to face the Reverend Silence again, trembling with anger at his betrayal, and his own stupidity.

'We have to stop this,' he said. 'I don't know what's happening here, but we have to stop it.'

Dr Ehrlichman pushed his way over to them and pulled at

the Reverend Silence's sleeve. To Dr Ehrlichman, of course, without Jim's spiritual vision, the Reverend Silence still looked the same as he had before, and not like the demon Sammael.

'What's happening? Why are my students all running away? You promised them Paradise, and so did I!'

But the Reverend Silence wrenched his sleeve free and said, '*What*? What did you expect? Who in their right mind thinks they can have everything they want, for nothing? What sane person thinks that they deserve Paradise?'

'Then tell me what is going on here, you charlatan,' said Dr Ehrlichman.

Jim smelled smoke, and it wasn't just the lingering smoke from Ba'al's departure. He suddenly saw orange flames around the side of the college buildings, in the direction of the sports stadium, and dense black smoke began to rise up into the sky.

Bethany tugged at his arm again and said, 'Daddy, we really should go!'

'She is right, *Señor* Rook,' said Santana, anxiously. Students were running in all directions now. '*Es hora para que nos vayamos – y tan rápidamente como sea possible!* It's time for us to go, as quickly as possible!'

William Rook came up, looking confused. 'I don't understand, Jim! I'm real now, aren't I? I'm not a ghost! This isn't a nightmare, is it? Tell me this isn't a nightmare, Jim! Tell me I'm real!'

At the same time, Simon Silence came gliding up to appear behind his father's right shoulder. He was smiling, but his face had become completely reptilian. Even his eyes had turned yellow, with black vertical slits instead of irises.

Jim understood who he was now, *what* he was, what he had been all along, ever since he had joined Special Class Two. Simon Silence was the serpent that Sammael had sent into the Garden of Eden to whisper into the ear of Eve, so that she would disobey God, and be exiled like Lilith. It was so chillingly obvious. Simon Silence had even given them apples – fruit from the tree of knowledge, and of memories that should have been forgotten.

'Well done, Mr Rook,' he said, with a nod of his head. 'You now have everything your heart desired, and so do we.'

Over toward the sports stadium, the smoke was piling up high into the afternoon sky, and now Jim could see that the eucalyptus trees were ablaze, with their tall trunks crackling and fiery leaves whirling up into the air.

Joe Chang and Jordy Brown came up to Jim, with most of the rest of Special Class Two close behind them.

'What are we supposed to do now, Mr Rook? Is this Paradise coming, or what? Don't look nothing like Paradise to us!'

Jim looked at the Reverend Silence and Simon Silence – Sammael and his Serpent – and said, 'No, Joe. Paradise has been canceled, due to devious lying bastards. Get yourselves out of here, all of you, fast as you like. But go to my apartment, OK. Five-seven-seven-five-one Briarcliff, right at the top of North Van Ness.'

'Why do you want us to do that, Mr Rook?'

'I want to have a headcount, just to make sure that all of you are fit and well. And we need to talk about what's happened here, and what we're going to do next. So – go! Go on, get out of here, and tell everybody else in the class where to meet up.'

'Yes, sir, Mr Rook!'

They didn't need telling twice. Urgently, they beckoned the class together and told them where they were going, and then they all ran off, past the science block, heading for the student parking lot.

'We're leaving, too,' Jim told Bethany and Santana and Ricky. His father, Billy, looked bewildered, so Jim took hold of his hand and said, 'Let's go, Dad. Everything's going to work out fine.'

'What – you're not staying to taste the fruits of your achievement?' asked the Reverend Silence. 'It's not every day that you get to witness an apocalypse of your own making!'

And Simon Silence, still leering over his father's shoulder, quoted his own essay on Paradise, word for word, '*For me Paradise will come on the day when the Fires are lit all over the world from one horizon to another and are stoked with Those Who Never Should Have Been.*'

'Come on,' said Jim. He held Bethany's hand tight, and started to walk quickly back to where he had parked his car,

with William Rook and Ricky and Santana following close
behind him. Other cars were already screeching out of the
parking lots, and speeding down the driveway toward the gates,
but there were still hundreds of students milling in panic around
the forecourt and the college buildings, and running down the
slopes, screaming. Fires were breaking out everywhere. Jim
heard a loud explosion, and glass splintering, and when he
looked to his left he saw a dragon's tongue of fire leaping out
of the window of the chemistry block, setting light to the
branches of the overhanging junipers.

Off to the right, from the top of the slopes, he heard even
more screaming, and it was then that he could see why all of
the students were running. Over the crest of the slopes, like
a tidal wave, came thousands of people, most of them wearing
what looked like dirty white robes. *Thousands* – even more
than the students – and they were pouring over the hilltop so
fast that they were easily catching up with the students and
overwhelming them, in the same way that a tidal wave would.

'What in the name of God . . .?' said Ricky.

Jim said, 'They're dead people, come back to life.'

'Like zombies? Is that what you're talking about? *Zombies*?
Get real, Jim! There's no such thing as zombies!'

They had reached the car. Jim took out his keys, dropped
them, and then had to kneel down and scrabble under the car
to find them again.

'I'd make it snappy, if I was you, Jim,' said Ricky. 'Whatever
those people are, zombies or not, they're headin' this way with
what you might call considerable momentum. And – *Jesus*!'

'What?' said Jim, standing up. The torrent of white-robed
figures was more than halfway down the slope toward them
now. They came rushing in complete silence, and they were
curiously out of focus, but there was no doubt about what was
happening to the students who couldn't outrun them. They
were engulfed, and disappeared, but after only a few seconds,
out of the depths of the furiously running horde, body parts
were flung up into the air – arms and legs and heads and torsos
that looked like bloody kegs, and long surrealistic loops of
intestine.

'Get in the car!' Jim shouted, but none of them needed to

be told. Bethany and Jim's father climbed into the front seats, while Ricky and Santana clambered into the back. Jim had just started up the engine when a young African-American student banged on the window and screamed, '*Take me with you! Take me with you!*' so Ricky opened up the door and let him in.

'They're tearing everybody into pieces, man!' babbled the student. 'They're tearing them all into pieces! My girlfriend! My girlfriend! Shit, man! Maria! They tore her into pieces, right in front of my eyes!'

Jim gunned the Mercury's 7.1-liter engine. The white-robed figures were less than a hundred feet away now, and he didn't have the time or the space to U-turn, not without colliding into them head-on. They were running toward the car so fast that they appeared to grow larger and larger with every second. Although it was so difficult to focus on them clearly, Jim could see that some of their soiled white robes looked like djellabas, with pointed hoods, but most of them seemed to be dressed in shrouds, heavily stained with blood and bodily fluids and yellowed with age.

They weren't zombies – not like Haitian zombies, or the living dead out of movies. But they were dead people, tens of thousands of dead people, Lilith's children, and the children of Lilith's children, all brought back to life, and desperate for their revenge on Eve's children, who had taken the lives that should have been theirs.

Just as the first of them reached the car, and thumped into the driver's-side fender, Jim shifted it into reverse and backed down the driveway at nearly twenty-five miles an hour, with smoke billowing out of the tires.

The white-robed figures came running after them, but Jim managed to spin the wheel and slew the car around, with its suspension bucking and bouncing, so that it was facing toward the college gates.

As he put his foot down again, though, he saw that the road outside the college gates was crowded with thousands more white-robed figures, like a huge marathon race, and that they, too, were running relentlessly toward them.

TWENTY

'What are we going to do now, man?' shouted Ricky. He twisted around to look through the Mercury's rear window, and already the white-robed figures were pouring down the driveway toward them. 'Coupla seconds and they're going to be climbing all over us!'

Jim slowed down for a moment. Bethany said, with her voice rising almost to a squeak, 'We can't just run them down, Daddy, they're living people!'

'I know they are, sweetheart. But what do you think they're going to do to us, if they get hold of us?'

'They'll tear us in to pieces!' said the African-American student. 'They tore off Maria's arms! They did it right in front of me! They tore off her arms!'

'The Reverend Silence promised me that I would get my life back,' said Bethany, and there were tears in her eyes. 'They wouldn't hurt me, would they? They wouldn't dare.'

'Maybe they wouldn't dare to hurt *you*, girl,' said the student, 'but nobody made no promises like that to me.'

Jim said, 'He's right. Hold on. Hold on *tight*. We're going to get ourselves out of here.'

Three of the white-robed figures flung themselves on to the trunk, drumming on it furiously with their fists, but Jim slammed his foot down on the gas pedal and the car surged forward with its tires skittering on the blacktop and its tail sliding from side to side. The white-robed figures tumbled off on to the ground, but they were immediately swallowed up by the hundreds more who were still running after them.

By now, the white-robed figures who were coming up the hill had reached the college gates. Jim kept the gas pedal flat on the floor and the Mercury was doing fifty miles an hour when it hit the first of them. The multiple collisions were thunderous, like an artillery barrage, one body bouncing off the hood after another. All Jim could see was white-robed figures, flying and spinning and flinging up their arms. Some of them came hurtling right into the windshield, and over the roof. Some were thrown to the side of the road. Others disappeared underneath the front bumper and the car rocked and swayed as its wheels ran over them.

'This *is* a nightmare, Jim,' William Rook repeated, over and over. 'My God, son, this *is* a nightmare.'

Bethany laid her hand on Jim's shoulder, as if to support him and reassure him, but all the same she kept saying, 'Please forgive us, please forgive us, please forgive us.' Jim couldn't tell if she were praying to God or to Ba'al, but then he thought: *Maybe it doesn't really matter.*

Santana had his eyes tightly closed and was gabbling Hail Marys in Spanish and repeatedly crossing himself. Ricky was still turned around, keeping his eye on the white-robed figures who were chasing them from behind. 'Bastards still comin', Jim!' he called out. 'Bastards still comin' thick'n'fast!'

No matter how many white-robed figures they knocked down, more came running toward them. But Jim kept his foot pressed hard down and the Mercury continued to plow through them – *thump*! *thump*! *thump*! – its engine roaring and its tires slithering on torn shrouds and skin.

As they forced their way further and further into the thick of the crowd, however, he began to realize that the white-robed figures were not only blurry, and that it was difficult to focus on them, they were not as solid as ordinary men and women. He had hit a deer once, when he was driving at night through the mountains, and the impact had broken his front tooth and wrecked his beloved Chevy Impala beyond repair. But although these white-robed figures were slowing them down, and they were jouncing wildly up and down as they ran over them, they weren't substantial enough to bring them to a stop, which the sheer weight of ordinary human bodies would have done.

'Keep going, man!' Ricky urged him. 'I think I see light at the end of the zombies!'

He was right. The crowd of white-robed figures was beginning to thin out, until there were only a few of them running up the road, and these few ignored them, or didn't see them, or maybe they had seen the slew of bodies that they had left

behind them, and didn't want to end their lives so soon after
they had been resurrected.

They reached Sunset, and Jim spun the wheel so that the
Mercury did a sideways slide and headed east. He handed his
cellphone back over his shoulder to Ricky and asked him to
call 911. Ricky tried again and again, but there was no signal.
The car radio was the same as before, nothing but the endless
shushing of white noise.

Jim was surprised how little traffic there was, although it
was crawling along even more slowly than usual. West Grove
college campus was mainly hidden now by buildings and trees,
but when Jim turned his head and looked back, he could see
that the main building was on fire now, as well as all of the
trees around it, including the giant cypress to which Santana
had been nailed. A thick column of whitish-gray smoke was
climbing hundreds of feet up into the sky.

'Looks like you'll be teaching in a tent for a while, dude,'
Ricky remarked, dryly. 'That's if there's anyone left alive to
teach.'

Bethany squeezed Jim's arm, and said, 'Daddy?' When he
turned to her, she tried to give him a comforting smile, but he
couldn't begin to tell her how remorseful he felt. What was
that old saying about 'he who sups with the Devil'?

'I'm OK,' he told her. 'Everything's going to work out,
you'll see.'

But they had only just passed the intersection with North
Canon Drive when Jim's father pointed southward, toward
Beverly Hills, and said, 'Would you look at that! The whole
darn city's burning!'

Palls of smoke were rising up everywhere, from Culver City
in the south-west, from the downtown area, from Huntington
Park, from Montebello. Helicopters were circling around,
glinting in the sunlight, and when Jim put down his window
they could hear the wailing and warbling and honking of sirens.

'I sincerely trust and hope that this is nothing to do with
us, man,' said Ricky.

As if to answer his question on cue, over a hundred figures
in shrouds and white robes came running down Benedict
Canyon Drive, from their left, and poured across the road in

front of them, before disappearing down North Rodeo Drive.
They rushed so fast, and they were so indistinct, that Jim felt
as if he had dreamed them, rather than seen them for real, but
he knew that they *were* real, and that it was his fault that they
were here.

'You think these dead-live people are only here, in LA?'
asked Santana. 'You think maybe all over the world? Maybe
Mexico? I have family in Rosarita, my mother, my grandmother. My two sisters.'

'I have no idea, Santana,' said Jim. 'The only thing we can
do is try to find a way to send them all back where they
belong.'

'*Love* to know how you're going to do that, man,' said
Ricky. 'When I was at college, we just about managed to
squeeze seventeen people into a Volkswagen. How do you
squash millions of people back into some freakin' three-inch
medallion?'

'I don't know, Ricky,' Jim told him. 'But let's get back to
my place and try to work it out.'

With that, he pulled out into the center of the road and put
his foot down. Other drivers blew their horns at him, but he
took no notice, weaving in and out of the creeping line of
traffic at nearly forty miles an hour. Torn shrouds were still
fluttering from underneath his car, caught on the muffler.

A Highway Patrol car flashed past them on the opposite
side of the road, with its lights flashing and its sirens howling
and whooping and wibbling, but the officers inside it didn't
even look at them.

'I think they chase after dead-alive people,' said Santana,
'not us alive-alive people.'

But then it must have occurred to him that he, too, had been
brought back from the dead, and he stayed silent until they
reached Briar Cliff Apartments.

Nadine was so shocked when she opened the front door of
her apartment and saw Ricky standing there that her knees
buckled, and both Ricky and Jim had to grab her elbows to
stop her from falling.

They helped her inside and sat her down on the couch. She

couldn't stop reaching up and touching Ricky – his hands, his face – and saying, with tears running down her cheeks, 'It's not possible. It's not possible. It's a miracle.'

Ricky sat down beside her. 'Nadine, sweetheart, I've learned today that a whole lot of things are possible that I didn't believe was *possibly* possible. I always thought that the world was full of weird shit before but it's weirder and shittier than I ever could have imagined. Haven't you heard what's happening?'

'What do you mean?'

'Didn't you see the news or nothing?'

'No. The TV's been on the fritz for most of the day, and I haven't been out.'

Jim said, 'I'd better get upstairs. I think I hear more of my class arriving.'

'OK, Jim. I'll tell Nadine all about it and then we'll come up to join you. I could really use a smoke.'

Jim left the Kaminsky apartment and climbed the steps up to the next landing. He stopped at Summer's door and rang the bell. He had rung it before, when he had first arrived back here, but there had been no answer. He guessed she must have gone for an interview, or down to Clawz to have her nails polished. There was still no answer, so he continued up to his own apartment. A large black crow cawed at him mockingly from the rooftop opposite. He didn't like crows. They reminded him of demons, and bad luck.

Apart from his father and Bethany and Santana, Joe Chang had made it here, with Hunni Robards and Jordy Brown. Jim had only just gone into the kitchen to get them all some drinks when there was a rapping at the front door and DaJon Johnson came in with Rebecca Teitelbaum. After another ten minutes, Al Alvarez and Jesmeka Watson appeared, and then Tommy Makovicka, carrying a motorcycle helmet with the red, white and blue flag of the Czech Republic on either side.

Soon, the whole of Special Class Two had turned up, with the exception of Simon Silence. Jim gave them all beers or sodas and filled three bowls with Doritos and giant pretzels and Dakota Farm potato chips.

Tibbles had come out of hiding and appeared to be enjoying

this unexpected company. He went around sniffing at each of them, and graciously accepting strokes and tickles under the chin. In the end, he walked across to the couch and jumped into Hunni's lap.

Before he talked to his students, Jim went out to see his father, who was sitting on the balcony, still looking edgy and disorientated.

'See that smoke behind the trees, son? Another house burning, by the look of it.'

'How are you feeling, Dad?'

William Rook gave him a quick, sideways glance, almost as if he were embarrassed to be here. 'I don't know yet. Glad to be back, I guess. But it doesn't feel like any time has passed at all.'

'Thirty-three years, Dad. That's a long time being drowned.'

His father reached out and squeezed his hand. 'I know. But the trouble is, I still feel the same way I did when I walked into the ocean. I still miss your mom.'

'I still miss you, Dad. But that's Old Father Time for you. Old Father Time is the meanest sneak-thief there ever was. Takes things away from you and won't give them back, no matter what.'

'You got *me* back. You got your Bethany back. Can't believe I'm a grandfather with an eighteen-year-old granddaughter! You got your friends back, too.'

'I know. But what has it cost? How many of those kids got ripped apart back there? How many more innocent people are going to get killed?'

His father shook his head, emphatically. 'That wasn't your doing, son. You were acting in good faith. You weren't to know what those Silence people really were, or what they were really after.'

'I should have. I didn't like them, I didn't trust them, and I had my suspicions right from the moment I met them. But I was only thinking of myself – of what *I* wanted. How selfish is that?'

'You don't have to talk to me about selfish. I left you alone on the beach, Jim, and walked off into the ocean.'

Jim laid his hand on his father's narrow shoulder. 'I know,

Dad. But it's forgotten now. I have something more important to worry about now. Sending those dead-alive people back to dead-dead land.'

'Jim,' said his father.

'What is it, Dad?'

'If you find out . . . well, if you find out that *I* have to go back there, too, then so be it. You know and I know that I shouldn't really be here.'

'I lost you once, Dad. I don't want to lose you a second time.'

A long moment of father-and-son silence passed between them; and then Jim went back inside his living room and smacked his hands together for attention.

'Listen up! I know how anxious you all are to get back home and reassure your parents that you're OK – and also to check that *they're* OK. But what happened today happened because of all of us, because of me.

'We were tempted into thinking that we could have everything that we had ever wanted, without working for it, and with no regard for the effect that it would have on other people. And we gave in to that temptation – me, just as much as you. In fact I'm far more responsible for what happened than you are, because I'm older, and I'm supposed to be wiser, and it's my job to take care of you.'

'You still a human bean, man,' said DaJon Johnson. 'You wanted your dead dad back and your dead daughter back. We can dig that. We ain't blamin' you or nothin'. We should never of listen to that wanksta.'

'I *believed* him,' protested Jesmeka Watson. 'And why shouldn't I? I got the voice, I got the looks, I got all the moves. All I needed was the breaks.'

Kyle Baxter put up his hand and said, 'I believed him, too, sir. When somebody tells you that he can give you happiness and bliss and contentment and good fortune and felicity and fulfillment, what are you going to say to him? You're not going to say "no, thanks," are you?'

'OK,' said Jim, 'we all got taken in. But what we have to do now is work out how to reverse what we've done, or at the very least how to salvage the situation.'

'Maybe we should hold hands in a circle and say all of those prayers backward,' Al Alvarez suggested.

'That's no good,' said Hunni Robards. 'I can't remember them *forward*, let alone backward.'

'Maybe we should go the Reverend Silence's church and exorcize him,' said Kyle Baxter. 'He's technically a demon, after all.'

'You need a priest for an exorcism, don't you?' asked Tommy Makovicka. 'You need a priest and holy water and all the right kind of prayers, whatever they are.'

Jim said, 'I have some books about demons with dismissal rituals in them. But I'm not confident that they would really work.'

'It could be worth a try, though,' said Rebecca Teitelbaum. 'My grandmother always used to put a spell over my crib when I was little – a piece of Kabbalistic paper, with garlic and rue and a little piece of mirror in it. She said that kept away demons, and it must have worked, because I never got possessed once.'

'That mangy old bear you keep totin' around, I reckon *he's* possessed,' DaJon Johnson retorted. 'I think he put the evil eye on me. My shoelace come undone, just after he look at me the last time, and I trip and fell down the stairs and nearly got killed.'

They all looked at each other, lost for any more ideas. Jim tried his cellphone again, but there was still no signal. His landline was dead, too, and there was nothing on his TV but snow. In the distance, sirens were still wailing, and they could hear the persistent throbbing of helicopters.

Jim said, 'There's a spirit who sometimes gets in touch with me, Father Michael. We weren't Catholics, but he used to be a friend of the family. After my dad disappeared, he helped us more than I can tell you. And after *he* died, himself, he still used to talk to me if I was in trouble of any kind, and he still does. I could try to get into contact with him – see if he has any ideas. He's a priest. He probably knows all about Sammael and Lilith.'

'You should talk to him, then,' Joe Chang nodded. 'It don't seem like none of *us* can think what to do. Well – we could go round to my cousin Gao's place and pick up his niner and then go after the Reverend Silence and blow his head off. That might work.'

'Give me a couple of minutes,' said Jim.

He went through to his bedroom and closed the door. The ceiling had been scrubbed since Ricky and all of those cats had been nailed to it, but there were still dozens of small craters in the plaster. He sat on the end of the bed so that he could see himself in the mirror on his closet door.

'Father Michael,' he said. 'This is Jim, Father Michael – Jim Rook. I need to talk to you, Father Michael.'

There was no response. Even if a spirit didn't want to speak to him, he could usually sense rustling and whispering in the spirit world, almost like party guests playing hide-and-go-seek behind the drapes. Now, though – nothing at all.

'Father Michael, I'm begging you here. I really need your help. I've made a terrible mistake and I don't know how to put it right.'

For a few seconds, there was silence. Then he heard a sound like a knife being scraped on a plate, one of those screeching sounds that sets your teeth on edge, and a haggard, bearded face appeared in the mirror, superimposed on his own face. He was sure that it was Father Michael, but before he had a chance to speak to him, the face disappeared, and all he could see was himself, sitting on the end of the bed.

He sat there for a while, wondering if he ought to try calling Father Michael again. But it seemed as the resurrection of Lilith's millions had not only interfered with radio and telephone and television, it had jammed all contact with the spirit world, too. Eve's children were cut off, unable to communicate with each other, or even with their dead friends and relatives. They could no longer call for help, either from this world, or the next.

He was still sitting there when there was a timid knocking at the bedroom door.

'Daddy? It's Bethany.'

He went over to the door and opened it. 'Any luck?' she asked him, but she could see by the expression on his face that he hadn't been successful.

'Ricky's here, from downstairs, with—'

'Nadine,' said Nadine, who was standing in the hallway right behind her. Nadine had tied up her hair now, and fixed her make-up, with purple eyeshadow and purple lip gloss to match. Ricky had changed into a black cowboy shirt with red piping, and skinny-legged jeans.

'Is Summer here?' asked Nadine.

'No. Why? I rang her doorbell a couple of times but she wasn't in.'

'Well, that really worries me, now that Ricky's told me what's going on. Round about one o'clock I asked Summer if she'd like to come downstairs and join me for a glass of wine – you know, so that I didn't have to drown my sorrows on my own. She said she'd love to. She had a hair appointment at Floyd's to have her highlights done, but she said that she'd be back before three thirty, easy. But look at it now, it's way past five.'

Jim said, 'Floyd's? Where's that?'

'Corner of Selma and North Cahuenga.'

'I should go look for her.'

'Hey,' said Ricky, 'I'll come with.'

'Daddy—' said Bethany.

'I have to, sweetheart. She's my neighbor and my friend.'

'Ricky, *you* don't have to,' said Nadine. 'Please, baby. I don't want to lose you again.'

Ricky took hold of both of Nadine's wrists and kissed her on the forehead. 'I'll be fine, Nadine. If there's one thing that being dead has taught me, it's not to be afraid of dying.'

'Come on,' said Jim. 'Let's go.'

TWENTY-ONE

They drove slowly along Hollywood Boulevard, keeping their eyes open for Summer. It was only 5.35 p.m. but already it was beginning to grow dark, not because the sun was going down, but because of the dense black smoke that was drifting across the street from all of the burning buildings.

Traffic had been unusually sparse when they drove back to Hollywood from West Grove College, but now the streets were almost empty. Now and then an SUV came rolling in the opposite direction, but nobody stopped and nobody put down their tinted windows. A few people were running along the sidewalks, and Jim slowed down as they came to Hollywood and Vine, because a young African-American man with green-dyed hair and a shiny green shell-suit had hesitated at the curb.

Jim called out to him, 'Sir!'

'*What*, man? What you want?'

'Are you running from something or are you just running?'

The young man looked anxiously over his shoulder and then started running again. Jim caught up with him and drove along beside him, keeping pace with him.

'Ain't you *seen* them?' the young man panted. 'You must of seen them! Like ghosts! Like a army of ghosts!'

'Ghosts?'

'Like, *thousands* of them! All dressed in sheets! But there's no way they ghosts! I seen them killing people! Pulling off their arms and their legs! Tossing them up in the air! Ghosts can't do that! And setting fire to everything!'

'Where are they?'

'All over, man! And they run so fast you can't get away from them!'

'You want a ride?' Jim asked him.

'Thanks – but no thanks! My friend – he has this music studio – just along here! Skream Records? I'm going to hide there! Shut myself up inside of the recording booth and not come out! Not until those ghosts . . . not until those ghosts is gone!'

He turned down Cosmo Street, a narrow alley lined with flat-fronted office buildings, and that was the last they saw of him.

Ricky said, 'Shit. Let's hope that Summer's found herself someplace to hide.'

Ahead of them, Hollywood Boulevard was miraculously clear of traffic, so Jim put his foot down until they reached North Cahuenga. He swerved left, and sped down the next block, until he saw Floyd's Barbershop on the opposite corner of Selma Avenue – a single-story building with a black-and-white mock-marble frontage. Apart from parked cars, North Cahuenga and Selma were completely deserted, although smoke and whirling black ash was blowing across both of them.

Jim pulled up outside Floyd's and both he and Ricky climbed out of his car. The sharp smell of burning made their eyes water, and Ricky sneezed twice and had to wipe his nose on the sleeve of his cowboy shirt.

Jim said, 'Listen!'

Not far away, they could hear sirens, but they could also hear people screaming.

Ricky said, 'Shit, man.' But that was all.

Jim approached the barbershop window and peered inside. The lights were on, but there was no sign of any customers or staff.

He tried to push open the front door, but it was locked. He rattled the handle, and then he banged on the glass and shouted out, 'Anybody there? I'm looking for a girl called Summer!'

There was no response, so he banged on the door again. 'Summer, are you in there! It's Jim!'

Again, nothing.

Ricky said, 'Might as well go back, Jim. If she's not here she could be anyplace at all.'

'Yes,' said Jim, reluctantly. 'You're right.' He backed away from the barbershop and looked up and down the street. It was then that he caught sight of Summer's powder-blue

Honda Civic, parked about two hundred feet away, half-hidden by a giant Land Cruiser. 'But her *car's* still here, look – so she couldn't have gone far. Not unless somebody gave her a ride.'

He went back up to the barbershop door and banged on it again. 'Summer! It's Jim Rook! *Summer!*'

Suddenly, a frightened-looking young man in a tight pink T-shirt and red velvet pants appeared on the other side of the door. Summer was close behind him, with her hair still folded up in silver-paper foils. The young man unlocked the door, top and bottom, and opened it.

'Summer!' said Jim. 'Jesus! We were just about to go off and leave you here!'

Summer came tripping out and hugged him and kissed him, and then hugged Ricky, too. 'We've all been hiding in the restroom! We heard you knocking on the door and we thought those terrible people had come back!'

'I don't know how they *missed* us!' said the young man, almost in a scream. 'There were *hundreds* of them! They came running down the street and they were tearing people to *pieces*!'

Jim took Summer's hand and squeezed it tight. 'I'm just glad you're safe, sweetheart. Let's get out of here.'

'They broke into Umami Burger,' the young man continued. 'They broke into Coffee Etc right across the street, they broke into Big Wang's, they even broke into the *Hookah* Lounge. They smashed all the windows and they were tearing the customers to *pieces*!'

'Well, try to keep safe,' Jim told him. 'And thanks for taking care of Summer. I mean it.'

'You're more than welcome. Summer's our favorite-favorite customer, aren't you, Summer? More than a customer, she's a dear-dear friend!'

Jim and Summer and Ricky climbed into Jim's car, while the young man closed the barbershop door and locked it and retreated into the back. Jim U-turned and then headed back up North Cahuenga. He could see now that most of the windows of the coffee shop on the opposite side of the street from Floyd's had no glass in them, and although it was too dark for him to be able to see very much inside, he could make out broken chairs and tipped-over tables and lumpy shapes that could have been dismembered bodies.

'Oh, Jimmy, you don't know how *scared* I was,' said Summer, lifting the armrest between them so that she could tuck her feet up underneath her and snuggle up close to him. 'When I saw those terrible people running past the window, I nearly *wet* myself. You're my knight in shining armor, you really are. Well, *both* of you are. You and Ricky. My knight in shining armors, plural.'

The black smoke that was billowing through the streets was becoming thicker and more acrid. Even though Jim's car was air-conditioned, the smell of burning made their eyes water and seared their sinuses. Ricky sneezed again, and again, and every time Summer said, 'Bless you, Ricks!'

Jim was already taking a right, back into Hollywood Boulevard, when Ricky said, 'Uh-oh! Shit! Looky there, Jim!'

About a half mile up ahead of them, another tidal wave of white-robed figures was heading toward them, completely filling the street from one side to the other. It was just passing Pantage's Theater, and it was surging in their direction, and *fast* – even faster than a real tidal wave.

Jim spun the wheel and steered the car back on to North Cahuenga. If they were lucky, the white-robed figures wouldn't have spotted them.

'It's *them*!' shrilled Summer, peering short-sightedly down Hollywood Boulevard. 'It's those terrible people! Like – who *are* they? Like – where are they, like, *from*?'

Jim didn't answer that. He was too busy speeding as fast as he could up North Cahuenga to Franklin Avenue. He could hang a right underneath the Hollywood Freeway and hopefully they wouldn't be confronted with another tidal wave of white-robed figures.

But as they sped past Yucca Street, with five hundred feet left to go before they reached Franklin, Ricky said, 'They've turned the corner *already*, man! They're coming after us!'

Jim glanced at his rear-view mirror. He could see the white-robed figures and there was no doubt that they were gaining on them. There must have been at least a thousand of them, pouring around the corner and running after them with grim determination. Jim wondered if they knew who he was, and that was why they were after him. Maybe the Reverend Silence had sent them to find him and tear him to pieces before he found a way to send them back to the spirit world.

In a way, he almost hoped that he had, because that would mean that there *was* a way.

'Oh my *God*!' said Summer. 'How can they *run* so fast? Nobody can run that fast!'

'These jokers can,' Ricky told her. 'Good thing they weren't around when we were holding the LA Olympics.'

'You think that's funny?' said Jim.

'Not at all. It scares the living crap out me, if you must know.'

Jim turned into Franklin Avenue without braking, and the Mercury spun through three hundred and sixty degrees, with Summer screaming all the way around. Even Ricky said, 'Jesus, man! You're going to kill us before they do!'

But Jim gunned the engine again and headed east, underneath the freeway. The only other vehicles on the road were a few abandoned cars with their doors left hanging open. All kinds of debris was scattered across the road, some of it groceries, some of it luggage and baby buggies, some of it bits of people. Jim made a point of not looking at it too closely, and steering around it whenever he could. He ran over one end of a woman's severed leg, and, grotesquely, it kicked up into the air, like a cancan dancer's.

They turned at last into Briarcliff Road, roaring up its steep, tight curve, and sliding to a halt in the parking space in front of Briar Cliff Apartments.

Jim said, '*Out*! And inside! They'll be here any minute!'

They ran up the two flights of steps to Jim's apartment. As they reached the front door, Jim looked back down from the landing and saw the first of the white-robed figures running up the slope toward them.

Most of them were young black-bearded men, but there were wild-haired women and children, too. Their shrouds and robes were even filthier than they had been when they had first appeared – smudged with smoke and spattered with fresh blood, as well as the centuries-old blood and fluids with which they had been stained when they were first interred.

They were still completely silent, and they were still blurred and out of focus, so that their eyes looked like shadowy hollows. Santana had described them exactly: they were the 'dead-alive'.

'Inside! Quick! They're here!' Jim shouted. He pushed Summer into the hallway in front of him and then slammed the door behind him, locking it and bolting it and sliding on the safety chain.

'Think that's going to keep them out?' asked Ricky.

'I don't know. Let's hope so.' Jim looked around and saw the heavy little oak bureau at the end of the hallway, which he used for storing receipts and screwdrivers and dead batteries and out-of-date credit cards and string. 'Here, give me a hand.'

Together, grunting, they pushed the bureau until it was up against the front door. DaJon Johnson came out of the living room and said, 'Wha's goin' down, man? That cholo just told me those scary dead dudes are right outside.'

'They are, yes,' said Jim, and as if to prove that he wasn't scaremongering, there was a deafening crash against the outside of the door, and then another, and then they heard fists beating against the kitchen windows.

Jim went through to the kitchen. The landing outside the windows was crowded with white-robed figures, and they were pummeling at the glass in a frenzy. Their mouths were stretched wide open, as if they were howling, but they made no sound. The left-hand window cracked, and then smashed, and then the right-hand window splintered.

DaJon Johnson and Ricky followed Jim into the kitchen. Joe Chang and Al Alvarez and Kyle Baxter joined them from the living room. Jim looked around and saw the girls all clustered together, and his father standing in the far corner, looking helpless.

'They're getting in!' said Al Alvarez. 'They're trying to pull out the whole goddamned window!' Six or seven white-robed arms came waving in through the left-hand window, like octopus tentacles. Almost all of their hands were sliced and cut by the broken shards of glass that remained in the frame, and blood sprayed all over the yellow-tiled window sill, but that didn't deter them. They seized the frame and started to wrench it violently outward.

Jim dragged the cutlery drawer out from under the worktop and crashed it down on to the kitchen table. He took out his ten-inch carving knife and said to Ricky and his students, 'Here! Grab what you like!'

They all picked up knives, except for Rudy Cascarelli, who chose Jim's double-pronged carving fork, and Kyle Baxter, who went for his Chinese cleaver. Jim went up to the sink, leaned over it, and started stabbing at the hands that were gripping the window frame. DaJon Johnson had picked up two knives, one in each hand, and he attacked the white-robed figures as if he were berserk, chopping furiously and relentlessly into fingers and knuckles and forearms and elbows.

But it was Kyle Baxter who inflicted the most spectacular damage. He lifted the Chinese cleaver high up behind his head, paused, and then swung it down so hard that it severed the hand of one of the white-robed figures at the wrist. The hand tumbled into the sink, and even though the white-robed figure didn't scream, he pulled his arm immediately out of the window and disappeared into the crowd, showering their shrouds and their djellabas with blood.

Kyle Baxter swung the cleaver again and again, hacking off at least five more hands and more fingers than Jim could count. Jim wouldn't have guessed that he could be so bloodthirsty, but he kept on cutting, and under his breath he kept repeating a whole thesaurus of killing and mutilation. 'Massacre! Execution! Cut to pieces! Decimate! Annihilate! Assassinate! Put to the sword!'

After less than ten minutes, without a sound, the white-robed figures suddenly withdrew their arms from the window, and disappeared back along the landing. Jim heard their feet pattering down the steps, and then there was silence.

He looked around the kitchen. The windows were all broken, but the draining board was dripping with blood and the sink was filled with hairy-backed hands, like a nest of dead tarantulas. Maybe the white-robed figures had simply decided that they had had enough, and that they were getting noplace.

'Think that's it?' asked Ricky. 'Think they got the message?'

'I couldn't tell you, Ricky. I thought they might be coming for me, personally, but I may be wrong.'

Summer came into the kitchen but Jim quickly pushed her out again. 'You don't want to see this, sweetheart.'

Back in the living room, Bethany said, 'They won't come back, will they, Daddy? Please say they won't come back.'

Jim said, 'I wish I knew.'

'What if they're still out there, waiting for us?' said Jesmeka Watson. 'If they're still out there, how are we going to get back home?'

'How do we know we even got homes to go back to?' said Al Alvarez. 'And there's no phones, so there's no way that we can check.'

Jim went out on to the balcony. Although the back yard was thickly screened by trees, he could see that fires were burning from one side of the city to the other. And there was such a silence. No traffic, on the freeways. No sirens. No helicopters. No passenger planes landing and taking off from LAX.

All he could hear was an occasional sarcastic caw, from that pestilential crow.

Bethany came out to join him. 'What are we going to do, Daddy? Do you think that Mommy's OK?'

Jim put his arm around her shoulders. 'Where your mom lives – sure, I'm sure she'll be fine.'

'But what are we going to do?'

'I don't know, Bethany. I really don't.'

'We can't stay here for ever, can we? Maybe we should try to get away. These dead people can't be *everywhere*, can they?'

'I don't know that, either. The Reverend Silence said there were millions of them. He said that God cursed Lilith's children, so that a hundred of them would die every day. If you believe that really happened, that adds up to thirty-six and a half million every thousand years, and how many thousands of years is it since Lilith was thrown out of the Garden of Eden?

'They could be everywhere,' he told her. 'Maybe there's no escaping them.'

DaJon Johnson and Rudy Cascarelli came out on to the balcony, too.

'You want to check this out, Mr Rook.'

'Oh, yeah? What is it now?'

'We eyeballed the road outside, to see if those dead-alives had taken a powder.'

'And?'

'Come and check it out for yourself.'

Jim followed them through the living room and out to the hallway. They had shifted the bureau to one side so that they could open the front door, although they had kept the door locked and Joe Chang was standing beside it with his arms folded like a nightclub bouncer.

He unlocked it, although he kept the security chain fastened until he had taken a quick look outside. 'OK, sir. It looks like it's clear.'

Jim stepped out on to the landing. He went to the railing and looked down. Hundreds of white-robed figures were assembled in the road, silent, unmoving, staring back up at him. When he leaned over a little more, he could see that they were crowded on the landing outside Ricky and Nadine's front door, too, and up the steps that led to Summer's apartment.

'Looks like they're prepared to wait for as long as it takes,' said Rudy Cascarelli. 'How soon before we run out of food?'

'Maybe a day,' said Jim. 'I haven't been to the store for two weeks. Seventeen people can't survive on two Hungry-Man Boneless Chicken Dinners for very long.'

DaJon Johnson said, 'This is really off the hook, man. Either they goin' to starve us out or else we try to make a break for it and they rip us to bits. I mean, how far do you think we goin' to get?'

Jim was still standing on the landing when Ricky came out. He saw the silent crowd of white-robed figures waiting in the road, and he said, 'Shit.'

'What is it, Ricky?'

'I'm in a fix, Jim. What in the name of God am I going to do now?'

TWENTY-TWO

'What kind of a fix?' Jim asked him. 'What situation could possibly be worse than this is already?'

'It's Nadine. She's diabetic. She's starting to go into a coma and she needs her insulin.'

'Oh, God. Well – there's a couple of cans of Mountain Dew Throwback in the fridge. That should help. It has real sugar in it.'

'She has to have her insulin, Jim. It's her type of diabetes. She didn't bring any up here with her because she didn't think that we'd be staying for long.'

Jim went back inside. Nadine was lying on his bed, with her eyes half closed, as if she were drowsy. Her cheeks were pale, except for those two lurid spots of rouge, and her forehead was glossy with perspiration. Summer was sitting on the bed next to her, holding her hand.

'Jim . . .' said Nadine, hoarsely. 'Sorry to be such a nuisance. All I need is my shot.'

'Don't you worry, Nadine. We'll sort something out for you. Bethany . . . would you bring me a can of that Mountain Dew Throwback out of the icebox? No, on second thought, Rudy, would you get it for me?' He didn't know if Kyle Baxter and Tommy Makovicka had finished clearing out the sink yet, and dropping the severed hands into the trash.

Ricky said, 'I got to do something, Jim. If she doesn't get her shot in twenty minutes she's going to go into a coma and then she could die.'

Jim went back through the living room and out on to the balcony, where Hunni Robards and Jesmeka Watson were keeping watch, and smoking at the same time.

Jim said, 'Any sign of those dead-alives back here?'

Jesmeka Watson shook her head. 'Not yet, sir, Mr Rook.'

He peered down into the yard, but it was deserted. Between the front of the apartment building and the back stood a ten-foot wooden fence, with a gate in it, but the gate was padlocked and the white-robed figures wouldn't have been able to climb over. He could still see Santana's shovel down there, next to a half-dug gopher hole, which he must have dropped when the Silences came to get him.

He leaned over the balcony even further, and saw that there was a drainpipe which ran down from the guttering around the roof, and down to the ground. It looked as if it were just within reach, and of course it was the same distance away from Ricky and Nadine's balcony on the first floor below them.

'This is what we do,' he said, beckoning to Ricky. 'We climb down, we get Nadine's insulin. We climb back up again.'

'Who do you think I am, man? Cheetah?'

'It's the only way, Ricky. We can't go out front because they'll rip us to shreds.'

Ricky looked down into the back yard and puffed out his cheeks. 'Guess you're right. OK, then – let's do it. But I fall and break my fuckin' neck I'm never going to forgive you. And Nadine's shots are in the bathroom cabinet, in case I do.'

Jim went to the very end of the balcony, dragged a chair across to the railing, and climbed up on to it, swaying backward and forward for a few moments like a high-wire walker to balance himself. Then he reached out with his right hand until he managed to get a grip on the drainpipe. He shook it, as much as he could, to feel that it wasn't too loose. Briar Cliff Apartments hadn't been built to a very high standard, and he didn't want the pipe coming away from the wall when they were halfway down it.

'Right,' he said. 'Ready or not.'

With that, he swung sideways across the wall and grabbed hold of the drainpipe with his left hand. The drainpipe lurched and his face was showered with dried mortar, and for a split-second he thought that the brackets were going to give way. He hung there for a few moments, not moving, trying to blink the grit out of his eyes and spit it out his mouth, but the drainpipe's fixings stayed firm.

'OK, Ricky,' he said. 'I think it's going to hold. I'm going down.'

Jerkily, he slid down the drainpipe, past Summer's balcony

and down to Ricky and Nadine's apartment. Even though Ricky and Nadine were on the first floor, there was still at least an eight-foot drop from their balcony railing to the stone-flagged patio below. Jim had to reach out with his left hand and get a grip on the edge of their wall, and then stretch out his left leg until his foot found the top of the railing. If he had fallen backward, he could have broken his spine or cracked his skull.

Ricky was clambering down the drainpipe, too, making blowing noises like a horse.

'Jesus, can't stop!' he panted, and the sole of his sneaker hit Jim on the top of the head. Jim pulled himself sideways and jumped over the balcony railing, landing on Nadine's sunlounger and toppling it sideways. He hadn't even managed to get up off the tiles before Ricky fell on top of him. The two of them lay sprawled there for a moment, trying to get their breath back.

The sliding door to Ricky and Nadine's apartment was already half open, so they stepped inside. It was a quarter of seven now, and beginning to grow dark, and the living room was gloomy. The kitchen door was ajar and through the Venetian blinds they could see the white-robed figures who were crowded on the landing outside. Some of them had rags or scarves tied around their heads, others had tall pointed hoods like Klansmen. None of them were moving or making a sound, just waiting.

Ricky sniffed and said, 'How in the name of hell are we going to get away from those creeps?'

'Let's think about that later, after we've given Nadine her shot.'

'But you don't have the faintest fuckin' idea, do you?'

'No, Ricky, I don't, and if that's your way of implying that this is all my fault, then, yes, it is, and if I thought that it would help if I went out there and gave myself up to them, then I would. But, quite honestly, I think it would only make things worse.'

Ricky slapped Jim's shoulder and said, 'Aw, come on, Jim. I'm not really blaming you. Most of us do things in life with good intentions that turn out to be shit.'

'We don't all do things that end up with hundreds of people getting killed and half of Los Angeles burning down.'

'Don't you worry, buddy. Sometimes we do things worse than that. My old man, he was assistant flight engineer on Bockscar, the day they dropped the A-bomb on Nagasaki.' He popped his fingers and said, 'Seventy thousand people killed, just like that – men, women and little kids.'

He crossed over to the hallway and opened the bathroom door. There was no window in the first-floor bathroom so he had to switch on the light. Jim waited for him in the center of the living room, looking at some of his paintings and his sculptures. The scratty red parakeet was still sitting on its perch, and when he came up close to its bars it made a harsh and hostile noise in its throat and screeched out, '*Silence!*'

'Oh, get stuffed!' Jim told it.

Ricky opened the bathroom door a little wider as he came out, and it was then that the light fell for the briefest of moments on the painting of The Storyteller, still standing on its easel.

To Jim's surprise, it no longer looked like Ba'al, with its horns and its gray gleaming skin, but he recognized the new face at once. It was an elderly man, with a neat white beard. His expression was serious, but there was something in his eyes which was both sympathetic and knowing. It was Father Michael, the same priest that Jim had tried to contact with no success when he was upstairs in his bedroom.

Jim approached the portrait slowly and stared at it. The eyes looked back at him with infinite compassion. However much Ricky grumbled or cussed or smoked, he was a brilliant painter. But how on earth had he managed to paint such an exact likeness of Father Michael? So far as Jim knew, Ricky had never met Father Michael, and he was long dead now.

He reached out and touched the painting with his fingertips. The paint was still sticky, so Ricky must have painted it only a few hours ago.

Ricky switched off the bathroom light and came over with a bottle of insulin and a hypodermic. 'Here we go,' he said. 'Now let's try to shin back up that fuckin' drainpipe!'

Jim pointed to The Storyteller with his thumb. 'When did

you paint this? It's so weird. It's an exact likeness of the dead priest I was trying to contact.'

Ricky squinted at the painting and said, 'Never.'

'What do you mean, "never"? It's here, I'm looking at it. The oil-paint's still fresh.'

'I never painted that, man. I never saw that old geezer before in my life. The last time I looked at that portrait, it was that devil guy.'

This is the only way open, said Father Michael.

Ricky turned to Jim and said, 'What?'

This is the only way open. They forgot that they had used this painting so that Ba'al could begin to make his reappearance. They remembered the smoke, they remembered the paintings in the classroom, they remembered the television and the door to the spirit world. But they forgot The Storyteller.

'Did you say that?' said Ricky.

Jim was staring at the painting of Father Michael in disbelief. Spirits had talked to him scores of times, both benign and malevolent, but they were mostly inside his own head. He had heard the wind blowing and birds singing in landscape paintings, and the sound of the ocean in seascapes; but he had never been talked to, out loud, by anybody's portrait.

You can defeat Sammael, said Father Michael. His voice echoed, as if he were speaking inside an empty room, and in a way he was. *There is a way.*

'Shit, man, I don't believe this,' said Ricky. 'Are you ventriloquiserating or something?'

Jim slowly shook his head, still staring at Father Michael. 'It's the painting, Ricky. It's the painting that's talking to us. Your Storyteller.'

'Aw, come on, Jim. You're putting me on. You're throwing your voice like that Achmed the Dead Terrorist guy. Look – let's go. We don't have time for this. We need to get this shot back to Nadine.'

'Ricky, I'm serious. Father Michael is talking to me through your painting because it's the only way that he can do it.'

'Father Michael,' said Ricky, with exaggerated skepticism.

'That's right, Father Michael. The priest who came to talk to us after my dad committed suicide.'

'Your dead dad who is now upstairs alive.'

'That's right. And that's the whole point. Life and death have been turned upside down.'

You have to make the ultimate sacrifice, Jim. That is the only way.

'What do you mean?'

'Jesus,' said Ricky, in despair. 'He's talkin' to himself now, for Christ's sake!'

You have to give up your Paradise. You have to give up the people you so desperately wanted to come back to life.

'You mean my father? And Bethany?'

When people die, Jim, they are dead. The only immortality is in heaven or hell. People cannot come back and walk the earth as if they were still alive. It is against all nature. It is against the will of God.

'Hey, what about me?' said Ricky. '*I* was dead, too, wasn't I? And so was Santana. You can't give *me* up, man. I don't want to be fuckin' dead. Not again.'

Father Michael said, *You know on whose behalf I am speaking, don't you, Jim? You cannot look upon His face, but you can hear His voice through me. He has seen the work of Ba'al and of Sammael, and of the serpent, too. He gave the children of Eve the chance to show their devotion to Him by resisting temptation. But again the fruit of the tree of knowledge proved irresistible.*

Again the blandishments of Ba'al proved too alluring for you to show self-restraint and consideration for others.

You have seen the result – the dead children of Lilith have risen from the grave as a great and murderous multitude, and are taking out their bitterness on the living children of Eve. Many hundreds are already dead, and countless more will die before Ba'al has taken them all down to his dominion, in hell.

'But what can I do?' said Jim. 'I started it. I allowed it to happen. How can I stop it?'

You must give up your Paradise and renounce your gift.

'What?'

You must renounce your gift to see spirits, and demons, and other manifestations, and you must renounce it for ever, for the rest of your life.

'What good will that do?'

The children of Lilith can only continue to walk the earth as long as you have the gift to see them – just like the people you have brought back to life. Ba'al gave you the power to bring them back, but power is meaningless without vision.

'Jim,' said Ricky. 'Do you believe this shit? Whoever this is, he wants me dead again, man, and you're not going to do that to me, are you? And – look – we have to get this insulin up to Nadine. We can't waste any more time talking to a goddamned *painting*. It's insane!'

Take your thirteen disciples and have them hold hands in a circle as they did before. Have them recite this incantation three times, Ba'al be gone, Sammael be gone, Lilith be gone. Then say, may my eyes be closed to the world of spirits for ever.

'And that's it? All of those dead-alive people will disappear?'

They will return to the graves from which you summoned them, yes.

'But what about all of those people that they've torn to pieces?'

The dead must remain dead, except only for the grace of God.

'But what if I can't decide what to do? You're asking me to sacrifice my daughter! You're asking me to sacrifice my father! You're asking me to sacrifice my friend!'

If you do nothing, your loved ones will stay alive for as long as they can escape the children of Lilith. But the whole world will be visited by the greatest human disaster ever known.

'But how can that be my responsibility? How can that be up to me? I'm only a goddamned English teacher, not a god!'

You are the only one who can see spirits. You are the only one who can talk to the dead. You are the only one who can make bargains with demons. That is your gift, and your curse.

'I didn't ask for it, though, did I?

Great musicians never ask for their talent. Neither do artists, nor scientists, nor writers. But whether you want it or not, every gift comes with the responsibility to use it wisely. A great gift, used selfishly, can cause catastrophe.

'I've had enough of this,' growled Ricky. 'You do whatever you like, Jim, but I'm not going to be lectured by one of my own fuckin' pictures, even if I didn't paint it.'

'All right,' said Jim. 'I'm coming.'

He looked back at the portrait of Father Michael and already he could see that it was beginning to change. The oil paint was thinning, and beginning to slide down the canvas, so Father Michael's face appeared to sag at first, and then to melt.

For a fraction of a nanosecond, Jim saw another face appear underneath it. A pale, ethereal face, quite oval, with the strangest olive-green eyes. It vanished instantly, but Jim stood in front of the easel, stunned, feeling as if he had been Tasered.

He thought, *I have seen God.*

In the corner, the red parakeet clawed noisily from side to side on its perch and screeched out, '*Silence!*'

'Come on, Jim,' Ricky urged him.

'Yeah, sure. Sorry.'

As he stepped out on to the balcony he took one last look back at the painting, but it had no face at all, only a brownish-gray smear of undercoat, waiting for the face of The Storyteller.

Climbing the drainpipe back up to Jim's apartment was a whole lot harder than climbing down, and it took them several attempts before they managed it, heaving and grunting and sliding halfway down again. DaJon Johnson and Al Alvarez leaned over to grab their shirts and drag them back on to the balcony.

Once he had rolled over the balcony railing, Ricky immediately went through to the bedroom to give Nadine her insulin injection.

Bethany came up to Jim and hugged him and said, 'Daddy – you're amazing!' and his father clapped him on the shoulder and said, 'Well, done, son! That was some climb!'

Jim gave them both a quick hug and then said, 'Give me a minute. I just want to make sure that Nadine's OK.'

He went into the bedroom. Nadine was propped up on two

pillows, and she had much more color in her cheeks. She gave Jim a weak smile as he came across to the bed.

Ricky was sitting beside her, smoking one of his skinny Peruvian joints. 'Thanks, Jim. You saved Nadine's life, no question.'

He offered the joint to Jim, but Jim shook his head.

'I'm sorry, Nadine,' he told her. 'Ricky and I have to talk.'

'That's OK. I need to get some sleep now, anyhow.'

Out in the hallway, with the bedroom door closed, Ricky said, 'I know what this is all about, Jim, and I know what I have to do. Of course I don't want to die, but what choice is there? Thousands more people getting killed? Or just me and Bethany and Santana and your dad – and your dad's been dead for more than thirty years already.'

'Ricky – you know that I can't ask you do this.'

'Too fuckin' right you can't. My dad had nightmares all his life about Nagasaki. Nobody asked of them Jap civilians whether *they* were willing to die or not. You know that Captain Chuck Sweeney dropped the bomb two-and-a-half clicks away from the intended dropping point, which meant that nearly half of the city was protected by the hills? That's where the famous phrase, "You fucked up, didn't you, Chuck!" came from. But my dad always used to wonder if Captain Sweeney did it on purpose.'

Jim leaned against the wall. He could see himself in the mirror opposite, unshaven, with his hair all scruffed up and bags under his eyes. His pale blue denim shirt had gray and brown skid marks on it from climbing up and down the drainpipe. He thought: *look at me. I can't believe I'm holding the fate of the entire planet in my hands. It just doesn't seem possible.*

Ricky said, 'You won't tell Bethany, will you, or your dad, or Santana? It's better if they don't know, believe me.'

Jim's eyes filled up with tears. 'I don't want to lose you, Ricky. I don't want to lose any of you.'

'I know that, buddy. But life's a shit and then you die. And then you come to life again and it's still a shit and then you die for a second time, sooner or later. I don't want to die again, Jim, believe me, but what's the alternative? Like I say, there *is* no alternative.'

'You're a brave man, Ricky.'

'No, I'm not. I'm pragmatic, that's all, and there's a whole world of difference between bravery and pragmatism, believe me.'

'Not from where I'm standing.'

Ricky put his arm around him and said, 'Come on, Jim. I'm reasonably high now so let's go do it before I change my mind.'

TWENTY-THREE

Jim went through to the living room where everybody was gathered and raised his hands to catch their attention.

'OK, everybody, listen up, please!'

Tibbles looked up at him from Hunni Robards' lap and he had seen that expression on Tibbles' face before: those narrowed eyes, those sloped-back ears. Tibbles could sense that something serious was about to happen. Something supernatural and scary.

Jim wondered: *Even if I give up my psychic sensitivity – will Tibbles keep something of his?*

Bethany came up to him and took hold of his arm and smiled up at him proudly and lovingly. *Jesus,* he thought, *why don't you just stick a knife in my heart?*

But he said, loudly, 'Special Class Two – everybody – I think I've found a way to send these dead-alive people back to their graves or their mausoleums or wherever they came from. It's a simple chant – but it's what exorcists call a dismissal. I have no idea if it's going to work, but right now I think anything is worth a try before any more innocent people get killed – before *we* get killed.'

'Sku me, how do we know this ain't goin' to make things *worse*?' asked DaJon Johnson. 'Last ritual we did was s'pose to give us Paradise but what did we get instead? We got *Day of the Dead,* that's what we got, with extra zombies to go!'

Jim said, 'I can't give you any guarantees, DaJon, but this ritual was passed on to me from somebody that a whole lot of people put their trust in.'

'We ought to try it, sir,' said Rebecca Teitelbaum. She hadn't brushed her hair since they had escaped from West Grove College, and it was looking spectacularly frizzy. 'You know what it says in the Talmud. "Whoever destroys a single life is as guilty as if he had destroyed the whole world, but he who saves a single life earns as much merit as if he had saved the whole world."'

'Yeah, whatever that means,' said Rudy Cascarelli. 'Right now I'm thinking we're all going to hell in a handcart!'

'Well, you Italians, you know all about handcarts,' said Al Alvarez. '"Get your tutsi-frutsi ice-cream!"'

Rudy Cascarelli gave him a shove. 'How'd you like some broken teeth, dude?'

Jim said, 'That's enough. We've got enough to worry about without losing our tempers with each other. Now, please – can everybody hold hands in a circle, the same way we did back at the campus.'

Self-consciously, everybody stood up and held hands. Rudy Cascarelli gave Al Alvarez another shove and Al Alvarez shoved him back.

Jim was holding Bethany's hand on one side and his father's on the other. William Rook turned to him and said, 'Whatever happens, Jim, you know that I'm real proud of you, don't you? And that I'm sorry for leaving you on the beach the way I did.'

Ricky was standing on the opposite side of the circle, between Jesmeka Watson and Joe Chang. He gave Jim a wink and a nod, as if to reassure him that everything was going to work out, and that he didn't feel resentful about the way that things had turned out. Jim didn't need Ricky to blame him – he felt guilty enough already.

'OK, then – say after me –"*Ba'al be gone, Sammael be gone, Lilith be gone.*" We have to say this three times.'

They recited the words – '*Ba'al be gone, Sammael be gone, Lilith be gone.*'

When they had done so, they all stood looking at each other.

'Anything happened?' asked Kyle Baxter.

Joe Chang pulled a face and shrugged. 'Nothing, dude – not so far as I can tell.'

'Maybe we should say them again, sir,' Rebecca Teitelbaum suggested.

'No, I don't think so,' Jim told her. 'I have one more thing that I'm supposed to say, and I think that kind of completes the ritual.'

He closed his eyes for a moment, summoning up the strength to lose Bethany and his father and Ricky and Santana. When he opened them again, Ricky was staring at him fiercely and mouthing the words, '*Go on, Jim! Go on! For fuck's sake, say it!*'

Jim cleared his throat, and said, 'May my eyes . . . may my eyes be closed—'

'*NO!*' screamed a voice. '*NO!*'

A dazzling crackle of lightning lit up the center of their circle, brighter and noisier than a thousand firecrackers. It was so bright that it left a blotchy red after-image floating in front of Jim's eyes, like a map of the world. It was only when he blinked, and blinked again, that he gradually began to see what had happened.

The Reverend John Silence was standing in front of them, with both of his fists raised up in fury. But this wasn't really the Reverend John Silence; this was Sammael, the Angel of Death, with his distorted, demonic face. His forked tongue flicked repeatedly out from between his lips as if he had a snake coiled up in his mouth, and of course he did. His son, Simon, who had tempted Eve, and Jim, too.

His clothing gave off an eerie, crawling fluorescence, and his shirt flapped and fluttered in a wind that Jim couldn't feel. He lit up all of the students' faces, and made their eyes glitter, so that *they* looked like demons, too, Sammael's minions.

'You are about to break your bargain!' said the Reverend Silence. 'If you speak those words, you will lose your loved ones forever!'

Bethany gripped Jim's hand tightly and said, 'Daddy?'

'Has he not *told* you, little girl? If he completes this ritual, you will die for a second time! *I* was prepared to sacrifice you, for the sake of Ba'al, but so is your own father!'

'Daddy?'

Jim swallowed, and swallowed, but couldn't speak. William Rook turned to him now and said, 'Jim? Is this true? You were going to give up on us?'

Shining and hurricane-blown, with his hair flying upward, the Reverend Silence came so close to Jim that their noses were almost touching, and grinned at him.

'Here is a man with no principles! Here is a man who is willing to betray the people who love him the most! Here is a man who betrayed the whole world!'

Jim could feel the Reverend Silence's spit flying against his face, and wiped his cheek with the back of his hand. He took several deep breaths, and then he said, 'Get thee behind me, Sammael. You cheated me. You lied to me. You tempted me. I was weak, I admit it. But not any more.'

'Daddy!' begged Bethany. 'Daddy, please don't! Daddy!'

'May my eyes be closed to the world of spirits—'

'*Daddy! Daddy! Daddy!*'

'NO!' roared the Reverend Silence, and seized Jim by the shoulders. His black fingernails were as sharp as claws, and they pierced his shirt and crunched into his shoulder muscles.

Jim shouted out in pain. The Reverend Silence shook him so violently that he lost his grip on Bethany and William Rook and dropped to his knees on to the floor.

'I would have protected you!' the Reverend Silence shouted at him. 'I would have protected you and your loved ones for ever! These children of Lilith outside, they would have taken everybody else – but they would never have taken you! You made a bargain! You made a bargain with Ba'al!'

Jim raised his head. The room was suddenly silent, except for the sound of Bethany sobbing. He looked at her, and she was so young and so beautiful, and she looked so much like her mother. She had been killed once, but now she had all of her life ahead of her. What he could no longer ignore, though, was that Bethany's life, like his father's, and Ricky's, and Santana's, had all been granted as a favor by the most evil being on earth.

Until the day they died a second time, they would always be indebted to the King of Lies and the Angel of Death. They would owe their existence to the massacre of thousands, and what kind of life would that be?

'No,' whispered the Reverend Silence. '*No.*'

'May my eyes be closed to the world of spirits for ever,' said Jim.

For a few long seconds, nothing happened, although the Reverend Silence was staring at Jim aghast. His forked tongue flickered and flickered, but he didn't speak, or couldn't. Jim had never seen anybody look so terrified, living or dead or demon, ever.

Suddenly, the Reverend Silence began to change. His demonic features softened and rearranged themselves – faster and faster, like a speeded-up movie run backward. His skin-color flushed pink. His eyes widened. Once again, he appeared in the guise which he had adopted so that he could enroll Simon Silence into Special Class Two. He must have stolen this appearance from somebody human, and now that human appearance was all that Jim could see.

His students were milling around and jostling each other in confusion. Summer was standing in the middle of the room with the foils still in her hair, her fingertips pressed to her lips, blinking in bewilderment. He looked for Bethany, but he couldn't see her. He couldn't see his father, either, nor Ricky, nor Santana. He took hold of the arm of the chair next to him, and pulled himself painfully up on to his feet. The Reverend Silence was still staring at him, but as Jim stood up he slowly backed away.

'Do you know what you've done?' he said. '*Do you know what you've done!*'

Jim took no notice of him and shouted out, 'Bethany!' but just as he did so the whole apartment was shaken by a thunderous explosion. His students screamed and shouted as the living room ceiling collapsed on top of them. Huge lumps of plasterboard crashed to the floor, followed by splintered wooden rafters and showers of shattered green tiles. Within seconds the entire apartment was choking with plaster dust.

The Reverend Silence's face was like a clown's mask, with sooty black eyes and a dragged-down mouth. He looked up to the torn-open ceiling and let out a long moan of despair, which gradually rose higher and higher into a scream.

Jim was no longer capable of seeing what came through the ceiling and seized the Reverend Silence. But he was lifted bodily off his feet and dragged through the jagged rafters and into the evening sky, still screaming.

His screams continued long after he had been carried away, but at last there was silence.

Jim looked around the living room, and at all of their dusty faces and clothes. Without a word, he clambered over the broken pieces of plasterboard and made his way to the front door. He opened it, and stepped outside on to the landing.

Briarcliff Road was deserted. Not a single white-robed figure in sight. The fires were still burning all across the city, but when he listened he could hear no more screaming, and no more breaking glass.

After a few minutes he heard sirens, and the sound of a helicopter.

Summer came out and put her arm around him. The shoulders of his shirt were still darkly stained with blood, and he winced.

'I want to tell you something, Jim.'

'What's that, Summer?'

'I think you're incredible, Jimmy. I really do.'

'I don't know why.'

Summer nodded, with a serious expression on her face. 'I don't know why, either. I didn't understand *any* of that. Like, who was that guy with all the fireworks? Where did he come from? And why was he so pissed?'

'It really doesn't matter. It's all over now, I promise you. At least I hope it is.'

'But your ceiling fell down! And where did that guy go? He, like, *flew*!'

'He didn't fly, Summer,' said Jim. 'Something came crashing through the ceiling and took him.'

He paused, and then he said, 'That's what happens when you let down demons. They're a bit like the Mafia. Not very forgiving.'

'A *demon* took him? A demon, you mean like a devil? I didn't see no *demon*.'

Jim gave her a tight, bitter smile. 'You know something? Neither did I.'

They were still standing there when they heard somebody trudging up the steps from the landing below.

Jim said, 'Jesus.'

Ricky appeared, looking as if he had just woken up.

'Ricky!' said Jim. 'You're still with us!'

Ricky came up to them, rotating his head as if he had a crick in his neck. 'Think I must have been sleeping in a draft.'

He peered inside Jim's apartment. The air was still thick with dust, and Special Class Two were still climbing around the living room, trying to drag aside the debris.

'What the hell happened? Looks like your ceiling fell down.'

Jim was overwhelmed. He pressed his hand over his mouth and there were tears in his eyes.

'What's the matter with you, man? You don't have to get all weepy about it. I know a good plasterer, fix that up at cost.'

'Thanks, Ricky. That's great.'

Ricky sniffed and said, 'You seen Nadine? Is she up here with you? I have to remind her to take her insulin shot.'

Jim stared at him. 'Don't you remember anything at all?'

'What do you mean? What am I supposed to remember? You know me. I'd forget my ass if it wasn't screwed on.'

'Nothing, Ricky. It doesn't matter. But I think that somebody's given me a reward that I don't really deserve.'

'Oh, yeah? Who's that, then? What did they give you?'

Jim thought of the face that he had seen on Ricky's canvas, in that nanosecond after the image of Father Michael had melted away. He could never know for sure. Maybe it had been nothing more than an optical illusion, a trick of the light, or wishful thinking. But he laid his hand on Ricky's shoulder and Ricky was real and solid and alive and smelled of turpentine and Peruvian grass and he had never felt such gratitude in his life.

He made his way back into his apartment, high-stepping over the rubble. As he did so, Rebecca Teitelbaum held up her cell and waved it and said, 'The signal's back! I'm just calling my grandparents!'

'Hey, mine's back, too!' said DaJon Johnson. 'I can call Na shortly, make sure she's still in one pee-ass!'

All of Special Class Two took out their cells and started furiously prodding at them. Jim stood and watched them, partly in fond amusement but mostly in pain. Bethany wasn't among them, and neither was his father, nor Santana.

As he stood there, though, his own cell started playing the

opening notes of Beethoven's *Piano Concerto Number Five*
– *da-da-da DAH*!

He tugged it out of his pants pocket and said, 'Jim Rook
here.'

'Jim? It's Jane – Jane Seabrook.'

'Jane! Are you OK?'

'I'm fine, Jim. We saw some of the riots in the distance but
they didn't reach up as far as Stone Canyon.'

'Jane—'

'I don't know how to tell you this, Jim. But somebody's
granted us a miracle.'

Jim couldn't speak, because he could guess what Jane was
about to tell him. *Thank you, God. Thank you, God. Thank
you.*

'It's Bethany. She's alive. About ten minutes ago there was
a knock at the door and there she was, just standing there.'

Jane took a few moments to recover herself, and then she
said, 'She's alive, Jim. I saw her dead, lying in the morgue,
but she's alive again and it's really her. I don't know how it
happened and I'm not going to question it.'

'Jane—'

'Before you say anything, Jim, one of the first things Bethany
said was that she doesn't want to see you.'

'She doesn't want to see me? I thought that was why she
enrolled in Special Class Two.'

'She hasn't told me why, Jim. But she's adamant. She doesn't
want to see you or hear from you or have anything to do with
you.'

There was nothing that Jim could say to that. He had been
prepared to sacrifice Bethany's second life so that the white-
robed children of Lilith would be sent back to their graves,
and no matter how many thousands of lives he might
have been trying to save, she obviously and understandably
resented it.

'All right, Jane. Tell her that I love her, would you? Tell
her that I hope she can find it in her heart one day to forgive
me.'

'Forgive you for *what*, Jim? You've never met her.'

'Take care, Jane.'

He snapped his cell shut and pushed it back into his pocket. All around him, his students were either talking to their parents or their friends, or desperately trying to get through to people who weren't picking up.

'I think I need some air,' he said.

Summer said, 'I'll come with you. All this dust is getting up my hooter.'

Together, they went down the steps to the road, Summer teetering on her high wedge sandals and Jim holding her hand tightly so that she wouldn't fall.

As they reached the parking area in front of the apartments, Santana appeared, trudging up Briarcliff Road in his short-legged dungarees.

'Santana!'

'*Hola, Señor* Rook! *Olvidé mi coche! Cómo podría olvidar mi coche?*'

'You forgot your car?'

Jim went up to him and shook his hand and clapped him on the back. 'Good to see you, Santana. I mean it. *Una larga vida y feliz.* A long life and a happy one.'

Summer turned her head and frowned at him as he went to unlock his car.

'I coulda *sworn* he was upstairs with us, before. How'd he get all the way down here? I think I'm going screwy.'

'Don't worry, sweetheart. It's been one of those nights.'

'*One of these nights . . . one of these crazy old nights,*' sang Summer, as they walked hand in hand down the steeply sloping curve to Foothill Drive. '*We're going to find out, pretty mama, what turns on your lights . . .*'

They reached Foothill Drive and ahead of them was North Van Ness, long and straight and utterly deserted, except for six or seven parked cars, all of them burned out. The evening air was pungent with the smell of smoke, and the wailing of sirens was growing louder and louder.

'*You got your demons, you got desires,*' sang Summer, softly. '*Well, I got a few of my own.*'

For no reason at all, going nowhere, they started to walk down the middle of North Van Ness, still hand in hand. Jim looked up at the smoke drifting south-westward across the sky. A quarter moon was shining, but occasionally the smoke blotted it out.

They hadn't walked far before Jim thought he saw a darker twist of smoke. It drifted much more slowly across the moon than the rest of the smoke, and for a long moment he and Summer found themselves walking in total darkness.

Jim thought: *I can't see you any more, Ba'al. Neither you nor any other demons. I can't see you and I can't hear you if you speak to me. Your days are over, and you're never coming back, because you have no one to help you any more.*

The twist of smoke cleared away, and the moonlight shone down on them again.

Summer put her arm around Jim's waist and kissed him on the cheek. 'It's just like we're the only people in the whole world, isn't it, Jimmy? Just you and me. We're like Adam and Eve, don't you think? Adam and Eve, in Paradise.'

TWENTY-FOUR

The one person who never reappeared was Jim's father, William 'Billy' Rook.

Over the coming weeks, the bodies of the dead were gathered together and buried, and the burned-out houses were either demolished or repaired and redecorated. Hollywood and the rest of Los Angeles echoed and re-echoed to the sound of piledrivers and construction trucks.

On several occasions, Jim thought he saw his father in the street, or in Ralph's supermarket, but each time, when he approached him, the man would turn around and look completely different, as if his father's spirit were repeatedly playing a trick on him, to upset him for what he had done.

One day, three weeks later, he drove to Santa Monica Beach with Summer and walked on the sand with her. Summer saw a red spaniel running around and went running after it, round and round in circles, laughing.

Jim stood with one hand shading his eyes, looking at the ocean. The wind whistled a soft, persistent tune in his ear, the way his father used to whistle when he was mending something, like gluing together a broken coffee-pot handle.

A small boy in a pale-blue T-shirt was sitting on a plaid blanket not far away. He was holding a pack of Oreos, and his blond hair was sticking up at the back. He was squinting at the ocean in the same way that Jim was.

'Are you OK, son?' Jim asked him.

The boy looked up at him, with one eye closed against the sun. 'I'm waiting for my daddy,' he said.

Jim turned back to the ocean. He stared at the surf for a long time, and then he said, 'So am I, son. So am I.'